TANGLEWOOD

BY

DAMON WOLFE

Publisher's Cataloging-in-Publication Data

Wolfe, Damon

Tanglewood / by Damon Wolfe

p. cm.

Summary: Twins Jen and Ben must help their bamboo creature Tanglewood or else he will be destroyed by a crazy cook who believes plants are mankind's mortal enemy.

ISBN 978-0-9907397-0-8

[1. Fiction, Juvenile — Action and Adventure]

[2. Fiction, Juvenile — Fantasy and Magic]

First North American edition, August 2014

ACKNOWLEDGEMENTS

I was lucky — my sister Laura connected me to the Iris Way neighborhood and its many young readers who consume books as fast as french fries. These kids were the first test-readers who had no idea who I was before they cracked open the book so I knew I could trust their feedback: Ben Antanow; the members of the "Book Nook" and "Anything But Pink" book clubs — Aruna Anderson, Charlotte Amspaugh, Mia Baldonado, Saayili Budhiraja, Allysa Leong, Zander Leong, Anna Mickelsen, Ryan Seto, and Lydia Wilson. Thanks also to Saray Aguilar, a first reader from the other side of the state who explained how the story connected to her personal outlook and creative ambition. To my own kids, Izzy and Jack, who teach me everything they know. And to my adoring wife, Meredith, who loves this sad and beautiful world as much as anyone I've met, and makes it less sad, and more beautiful.

CONTENTS

PART ONE—SPIRIT

PART TWO—WOODS

PART THREE—SPIRIT OF THE WOODS

PART ONE

SPIRIT

BAMBOO

Jen hid within the bamboo. The light filtered by its canopy cast a dappled pattern on her skin, a camouflage that moved with the breeze. She felt leaves brush her neck. She felt the wristband on her right arm, taut, as always. She heard feet running toward her, took aim using her ears more than her eyes, pulled back on her bow and let the arrow fly at the same moment as rapid click-click-clicks came from the direction of her target. A dozen darts came at her, half of them halted by the bamboo, the other half snagged in her hair.

"I got you first!" Ben said as he stood on the lawn just beyond the edge of the bamboo, clutching an emptied Nerf dart pistol in each hand. Jen's arrow was stuck to the middle of his forehead.

"Maybe," Jen said as she emerged from the bamboo. "But I got you best."

Ben looked upward and cross-eyed. He saw the arrow's shaft angling upward from his forehead, like a long, thin horn. "How come it didn't just bounce off like it usually does?" He asked.

"I spit in it first. It sticks really good that way," Jen said. The suction cup made a satisfying POP as she yanked the arrow from her brother's head.

"Ow." Ben rubbed his forehead and checked his fingers for spit. "You can be really gross," he said to his sister. Jen shrugged and kissed him on the red spot left by the arrow's suction cup.

"That should be gone by the time we get to school," Jen said.

"JayBee! Breakfast!" Dad called to them from across the street. Jen and Ben dropped their toy weapons and left the bamboo-enclosed yard that wasn't theirs; its house had been empty for several years now.

As she always did when departing their secret space, Jen ran her fingers through the branches and soft leaves of the bamboo, which sent a tingling up her arm, a sensation that reminded her of holding Mom's hand when she was very young. But Jen didn't think back to when she was little that often. If anything, she was impatient to be older and stronger. Impatience was Jen's thing, and now that she and Ben were eleven, her impatience had intensified — except when the bamboo was next to her, or even better: when she stood within it. Then her restlessness vanished and she experienced an almost perfect calm, as if she could take the time to notice everything — not just the things you can see, but also the things you can't see. Although it sounded a little crazy, Jen noticed something within the bamboo. It had a personality and a strength she admired. Jen wished the bamboo could follow her wherever she went.

The kids entered the kitchen where their father, Ross, was whipping eggs. "Hey there! Go get your Mom — she's been working since before dawn. She needs to eat."

BAMBOO

Jen and Ben went out the side door and crossed the driveway. Before heading up the stairs to the studio workshop over the garage, Ben asked his sister, "Should we, do you think?"

Jen scrunched her mouth to one side. "Yes, definitely. She's been working too hard, and it's been a while since we reminded her we were here first, and in charge."

They ascended the stairs taking light steps. Ben turned the doorknob slowly, then Jen pushed open the door just as carefully. Sylvanna, their mother, was bent over her worktable deep in concentration marking lines on a long stretch of fabric. The kids crouched low, and silently made their way toward Bonesy, the dress mannequin that faced Sylvanna from the opposite side of her worktable. Bonesy was not an ordinary-looking mannequin. Its torso was made of tightly woven wicker; its limbs, formed by squared-off wooden slats, had hinged joints; its elbows, knees, ankles and wrists could bend and be posed. Even its fingers could bend. Someone had put a lot of work into making Bonesy.

Jen and Ben, completely undetected by Mom, were now positioned behind the mannequin. Each held an elbow with one hand, and a thigh with the other. Jen winked at Ben.

"Kill the humans!" The kids blurted as they tilted Bonesy toward the worktable and extended his arms directly at Mom, who startled more than she usually did for this attack. Sylvanna quickly recovered then did her part, which was to faint, dramatically. This time, however, she only dropped her head onto the top of the worktable.

"Aw, how come you don't faint onto the floor anymore?" Jen asked.

"I can't do that stuff again until after the baby is born," said Sylvanna.

Just then Bonesy's limbs, which had become very loose and wobbly over the years, all popped out of their sockets. Jen and Ben stood there, each holding a disembodied arm and leg. This wasn't the first time, and it didn't faze them.

"Is the baby going to be a girl?" said Jen.

"No. A boy. We need a boy," said Ben.

Sylvanna said, "We'll find out in two months."

"But, you must know. Everybody finds out whether they're having a baby sister or brother beforehand. Tell us!" Jen insisted.

Sylvanna said, "You're going to love it the same, no matter what it is, I guarantee it."

"That doesn't make sense," said Jen.

"It will make sense," said Sylvanna. "It better."

Sylvanna felt the baby inside her kick as she looked at her two children. She marveled how much they still looked identical for fraternal twins, which she knew would change over the next couple of years. Their faces were sweeter than ever, even with Bonesy's dangling limbs clutched in their hands. "Just drop the arms and legs and I'll deal with them later. We've all got a big day ahead of us," Sylvanna said.

"Yeah, 'cause it's the last day of fifth grade!" Ben whooped.

"Yay, yay, yay," Jen sang. "And it's a half day!"

* * *

Twenty minutes later Ben stood on the front porch waiting for Jen, who stumbled out the door buckling her belt with one hand while trying to put her hair up in a ponytail with the other. It would be a messy ponytail even if she used both hands, Ben knew, because Jen didn't care about neatness as much as he did, not by a long shot. Ben's collared shirt was buttoned all the way to the top, and his hair, not quite as long as Jen's, hung straight to his shoulders — long for a boy, but he enjoyed the way it felt against his neck, and he liked being able to cover his eyes with it when he wanted a moment to himself. Today, like every day, Jen wore straight-legged jeans, a T-shirt and slouchy high-tops that she had scribbled all over with permanent markers. And her wristband, of course, was always on. She had been wearing it day and night since last Halloween when she dressed up as her hero, Xena the Warrior Princess.

Ben tugged Jen by the arm and she followed. He sounded worried as he led her off the porch. "There's something new on the sign," Ben said. They dashed across the street, halting at the "For Sale" sign that had been stuck in the ground for so long they had learned to ignore it. The sign stood in front of the wall of bamboo that hid the empty house, the house that, as far as they were concerned, belonged to them. At least, its yard did. A sticker across the sign said "SOLD".

"Maybe the new people will let us come over and play in the yard," Ben said.

Jen didn't want to think about this right now, or ever, really. Besides, it was just a sticker. "It said that once before, and after three weeks the sticker disappeared and nothing happened," Jen said. But as they started toward school she ran her hand gently through sprigs of the bamboo. "I wish it could just walk across the street and live with us," she said.

* * *

Jen and Ben's mood lifted when they arrived at school because it would be nothing but recess and cupcakes for three and half hours, then, at noon, it would be time to go home for three months. The yard and field were bathed in sunlight and buzzing with kids.

Ben, the only boy jump-roper in the school, ran to his crew. The jump-rope girls were thrilled to have Ben because he came up with wild variations on what you could do with jump ropes. Today he tied five ropes together at one end, then laid out the untied ends, radiating them outward from the center, like a starfish. Ben sat in the middle holding the central knot above his head, while five spinners had to coordinate their rope spins so that the jumpers could hop from one to the other to complete the circle without blocking a rope. After fifteen minutes no one had made it through, but everyone was laughing so hard it didn't matter.

Not far from the jump-ropers a crowd had formed around the tetherball pole. This was Jen's turf. Tetherball had speed, smashing, and required both fists and wrists. For Jen, few sensations had the thrill of backhanding a tetherball, a righteous blow that delivered justice without anger. Well, there was some anger involved, but she usually directed it at the ball, not at her opponent, who she definitely wanted to crush, but not kill. Winning mattered to Jen, at some times more than others, and this was one of those times.

"Beat him, Jen!" shouted Rudy, a fourth grader. Jen's opponent was a boy named Stones. If that was his real name it was perfect. Every angle on him from his jaw to his ankles looked sharp and rocky. Stones was the meanest kid in sixth grade, and even though Jen didn't have to suffer having him in her class she felt as if beating Stones at tetherball would be like arriving at a village in the mountains and slaying a monster so everyone could live their lives without being afraid all the time.

"Beat him, Jen!" Rudy shouted again. He wanted to see Stones defeated, as did many others who kept their cheering to themselves during this best two-out-of-three match. Stones won the first game, and Jen won the second. The third game had been going on for a while, the tether having wound one way, then the other many times, and now it was circling against Stones. Stones let out an ugly grunt as he punched the ball with his fist. From Jen's perspective the ball looked as if it wasn't tied to a rope anymore; it flew in a straight line at her head, like a cannonball. Instinct took over, so she ducked.

"No!!!" Jen yelled at herself for choosing safety first. She rose, pivoted on her left foot and smacked the ball back at Stones on the next wraparound, but he was ready with an open hand and slapped it back, this time shot-gunning words instead of animalistic grunts.

"You dress like a boy!" Stones blurted. Jen kept her cool and batted the ball back giving it a high arc. Stones, taller than Jen by half a foot, reached up and reversed the ball with a downward smack as he snarled, "What's your gender, Jen-derr?"

OK, now she was mad. Jen shifted, clasped her hands and spun, her arms fully extended. She felt the wristband tighten around her forearm as her muscles tensed and BAM! Her backhand sweep put so much speed on the ball that the next thing everyone saw was the ball bouncing off Stones's face, which was both good and bad. Stones's hard face had returned the ball her way, and with such velocity that the tether wrapped around the pole against her for three full revolutions before Jen could reverse it with a swat that finally won the game.

Stones hadn't been able to open his eyes after the direct hit to his face. He growled as the crowd of kids cheered his loss — all but his two underlings, who twitched, unsure what to do.

Jen felt doubly good. She had beaten Stones and made other kids feel they had won along with her. Rudy the fourth grader ran up to give her a high-five. "Yeah!" Rudy shouted at Stones, "You were beaten by a girl!" A giant splotch with an imprint of the ball colored half of Stones's face, and his eyes, icy blue, wide open, looked like they were about to shoot flames.

Stones stalked menacingly at Jen and Rudy, so Jen put herself between him and Stones, who then shoved Jen's shoulders, forcing her to stumble backwards. "I bet you pee standing up," he said so everyone could hear. Others began to stare, even kids who hadn't watched the tetherball match.

Two more shoves from Stones and Jen was no longer able to keep Rudy behind her, so she pushed Rudy to one side while counterbalancing to stay on her feet. She collided with Mei, one of the jump-ropers, and now Ben stood right next to her.

Stones's head blocked out the sun. "Ha! You play tetherball and your brother plays jump-rope? Which one of you is the girl and which one's the boy? Is Jen-der the boy? Is Ben-der the girl?"

Stones then began to chant, giving his two underlings a direction to follow, so they joined in. "Jen-der Ben-der!, Jen-der Ben-der!" Over and over until kids who otherwise remained neutral began to give in to the rhythms of cruelty, and in Jen and Ben's minds the happy music of the last day of school degenerated into a bombardment.

Ben lurched at Stones, but Jen stopped him by side-stepping, again using her whole body as a shield. "Ben, don't!"

"Jen-der protects Ben-der! That proves she's the boy!" Stones cackled to the gathering crowd. He shot an acid smile at Ben. "That's a very nice blouse you're wearing today, Ben-der." Stones's words scraped at Ben's feelings like car tires crunching over gravel.

Jen's arms shot out. She grabbed as much of Stones's hair as she could and pulled hard while Rudy, Jen's biggest fan, whooped, "Beat him again, Jen!"

Stones whipped his head until he broke free, and then, like every nasty kid in front of a crowd, went after the weakest one. He grabbed Rudy by the collar with one hand as he clenched the other into a fist that was all knuckles. Rudy whistled, a loud whistle that stopped Stones for a second, and within that one second a seventh grader descended into their midst like Batman. The seventh grader pulled Stones backward, dragged him to the tetherball circle and lashed him to the pole with the tether. It happened fast.

The crowd migrated back to the tetherball pole, becoming very quiet as the seventh grade hero leaned toward Stones until their eyes were just an inch apart. "You touch Rudy again and I will end you," the hero said. Then he walked away while everyone stood there, stunned.

Rudy shouted, "Thanks, Rick!" He turned to Jen with a proud smile. "That's my big brother."

Jen and Ben looked at one another, sharing the same thought. They both knew what it was like to have a sibling, but neither Jen nor Ben knew what it was like to be an older sibling, or, more importantly at this moment, to have one. In times of confusion or trouble they knew they could rely on each other, but it was always obvious that neither of them had the advantages of greater size, age, or experience.

Beyond that mutual thought, however, Jen and Ben reacted very differently to the moment when Rick the older brother flew in to save the day. Ben felt a twinge of disappointment, a belief that he was supposed to be able to defend his sister better. Jen, however, just felt jealous, jealous of both Rudy and of Rick. Her jealousy was complicated, colored by a sadness that Jen didn't understand, and just hated.

After he had freed himself from the tetherball pole, Stones marched up to Jen and Ben to announce that he blamed them and they would pay for it. They stared at one other silently as the tension built. Then the teachers called everyone back into the classrooms for cupcakes.

* * *

At noon when the final bell of the year rang, Jen and Ben bolted out their classroom door and ran, but not with summer on their minds and a song in their hearts. Instead their hearts pounded boom boom boom as they put distance between themselves and Stones, assuming he would be lurking nearby to chase them to do who-knew-what once he caught them. They ran for a solid ten minutes and didn't stop until they turned off Elm onto Sycamore, their street.

Ben leaned onto his knees to catch his breath. He even unbuttoned his top collar button, which he didn't like to do because it looked sloppy. Jen took a peek back down Elm, where they had come from, but saw no one.

"Worst day of school ever!" She used her forearm to wipe the sweat off her face; the wristband left a streak of dirt across her cheek.

"Maybe by the fall everyone will have forgotten," Ben said to himself more than to Jen. Ben hated that it bothered him, the accusation of being a girl. Personally, Ben didn't take it as an insult because the whole idea was silly. It was obvious he was a boy, so who cares? But Ben knew that other kids would see it differently, no matter how stupid the idea was. Ben just wanted people to see him as competent and capable. Why anything else mattered, he had no idea.

Jen resumed fuming. She yanked her elastic ponytail holder all the way off. By now it barely held hair in any kind of ponytail, anyway.

"I'm sorry, Jen," Ben said.

"For what?"

"That I wasn't born before you. I mean, technically I am five minutes older. But I mean, by a year or two."

"Yeah, I wish I was older, too," Jen said. "But the fact is, you and me, we're just twins. How awesome would it be to whistle and WHAM, all your problems are solved! We both could have used someone like Rick today."

"Well," Ben said, "we did have someone like Rick today."

"I mean one of our own." Jen's wish to be older was shadowed by her wish that she had an older sibling. Someone like Xena, an intense warrior, would be perfect.

As they began walking the block toward home Jen put her arm around Ben and pulled him close for a sideways hug. "You're OK, Ben," she said, and Ben smiled, until he looked ahead and said, "Oh, no."

A workman was digging out the For Sale sign.

They ran to the workman. Jen arrived first. "What's going on?" she asked.

"When they ask me to take these things out it usually means the new people are moving in the next day or so. Was this your house?"

"Kind of," said Jen.

"Not really," added Ben.

"Not for long enough," Jen said.

As they crossed to their house Ben said, "That means we have to get our stuff out of there today."

"After lunch," Jen said. "Dad promised burgers." Jen needed a burger. Really bad.

DOWN

Stones left school in a bad mood, troubled by thoughts worse than tetherball, Jen, Ben, Rudy, or even Rick. Those people and this morning's events — he would have to forget these some other time. Right now he applied his energy to stop thinking about the remainder of this wretched day. If only he never had to think. That would be nice.

Stones wandered as slowly as possible to the school's back parking lot and saw Nash fussing with something in the truck bed. Stones approached the truck without saying a word, just got into the passenger seat of his father's pickup and sat there glumly, pressing the soles of his shoes against the glove compartment while he waited for Nash.

Stones called his father by his first name, only. Years ago Nash had told him, "I don't want to hear you calling me, 'Dad' unless you have a problem so big, it'll kill you. You got that? A man calls another man by his name. So be a man." Nash repeated that speech every time Stones acted like there was a problem, but it had been years since Stones had heard it. Not because Stones didn't have any problems. Stones just stopped talking to Nash about anything that troubled him. Which left very little to talk about. Nash appreciated how quiet a boy Stones was.

The driver-side door opened. Stones felt the bench seat tilt from Nash's weight. "Here," Nash said as he handed a crumpled sandwich bag to Stones. Stones took it, didn't open it.

"Snacktime. Chew up. You're going to need extra skrunch in you when we get there." Nash liked the word "skrunch." He flexed his biceps whenever he said it.

Stones opened the bag. A raw turnip root cut in half. Stones didn't feel like turnip root. The inside tasted like bitter chalk, the outside tasted like dirt, flavors he was tired of. "I don't want this," Stones thought to himself. But all he did was click his tongue and re-close the bag.

"Fine, eat it later," Nash said. Then he stepped out, reached into the truck bed once again and returned with another bag, this one long and flat. The bench seat dipped. "This should make you feel better." Nash handed Stones the bag, which had a black handle sticking out from its top. He wrapped his hand around the handle and withdrew a machete.

Stones didn't want to admit it, but the sight of the machete did make him feel better. The heft of it almost made him smile.

"We have a couple of errands to run first, but as soon as we get to the new house, you'll put that baby to use," Nash said as he pulled out of the lot and roared into the street.

* * *

Ross served the lunch he had promised Jen and Ben. He laid plates in front of them as they sat at the dining room table. "One burger with mayo and ketchup on the top, the other with ketchup and mustard on the bottom." He hadn't fully let go of the plates when both kids had their burgers scooped up in their hands, their mouths angling in for the kill.

"Hey! Wait for Mom. You two are like lions at the zoo."

"Dad! Burgers." Jen said.

"Sure. But Mom's joining us for lunch today." Dad said, as he put one salad plate in front of the kids, with salad. Ben brought his bangs in front of his eyes as Jen pushed the salad plate to the other side of the table, as far as her arm would reach.

"Not today, huh, kids?" Dad wasn't mad or disappointed, just matter-of-fact.

"Nope," said Jen.

"Vegetables. One day, kids, you will eat them. It's inevitable. They're good for you."

Jen and Ben couldn't imagine any of that.

"It's summer, now, Dad," Ben said.

"Yeah, why wreck it so soon?" said Jen.

Sylvanna entered the room cradling Bonesy the mannequin's disembodied arms and legs.

Ross said, "Are you trying to send some sort of message, honey?"

"Ha." Sylvanna held the limbs toward the kids. "Bonesy's arms and legs are out of their sockets for good, so they belong to you two, now."

"Eww," said Jen. "Creepy," said Ben.

"The first thing I'm going to do with that money is buy a new mannequin," Sylvanna plopped the limbs on the floor next to Jen and Ben before leaning on Ross's shoulder as she sat down.

"Can we eat?" Jen asked.

"Go for it," said Mom. And they did.

After about a minute of chewing, and forks tinkling against plates, Dad cleared his throat. "So, we have some news to share with you both."

Jen had just taken her next bite. Something about her father's voice caused her to stop chewing. She looked up at her parents and paused while she scanned their faces. "Are you giving our room away to the baby?" she said, with food in her mouth.

Mom answered right away, "No, of course not." Jen smiled and began to chew again.

"You both know how amazing your mom is at designing and making clothes," Ross began.

"You're the best, Mom." Ben said.

"Well," Ross continued, "an important woman in the fashion world agrees." Ross turned to his wife. "This is your news. You should tell them."

"OK," Mom said, "This summer I am being paid to create a whole line of women's clothes."

"Wow!" Ben put his burger down. "Casuals?"

"More fun than that," Sylvanna answered. "Chic and classy, like for a special date, or a weekend in the city with someone you love." She reached over to Ross and touched his cheek with the back of her fingers.

"Go, Mom!" Jen raised a fist between bites.

Ben thought he saw a look of doubt flash across his mother's face. Or something.

"It's a very short schedule," she said. "Less than six weeks."

"You can do it, Mom." Ben had absolute confidence in his mother's talent. His earliest memory was of watching her turn flat, lifeless material into clothes that seemed alive all by themselves, even without people inside them.

"Well, it's summer," Dad began, "which will make things a little tricky...."

"Don't worry," Jen said, eagerly, "we'll keep the volume low, and, besides, during the day we'll probably be playing, um, at other places—" She cut herself off, remembering the workman removing the sign. She felt a knot in her chest.

"No, kids, my project is going to take real peace and quiet," Sylvanna said, and then inhaled in a way Jen could tell was the beginning of something she didn't want to hear. As soon as her mother began talking Jen couldn't make out the words. She swam inside the sensation of being in a dream she knows is a dream, waiting to wake up. Like being under water. She gave up trying to understand the conversation and noticed that a half a hamburger lay on her plate in front of her, which was weird because she couldn't remember putting it down. Her appetite disappeared, as if she had never needed an appetite.

Ben's voice began to shake her back to reality, slowly at first, until he blurted out, "Sleep-away camp?!" Ben sounded almost outraged. "But we're not camp kids!"

"You'll love it, I just know you will," Dad said.

"Have you been there? Have you seen it?" Ben said.

"Well, brochures," Dad answered. "It isn't easy to find a camp that has openings this late, but I'm sure it's going to be great."

"Why?" Ben wanted to know.

"Because it's in the mountains!" said Dad. Ben wondered if his father's enthusiasm made him overlook certain details from time to time.

"Mountains means it's a bunch of trees and dirt! We want to be here. We like being at home. Don't we, Jen?"

Jen didn't respond.

"I know that once you're up there," Dad began to say. Ben slumped deep into his chair. Sylvanna squeezed her husband's knee, a signal that he needed to let her do the talking.

"Kids," she said, "We know that camp is an entirely new thing, and that we're springing it on you all of a sudden."

"We feel bad about that," Dad said.

"We do. And if there were any other way, but this opportunity is something I've been working toward for a while."

"And the baby," Dad said, "is almost here."

Mom cut him off. "We just all have to make it work. Like we always do, even if it sucks for a little while."

Jen finally said something. "I knew that baby was going to cause us problems."

Mom and Dad stopped talking. They looked like they were forcing themselves to not look sad.

Ben broke the silence after what seemed like an eternity of awkward. "She didn't mean it," Ben said.

Jen knew that was a cue, but it took her a minute. "Sorry," Jen said. "I didn't mean it."

* * *

The kids sat in their shared bedroom eating a one-pound chocolate bar that Dad gave them after lunch.

This summer camp thing, as much as they hated the idea, left them both feeling sorry for themselves much more than being mad at Mom and Dad. Being mad at their parents was such a foreign feeling that neither Jen nor Ben knew how to sustain it. And at least they had the built-in safety net in one another, so neither of them would have to be away from home alone. So after listening to Mom and Dad explain a few details about the camp — it had a strange name, "Triple-Bar" — and looking at a few pictures, both kids were able to turn their minds back to where things were before lunch.

Which actually wasn't great. There had been enough unpleasant surprises even before the news about going to camp. But chocolate's soothing flavor helped Jen settle down, and in that calm she remembered that she had wanted to talk to her mother, alone, about what happened that morning.

She said to Ben, "Before we go, you know," she gestured out the window to the bamboo across the street, "to get all our stuff from our place, I have to go ask Mom a question. I'll be down in a little bit."

Ben nodded. "I'll get the stilts from the garage in a few minutes," he said.

Jen climbed the outdoor staircase to the workshop where she found her mother at her drafting table, immersed in a sketch. On the wall next to the drafting table Jen noticed a new piece of artwork, a large, embroidered clothing label that said, "Fit Yourself," in letters that were both fun and elegant.

"Mom," Jen said.

"Hmm."

"Is it OK the way I dress?"

Sylvanna stopped sketching and looked directly at her daughter, who was sidling toward her. Sylvanna licked her thumb and wiped at a small streak of dirt on Jen's forehead. Jen's eyes looked rounder and sadder than usual.

"Jen, you march to your own drummer. It's a good beat. Keep marching."

Jen put her head onto her mother's lap. She faced the wall, chockablock with her mother's sketches, most of them women in dresses.

Jen said, "I don't dress in clothes you like."

"What?" Sylvanna was as surprised as she sounded.

"You know, girlier clothes. People think I'm a boy sometimes. Someone even said it, once. Today."

Her mother lifted up Jen's drooping head so she could lock onto her eyes as she spoke. "Baby," Mom began, her voice soothing and warm, "you are definitely a girl, up and down, inside and out, and it's only going to get more obvious. You dress great. You dress like someone who isn't afraid of 'The Other'."

Jen raised an eyebrow. She wasn't sure what her mother had just said — it sounded like the name of a horror movie. "The— What?"

"Every thing is mostly itself," Sylvanna explained, "but there are always little bits of whatever you might call the opposite thing mixed in. It's not really the opposite, though; it's the other side of the same thing — like the sides of a coin. We call them the opposite, but they're attached to one another. 'The Other' is different from you, but still connected to you."

Jen had no idea what her mother was talking about.

"Men and Women, Boys and Girls, for example," her mother said.

Well, Jen thought, it is true that boys and girls weren't opposites when you thought of them both as "people". She wondered what the opposite of "people" might be.

Jen said, "Ben always pays attention to what he's wearing, and sometimes he looks almost as stylish as one of your sketches." She looked downward, at her own left knee where a streak of dirt began that didn't end until it reached the middle of her T-shirt.

"I think we got mixed up when we were inside you," Jen said in a very small voice. She put her head down again, this time pushing it into her mother's stomach, like a small child who wants to go back to before they were born. Jen felt the new baby stop her head from going very far, and then felt her mother's fingers running slowly through her hair, untangling a few knots along the way.

"You're gorgeous and caring and kind and tough. Tough is important to you. It always has been. You dress tough because you like to feel tough. There's nothing wrong with that."

"I dress like a boy."

"No. When people lived in caves they dressed in the skins of strong animals so they could feel like they had the same kind of power."

"Mo-omm! Don't make me learn new stuff! School is over."

"Hush. This is a very short and simple lesson: You don't dress like a boy. You dress tough."

Jen still believed her parents knew everything there is to know, even though her suspicions were growing that they might not. "Growing up is too confusing," Jen said.

"Boys don't own 'tough,'" Sylvanna continued. "Boys dress the way you like to dress because they want to look tough, not because they want to dress like boys."

Jen looked at her forearm, at the wristband, and everything her mother just said, made sense.

"Xena," Jen whispered, forming a fist, feeling the wristband tighten.

"Exactly," Mom said. "You've been wearing that wristband since Halloween. And now that you understand why it's so important, maybe it's time to wash it."

"No way," Jen said. "The wristband is part of me, and I am part of it. Washing could ruin what we've got going."

"Well," Sylvanna said, "a permanently filthy wristband is a small price to pay for having a happy daughter."

Jen's mood lightened swiftly as her mother's wisdom and kindness sank in, and even dark thoughts became bearable, almost funny. She held up her fist to admire the wristband as she let out a comically sinister laugh, "Heh heh heh. The power of The Other is in me, and on me! It is mine!"

"OK," Sylvanna said, "you're obviously feeling better, so Momma's gotta get back to work."

On her way out Jen said, "Hey, what about animals and plants? Are plants "The Other" to animals?"

"Yes," Sylvanna said. She hadn't really thought about it, but wanted to keep things moving along.

"But I'm an animal and no part of me is like a plant," Jen mused.

"Maybe if you ate vegetables, even once, you would find that part," Sylvanna said, as she turned her full attention back to drawing. Jen shut the door quietly and took the stairs two at a time down to the driveway where Ben waited, teetering on the stilts with the last hunk of chocolate bar hanging out of his mouth. He broke off half and handed it to his sister.

* * *

The only "normal" way into the bamboo-surrounded property was a narrow, decorative front gate that was locked and partially covered by encroaching bamboo stalks. Other than the tiny gap at the entry gate the bamboo hid the entire lot. An overgrown path ran between the right-hand side of the lot and its next-door neighbor. The kids snaked down the path, squeezed into the bamboo and arrived at a secret gate deeply embedded within. This gate was obviously a remnant of a wooden fence that had long ago been taken over by the bamboo. The only continuous stretch of fence around the yard, now, lined the back edge of the property, separating the bamboo from the lot behind it.

Using the secret gate wasn't strictly necessary — there were sections of the stand they could shimmy through — but using the secret gate meant something to Jen and Ben. For Ben, it helped him feel more like he had permission to enter the yard. For Jen, it served as a comforting reminder. The very first time she had pushed the gate open she needed to force it over some of the bamboo's roots, scraping several stalks at their base. When she saw the wounds she wondered if the bamboo felt pain the same way she did when she skinned a knee or elbow. Just because the bamboo couldn't talk or move, she thought, didn't mean it couldn't feel pain. She had kept an eye on the scrapes she had caused, checking them every day. She noticed that a scab formed over them, which then became a more permanent-looking scar, and the scars at the secret gate reminded Jen that the bamboo was strong, and could heal itself.

Jen entered the yard, noticing details she had ignored for a while, or maybe had never seen before. The bamboo had grown a lot this spring and reached higher than ever. The breeze fluttered the topmost leaves, making a *shishhh* sound like ocean waves bubbling after hitting the shore. The lawn was the greenest it had ever been. It grew to the very edge of the bamboo so that the transition from grass to bamboo formed a swooping wave that crested high above their heads where the blue sky went on to forever.

The house within the bamboo waves was almost inconsequential. This was a yard that had a house, not the other way around. "The house sure is tiny," Jen said.

"It's a little egg inside a big nest," Ben said.

Jen hadn't thought of it that way before. "I guess we're the birds who have already hatched, and it's time for us to leave."

Jen and Ben pushed away the sadness of their words by focusing on the work at hand. Ben picked up the Nerf pistols, shoved them in his jacket pockets and went after the innumerable darts.

DOWN

Jen used her feet to knock the soccer ball to the center of the lawn. Same with the Frisbee and the plastic baseball bat they used as a sword more than as a bat. Then she picked up the bow and slung it over her shoulder as she began to seek the many suction-cupped arrows, most of them cradled in the bamboo. After recovering the ones in low-lying branches Jen hopped onto the stilts to reach higher up. She tottered from the back corner forward until she faced the thick wave of bamboo that lived at the front of the lot.

She hooked her left arm around both stilt tops as she reached in with her right to grasp hold of a hefty bamboo stalk that grew in the middle of the stand. She leaned inward to scan for arrows hidden within the canopy, and as soon as the bamboo enveloped her she became immersed in the realm of her senses, as if the physical part of her dissolved into the criss-cross pattern of the inner branches, into the gentle curvatures of the leaves, into the dappled sunlight as it filtered through, and into the tickle of the twigs against her cheek, as the sweet scent rose from the roots where the bamboo tied itself to the earth. She felt light-headed, and tightened her grip on the stalk, and as her grip tightened she felt a presence, a vibration coming from somewhere within the bamboo, or maybe it came from within her own wrist, the pulsing of her own heart, and she had the oddest sensation that her hand and the bamboo were no longer separate things. Then, she froze.

Deeper into the stand stalks began to shake. A low voice, almost a growl said, "Start here." The voice came from the other side, from the sidewalk out front. The growl became a rumble that wound itself up into a deafening whine that began to shred: the most horrible sound Jen had ever heard. Crunching, grinding, tearing, all at once. The bamboo shuddered violently; the spasm spread to the stalk she held tight. She didn't want to let go but the stalk popped loose, as if its connection to the earth had disappeared.

She flapped her arms, struggling to regain control of the stilts and she stutter-stepped backward to the grass. The stalk she had held onto continued in a downward arc, falling toward her, then halted as it jammed into bamboo spires that still stood tall as they began to convulse. More stalks slanted their way down toward her, their branches dangled above her head, unsteady, unstable, their leaves flopping loosely, almost falling, but slowly, like tears stuck to a cheek.

"Jen, for God's sakes MOVE AWAY!!" Ben's voice penetrated the incessant crunching and tearing. Jen felt a firm yank on her belt loops and her feet left the stilts but she kept her grip on them, wishing the stilts were swords or guns she could use to fight back the monster that ripped the bamboo apart. The bamboo now collapsed in clumps, stopped by the ground but having seizures every time another fell onto a pile that splayed at every angle like pick-up sticks.

"Jen!" Ben yelled again, and she finally turned to run with him, but he was heading toward the secret gate so she pulled his shirt to redirect him to the very back of the yard instead.

"We're not leaving!" she shouted above the din.

They shoved their skinny bodies into the back stand of bamboo, an enclosure deep enough to keep them hidden as they watched.

At the front, where Jen had stood, a gap widened, a hole where bamboo stood, and through the hole stomped a large man using a chainsaw to tear through another swath of bamboo stalks. Then a boy appeared through the hole swinging a machete with reckless energy. The destroyers each wore breathing masks that covered their mouths and noses, wraparound goggles, heavy jackets with the hood pulled tight around the head: monsters from outer space in cheap costumes.

DOWN

The man turned off the chainsaw, unclipped his breathing mask and whooped, "What do you call a hundred bamboo stalks cut down at the root?"

The boy unclipped his mask. "A good beginning!"

Jen and Ben's jaws dropped. It was Stones.

"You are so RIGHT!" the man hollered. "This is a great day!" The man grabbed a plastic bottle filled with bright orange liquid, downed it all then crushed the bottle as he carelessly tossed it onto the pile of fallen bamboo. He clipped his breathing mask back on, fired up the chainsaw and slashed into more bamboo.

Ben prepared himself to hold Jen back, thinking that she was about to bolt out there to stop the big man and Stones. Jen's face was contorted into a look Ben had never seen, on her, or on anyone. She was there, but she wasn't. She was herself, but she wasn't. Jen seemed to have come to a grinding halt. But her eyes flickered, and her jaw jutted. He wasn't sure if that meant she was staying put or was about to go ballistic. So he acted fast.

"Jen," Ben shook her. "Jen we have to leave. Now!" He coaxed the stilts from her white-knuckled grip and propped them up against the fence that separated the bamboo from the neighbor behind it. He aimed his sister at the stilts and then shoved her up and over the fence. She was dazed, but she did what he told her, and they were safely out.

They walked through the neighbor's yard without being seen, and onto the sidewalk one block over.

As they walked back home Jen said nothing, and for the first time, ever, Ben worried about his sister.

VACANT

Jen spent the rest of the afternoon on the steps of her front porch. Ben tried to distract her but she was in a daze.

Another hour of sawing and hacking across the street left all the bamboo flat on the ground. A truck pulled up; its driver unloaded a small bulldozer, then drove off. Chainsaw Man got in the bulldozer. He looked stupid, Jen thought, like a grown kid sitting in a toy car that hasn't fit him since he was four. He and his little bulldozer scraped the bamboo into piles and then cut into the ground to tear out their roots.

The bamboo had always looked particularly beautiful at this time of day, from late afternoon to twilight. The lowering light would stream through the bamboo, setting aglow its golds and greens before they faded to a wispy, purple silhouette once the sun had set. But tonight the low sun shone right into Jen's eyes, and all she saw across the street was a harsh, blown-out glare smeared over ruination. The little house looked lonely, an egg whose nest had been taken away.

Jen wondered how to make sense of bad things when so many happen at once. A pit formed in her stomach as she realized there was no rule forcing bad things to stop happening once they began. The next worst thing could be just around the corner, ready to unfold at any minute.

And here it came, another truck. Stones and the Chainsaw Man unloaded boxes and furniture, and then the driver drove the truck away while they stayed to unpack: They hadn't come just to destroy the place — they were also moving in! Chainsaw Man had to be Stones's father, Jen thought, which made cruel sense.

The tiny house had lots of windows through which Jen could see Stones and his father unpack. Stones excitedly jumped up and down as they set up a drum kit in a room that faced hers. Stones began flailing at his drums with the same overkill he used swinging the machete. Or playing tetherball.

"You suck at tetherball, too," Jen said, under her breath. Ben was standing behind her in the front doorway doing his half-hourly check to see how his sister was doing. Now that she had started muttering to herself he hoped she was ready to talk.

"It's hard to know which is the worst part of all this," Ben said.

"My bamboo," she said, "is gone."

"I liked it, too," Ben said.

"Our bamboo," she agreed. Ben watched closely to see if she was about to cry, but she looked too angry to cry.

"Something about this is very wrong," Jen said.

"Having Stones as a neighbor is definitely bad," Ben agreed.

"No," Jen said. "It's worse than that. This is like—" She trailed off.

"Like what?" Ben asked.

"Like murder." Jen said. And as soon as she said it, she wondered why she was taking it this hard. She was used to being able to find silver linings and bright sides, but now she drew a blank, and felt as if a new part of herself had just been added on, one that pushed against her old ways.

The sun was gone. Stones slashed away at his drums, creating a jagged beat that could be a song, but only to a twisted soul. A dog began to howl.

Jen rose up to head inside the house with Ben. "I don't think I'm upset about going to camp anymore," Jen said.

* * *

At the dinner table Jen fidgeted with her wristband while waiting to be served. She unsnapped it, found a bamboo leaf pasted to her skin held there by sweat. She smoothed out the leaf but left it on her, and snapped the band shut.

Mom sat down. Dad put hotdogs in front of the kids and served salad onto a couple of plates. Jen and Ben both shot their father a look.

"Don't worry. These are for Mom and me," Dad said.

Dad asked, "What happened across the street?"

Neither of the kids wanted to talk about it so they were happy Mom jumped in with an answer. "The new people drove up, and fwoosh. Good-bye, bamboo."

"Maybe one them is a landscape architect?" said Dad, always looking for the positive angle even when none existed. Ben thought to himself that the man with the chainsaw didn't seem like the type of person who was capable of making things look nicer, or capable of *making* anything at all.

Mom asked, "Did you two see if there's someone your age?"

"He's a butt," Jen said.

"He probably needs time to adjust to his new neighborhood," Dad said.

"No," Ben said, "We know him. He's a butt."

"Look, I believe you," Dad said. "All I'm saying is, let's be neighborly."

The doorbell rang.

Dad stood up, "Keep eating, I'll get it."

Sylvanna looked at her kids, knowing that both of them were down in the dumps deeper than they were used to. She said, "You guys are usually on your second hot dog by now."

"Not that hungry," Jen said, quietly.

"I know you really liked that bamboo," Mom said.

Ben nodded.

"Maybe later this summer before school starts we can plant some in our yard," Mom said.

Jen and Ben appreciated the gesture even though their mother had just committed the biggest no-no of summertime by mentioning that school would, someday, start again.

"Thanks, Mom. Yeah. Maybe," Ben said.

Jen had the sad thought that it could never be the same, exact bamboo, so what would be the point? But she kept her mouth shut.

Dad returned. "That was our new neighbor, Nash, and he invited us to a barbecue tomorrow at his place. All of us!"

* * *

After dinner, in their bedroom, Ben said to Jen, "I don't think I've ever heard you say NO so many times in a row."

"I was making up for all the NO's you should have said."

"I don't want to go! I said that," Ben shot back.

It was true, he had protested, but no amount of protesting would have satisfied Jen. The idea of going to eat at that place, with those people after what they did — it broke through her thin shroud of numb acceptance, and intense frustration began to spray out between the seams.

She picked up the bamboo stick that lay on her bed, a pretend sword she had found across the street last year, a gift from the bamboo. She repeatedly thrust it at the air in front of her, grunting with each lunge.

"Exactly who do you want to stab with that?" Ben asked.

"This day sucks!" she said. "Revenge!"

Then she dropped the bamboo stick-sword to the floor flung herself onto her bed, and kicked her feet into the mattress while she screamed into her pillow.

Ben was as upset as his sister. He had the same need to dissipate his agitation through movement but instead of theatrics, Ben's trick was to keep his hands busy. He had been sitting at his desk building a plastic model from a kit, a giant robot named the *Gundam Deathscythe*. It had lots of parts. He put all his energy into gluing tiny pieces together that made the head and helmet.

Their father knocked on the half-open door and entered. "Hey guys. It's getting kind of late." Jen sprung up from her bed and huffed into the bathroom attached to their room, sat down on the toilet and peed with the door open. Jen always peed with the door open.

Ben rolled his eyes and shook his head. "She'll start closing the door after she's twelve, I guarantee it," his father said, but Ben wasn't counting on it.

"Dad," Ben said, "is Mom all right?"

"She's great. I mean, she knows you two are upset and she doesn't like that but she's really excited about designing those clothes."

Ben felt ashamed. "I forgot about that news."

"Don't sweat it. A lot got dropped on you today."

Ben said, "Yeah. This camp we're going to, does it have, like, arts and crafts?"

"Those were definitely listed in the brochure," his father said. "Your mother insisted on a camp that offered art. If all you want is arts and crafts, they'll be fine with it. They let kids choose what they want to do."

"What about sword fighting?" Jen said, from the toilet.

"Well, archery," Dad replied.

Jen came out of the bathroom. "With real arrows?"

"Actually, yes."

Jen gave her father a hug.

"Go kiss your Mom," Dad said, and both kids went to do just that.

When they lay in bed with the lights out, Jen looked out their front window. Ever since she could remember she would fall asleep to the sight of the bamboo across the street. The window had framed it perfectly. The bamboo would shimmer with moonlight, or, on moonless nights, shimmer from porch lights, as if it wanted to catch hold of all light no matter where it came from. Five minutes watching the bamboo through the window would transport her to a restful slumber. But tonight she saw nothing but black sky and a lonely street lamp that stood on the next block.

"An empty window." Jen sighed. She felt a tear build up in the corner of her eye.

It took over an hour for her to fall asleep.

DIRT

The next afternoon Jen, Ben, and their parents left for the barbecue. From the front porch the sight across the street hit Jen and Ben equally hard. The bamboo was lashed into bundles that lay in a four-foot wide gash surrounding the lot — a shallow grave. Muddy streaks zigzagged the edges of lawn where the little bulldozer went back and forth to gouge out the roots. The bulldozer itself was parked to one side, its front scoop lifting a wedge of the bamboo's root structure. The scene reminded Ben of a diorama he knew from a museum: a life-sized model of a dinosaur in the act of ripping up a tree and eating it, surrounded by a forest painted on the walls, its paint so faded that the trees in the background looked like ghosts who could do nothing to stop the monster from devouring one of their own.

The family now stood on the tiny slab porch of the naked house. Ross rang the bell. He carried a box that held a pecan pie.

Nash answered the door. He looked part human, part rock. His smile was huge and crooked, his teeth like chisels capable of tearing open tin cans. He extended a hand, a slab of meat at the end of an arm that looked made for breaking things.

"Ross, right?" Nash said. The kids saw their dad wince as the brute shook his hand.

"Name is Nash, ma'am," Nash said directly at their mother, who looked perplexed. She fixated on Nash's right biceps where a tattoo stained his body with an image of a tree on fire.

"Like it?" Nash asked as he flexed his arm causing the flames to expand as if flaring to engulf the tree. Ben could tell by the look on his mother's face that she wasn't thrilled with the artwork. Ben knew his mother's taste, and tattoos on fire wasn't it.

The family entered the house, Jen and Ben sticking close to each other. Nash shot them a glare that felt as if he wanted to catch them doing something wrong. "Kids?" Nash asked, pointing at them as if he wasn't sure what they were.

"This is Jen and Ben," Ross introduced them.

"Two of them?" Again it sounded like a question. Was his eyesight bad, Jen wondered.

"Not identical twins. Fraternal twins," explained Sylvanna — somehow their mother knew what the boulder-brained bruiser was asking.

"That's the only way to get a boy and a girl that are twins," Jen said. She hated this man but there was no way she was going to be scared of someone who seemed stupid.

"Huh. Which is which one?" Nash asked.

Jen rolled her eyes. Ben thought to himself "Does this problem run in their family, not being able to tell a girl from a boy?"

"Stones!" Nash's voice rattled the window just behind Jen and Ben. Stones appeared, and the three kids glowered at one another as Nash slid open glass doors and escorted Sylvanna and Ross to the back yard.

"This stinks," Stones said.

Jen and Ben couldn't agree more, but they had discussed before coming over that the best way to deal with Stones is to give him dirty looks and say nothing. Jen tugged at Ben's sleeve and they walked to the back yard.

In the middle of the yard was a stainless steel coffin; at least, that's what it looked like. When Nash opened its lid they could see that it was actually a very long grill, shiny on the outside, black on the inside. Next to the grill a stainless steel table held whole vegetables, a chopping board, and a machine that looked like a small outboard motor.

Nash twisted the knobs on the grill. A hiss, several clicks and FOOMF! The burners ignited. He moved to the outboard motor, which was a juice machine.

"Drinks!" Nash announced. "Carrot Shake, Parsnip Punch, Green Beet Cocktail — anything that can be ground to a pulp, you can have."

He picked up a turnip and shoved it into the juicer's top feed chute, hit a switch and pulled a lever. The grinding sound made Jen feel sick. Ben was trying to figure out what the machine would do to the turnip when a cloudy liquid sluiced out a bottom chute and streamed into a plastic cup.

Nash grabbed the cup and downed the turnip juice in one gulp.

"Ahhhh. Smooth. What'll each of you have?"

Sylvanna and Ross didn't have an answer ready. Ben looked as if he had just stepped into a wet pile of something. Jen spoke first.

"What about the bamboo," she said. It was an accusation, not a question.

One of Nash's eyebrows arched its way through all the ditch-like creases of his forehead. "I admire a boy who likes drinks you can chew, but I don't serve weeds to guests," Nash said.

Sylvanna said, "Nash, that's Jen. Our daughter." She didn't sound annoyed but Jen could tell that her mom was a little irritated on her behalf.

"That's what I meant," Nash's face cracked into a smile. But Jen's comment about the bamboo was ignored. Ben marveled at grown-ups' ability to pretend everything is fine when, in fact, everything is awkward. Ross changed the subject.

"This yard is huge," Ross said. "Do you have plans for it?"

"Flagstone, when I have the money," said Nash, "But until then, concrete."

Jen became distracted by an unpleasant crackling, and saw Stones hopping from bundle to bundle of bamboo making his way to the front. Jen caught up and, making sure that the house blocked the view from the back yard, pushed Stones off as he landed on the next bundle.

"You think I won't pound you because mommy and daddy are here?" Stones said, cracking his knuckles.

Jen wasn't sure, but didn't care. She stared back, watching, daring. Ben, noticing Jen wandering off, had positioned himself halfway between the front and back yards to keep an eye out, hoping that Jen and Stones had enough sense to keep a low profile.

Stones defiantly hopped back onto a bundle and started rocking his body as if he were steadying himself on a log in a river. The back-and-forth motion ground the bamboo into the mud, which added squishing to the muffled crackling of small branches that fractured under his weight.

"Quit it!" Jen hissed through her teeth. "You're hurting it!"

Stones halted but only to laugh at her. "It's already dead!" He said. "We killed it."

Jen felt her wristband tighten. Quick as lightning her fingers clutched Stones's throat. "I will bring it back to life," she heard herself say. "And it will end you." Her words caused Stones to look more frightened than she had expected. He looked terrified.

"Jen!" Ben hissed, "Not worth it!"

Ben was right. She let go of Stones and backed away.

"Kids," Mom called, "come here."

Nash stood at the grill pouring oil onto sizzling food. Flames shot up. He turned away from the heat.

Is that a cigar jammed in his mouth? Ben wondered. Then Nash clamped down, his jaw muscles flexed, and Ben knew that whatever was in Nash's mouth was done for. KRUNCH! It was a carrot.

Ben sat down at the table made of metal and plastic.

Nash scraped yellow, green and red strips off the grill that glistened like tongues. He presented a plate of them to Ben's parents. "Try these."

"Mmm," Sylvanna said, "these peppers taste great."

Ross agreed. "What's your secret, Nash?"

"I'm a cook."

"So is it like with magicians?" Ross asked. "You never give away your secrets?"

Nash just smiled, Ben noticing a sinister edge to it. The carrot held in Nash's back teeth, went KRUNCH once again as Nash's jaw snapped down. Then the shortened remains of the carrot rolled deeper into Nash's mouth as if transported by a mechanism. Maybe Nash had gears as well as teeth in his head. Maybe Nash and that juicer came from the same factory, Ben thought.

Jen sat on the bench and slid close to Ben.

Sylvanna took another pepper. "Wow, I'll bet you do amazing things with ribs," she said.

The next crunch from Nash sounded disapproving. "Meat's not for eating. Only vegetables."

DIRT

Jen and Ben didn't understood what "only vegetables," meant, both of them too immersed in having a bad time to decode weird sentences. Nash swung around from the grill holding a platter piled with burgers in buns. That's what they looked like, so Jen and Ben, desperate for anything good, perked up. Hamburgers: a gateway to at least five minutes of happiness.

"Dinner!" Nash said. Ben and Jen lifted burgers off the platter and in no time each had taken a huge bite.

Ben looked as if he had just eaten ashes.

Jen spat hers out.

"Portobello mushroom patties, my specialty," Nash said. Fortunately for Sylvanna and Ross, Nash had already turned to the grill and didn't see their kids eject and scrape the food from their mouths.

"It's like dirt." Ben's comment was covered over by Stones's grunting as he plunked his bony butt on the bench as far from Jen and Ben as possible. Stones grabbed one of those horrible things from the platter and ate it quickly, nervously, like an unbalanced chipper-shredder about to fling parts everywhere.

Nash served food onto people's plates — something as gray as it was green and slimy, and globs that looked like sponges oozing purple blood.

Ben had been in this kind of inedible food situation at a friend's house, where he solved the problem by making a Labrador retriever very happy. "Do you have a dog?" Ben asked Nash.

"No meat eaters get to live in my house," Nash said.

Stones ate his food fast, but not happily. It was difficult to imagine Stones looking happy, and, as far as Jen was concerned, Stones deserved to eat dirt burgers, snot glop and blood sponges for the rest of his life.

The adults were just starting to eat when Stones stood up. "I'm done," he said.

"You cleared your plate," Nash said without looking up, "so go ahead and have movie time. Watch the new one I got for you, it's a classic."

"Did you get the funny one I said I wanted?" Stones asked.

"You know the rule: I pick the movies. Go watch it."

Stones stomped into his house. Ben, who loved all movies, couldn't imagine being upset by having to watch one.

Jen and Ben looked down at the mess waiting on their plates. They breathed through their mouths, wishing they didn't have noses.

"Nash," Ross said, "if you don't mind I think my kids are done, they've both been fighting something that's killed their appetites."

Nash shrugged and said, "They're your kids."

"Go on, you two, watch the movie," Sylvanna said.

Ben and Jen resigned themselves to the least worst option. Being in the same room with Stones would be unpleasant, but the food was disgusting.

* * *

Jen and Ben entered Stones's living room. Cardboard boxes lined the walls. Two metallic chairs faced toward a television on the bare floor, a DVD player messily wired to it. Stones upended one of the boxes. Plastic DVD jackets poured out. He scrabbled through them, grabbed one and cursed under his breath as he struggled to get a fingernail underneath its shrink-wrap.

Ben squatted to glance at the pile of DVDs. One was called, The Day of the Triffids, another, Attack of the Killer Tomatoes. He picked up two more. Tulips of Death, and The Man-Eating Plant from Planet Twilo.

Stones tore open the new disc, a movie named *Little Shop of Horrors*. On its cover: a giant, red, polka-dotted plant with teeth.

"What's with all the movies about monster plants?" Ben asked.

"I just hope you hate scary movies as much as I do," Stones muttered, "because that's all I got."

"Why watch them if you don't like them?" Jen asked, sincerely. Jen didn't expect Stones to answer her, but he did. "Because they're good for me," Stones said as he shoved the disc into the player. He slumped into the metal chair, aimed the remote and squeezed the play button.

* * *

In the back yard Nash spoke with food in his mouth.

"We moved into this place, the first thing I did is show the bamboo who's the boss. You have bamboo in your yard?"

"No, but we're thinking about it," Sylvanna said.

"You ever see what bamboo does to sidewalks and driveways?" Nash replied. "Crack them to pieces. Next comes the house, then, before you know it, the tables are turned. Plants are vicious. All they need is time and they can destroy anything. Little tiny acorn with little tiny roots? Not for long. They grow! And then those roots become tentacles, gripping and crushing, turning boulders into dust. We have to eat them before they eat us." Nash gnawed through another mouthful of food.

Ross said, "Most vegetarians I've met say they eat vegetables for health reasons."

"Survival is a health reason," Nash dredged his fingers through Jen's plate now that he had eaten everything from his own. "People think mankind rules the earth. People want to save the trees but they've got it all wrong. Plants are the ones who have all the power.

We have to eat through them as fast as we can, to absorb their power. What you eat is what you become."

"You mean, become a vegetable?" Sylvanna said with a giggle hoping to lighten the mood. Nash's upper lip curled, his teeth reddened by beet fibers, and his eyes flickering yellow from the flame of a candle that oozed wax onto the table.

"Stones's mother loved plants," Nash continued. "Called them the most intelligent life on the planet, smarter than people, better than people, talking nonsense about new life forms, sounding crazy. So she leaves, goes to the Amazon, a place that's nothing but plants, weeks later they find her in a cocoon of vines, her head inside a giant Venus fly trap."

Sylvanna felt conflicted. Nash's story was horrifying and sad. On the other hand it sounded too strange to be true.

"Wow," Ross whispered softly. "Nash, that's terrible. We're very sorry."

"Forget it. I have. It's in the past. The past is dead. We should erase it and everything that made it happen. Focus on the future, I say." Nash flipped open the bun on Ben's plate, and stuffed the portobello mushroom patty in his mouth. "Looks like your kids could use a few lessons about eating their vegetables," he said.

* * *

Jen and Ben each took a turn sitting on the second metal chair in the living room but it was so hard and cold they returned to the bare floor to watch the movie. The movie was okay, and not really scary. Mostly it was silly. There was this nerdy character named Seymour who had to feed a plant named Audrey Two. The problem was that the Audrey Two needed blood to grow, which was fine when it was little because just a few drops of blood did the trick.

But now that it was bigger than a man it needed to eat whole people.

A character named Mushnik, not suspecting a thing, walked in front of the ten foot tall Audrey Two who opened her mouth, a big flower with teeth. And—

Stones yelped, "Watch out! Watch out! Oh no!" his eyes wide with fear.

CHOMP! Audrey Two devoured Mushnik.

"Wait," Ben said, confused, "this isn't scary. Is it?"

"That plant looks like a cartoon puppet," Jen agreed.

"Evil! Plants are evil!" Stones yelled at the television.

"How can they be evil? Plants don't have brains," said Ben.

"You don't have a brain," Stones fired back, grabbing Ben's hair.

"Leave him alone!" Jen went for Stones's throat. He released Ben to deal with her. Stones had blocked her arm before she made contact but Jen continued pressing toward Stones until her face was just inches away from his.

"What's it gonna take for you to stop being such a butt-head?!" Jen said through her teeth.

Stones shot back, "What's it gonna take for you to dress like a girl?"

Jen went nuts, flailing with her free arm until she had a grip on Stones's shirt. Ben moved in to pull them apart and the three of them became a snarl of yanking limbs that hit a wall, rolled into the kitchen, then bounced off the refrigerator out the open door and into the back yard. By the time they were outside Jen was on Stones's back clambering toward his neck. Ben's legs were wrapped around Stones's ankles. To the grown-ups they looked like they were horsing around and having fun.

"Hey kids!" Ross sounded excited.

The kids unhooked themselves from one another, said nothing and tried to act normal.

"You guys will never guess what Nash and Stones are doing this summer," Sylvanna said.

Nash tapped his own chest with a turnip. "Head cook for Camp Triple-Bar, right here," Nash said. He then pointed the turnip at Stones, "with my kitchen assistant, Mr. Stones."

Jen said nothing. Ben said nothing.

Nash's smile dilated to a full blaze, "This summer you two will learn to eat right!"

Stones whispered, his lips unmoving, "You guys are gonna die."

HANDMADE

Every kid reaches a point where they start to take matters into their own hands.

Jen got into bed that night exhausted from two days' worth of being shoved and shaken. After lights out she looked through the front window and its emptiness sank her, so she turned to their other window, which faced the back. She hadn't taken in the view through the back window in a long time. The moon illuminated a large oak tree that grew in a neighbor's yard, the oak taller than everything around it except the clouds rolling by as they changed shape with the force of breezes that also caused the oak's heavy, crooked branches to sway. Swaying oak trees weren't as calming as bamboo, especially in the dark.

She looked at her poster of Xena, the warrior princess on the wall above her bed. She picked up the bamboo stick she used as a sword, held it up to the ceiling.

"I have many skills."

"What?" Ben asked.

"I wish we had a big sister."

"Big brother would be better. Or a giant robot."

Jen liked the way her brother saw the world. A giant robot would be cool, especially if you controlled it.

"I wonder what it will be like to have a little kid in the house?" Jen wondered aloud.

"Noisy and smelly, I guess."

"Not as smelly as that food, if that was food. How are we going to make it through camp with Stones there and food that isn't food?"

"Maybe we'll starve to death before Stones gets a chance to kill us."

Ben was the only person who could say horrible things like that in a way that made Jen laugh. She scrunched up her pillow and lay on her side keeping the bamboo stick next to her on top of the blanket, holding onto it as she drifted off to sleep and fell into a dream.

Jen's hair tossed around her as she walked through a forest. The moon and clouds shone silver, and the trees, black silhouettes against the moonlight, stood unmoving until the breeze became a strong gust that sent their branches bouncing up and down. She stepped lightly, watchful, listening. Her wristband tightened around her forearm as she clutched a sword made of bamboo. Her hair covered her eyes, its moving black strands mixing with the black bouncing trees until she couldn't tell them apart. She stopped, cleared the hair from her eyes — and the trees were gone, all of them gone but one oak tree whose branches, pushed by a new gust of wind, moved in ever-widening arcs until they became arms and legs, gnarled and strong. The oak tree rose, as if it had been hunched and folded but now stood its full height, a towering giant. The giant turned, faced her, lifted its arms, one wielding a large, steel sword, the other a mega rifle, a cannon of destruction. The giant raised a leg and swung it forward, taking a huge step toward her. Jen whipped around to run and saw Ben standing there playing with a yo-yo as if none of this was happening. She grabbed him, pulled him with her as she ran and yelled, "We can make it!" Her heart pounded, the earth shook as the tree-giant's feet hit the ground with each step. She ran faster, pulling Ben. "We can make it. We can make it! We can make it!!!"

"We can make it!" she heard herself say as she woke up, her heart pounding, almost exploding. The oak tree outside the window stood where it always stood, its branches swaying gently. Her hand hurt; she was clutching the bamboo stick so tightly that she had to force her mind to tell her hand to let go. She looked at the bamboo. She looked at the almost completed *Gundam* robot model on Ben's desk.

"We can make it," she said.

She hopped out of bed, moved to Ben's side of the room and shook him.

"Ben, wake up."

Ben was a heavy sleeper. She shook him harder.

"Wake UP!"

* * *

"What in the world are you talking about?" Ben sounded a little irritated, which Jen understood because nobody likes to be shaken in the middle of the night then having a light shined directly in his eyes to be woken up.

"The big sister we want..."

"Big brother." Once Ben was awake his mind worked fast.

"OK, like the kid at the school yard, what's his name? Rudy? He whistled and *wham*, there he was, his older brother, right? We want that. Or like Xena. Xena would be perfect. But we can't have it like that..."

"Jen—"

"...so this will have to do." She held the bamboo stick toward him, with an outstretched arm, not like a sword but straight up and down, like a cross held before a vampire.

Had Jen snapped from the past two days of insults, bad news, losses, and the prospect of a month in the woods with a menace and only slime mold to eat? Their situation was pretty bad, Ben thought, very bad, but he couldn't see going crazy from it. On the other hand, Jen was different from him.

He spoke quietly. "Jen, are you...?" He paused when her left eyebrow arched, higher than it had ever been. Ben's eyes shifted back and forth between her eyebrow and the bamboo stick she held. He felt a little scared, but he asked his question. "Are you awake?"

It had only been about a minute since she had leapt from her bed. She knew that what she had seen was in a dream but she had forgotten that Ben wasn't actually in it with her, so she began to explain what the dream revealed to her a little more carefully, but still fast.

"Tonight, when we were over there, the way he looked when I pulled him off the bamboo saying I'd bring it back to life. He's afraid, Ben. He's afraid of plants."

"You had your hand around his throat."

"He's not afraid of me. That movie. It freaked him out and it wasn't even scary, it was funny."

"All his movies seemed like they were about monster plants," Ben recalled.

"But he hates scary movies."

"And he has to watch them because they're good for him? I don't get that."

"I don't either, but the point is, he's afraid of plants."

"Do you think that's why they cut the bamboo?"

"They killed it, Ben. They killed our bamboo. And we're going to bring it back, only this time it will be the big sister — or brother — we always wanted."

"From dead bamboo?" Ben said.

"We can make it." Jen said it emphatically, raising the bamboo stick, again wielding it as if against a vampire.

"Take this," she said. She handed it to him.

Ben looked confused, but he took the bamboo.

"It's just one stick," Ben said.

Jen walked into their closet. "There's a lot more across the street. Plus we have all these parts we can use."

Jen backed out of the closet. She held Bonesy's right and left arms by their wrists. "The legs are still in there."

"Jen, I don't want to say it but you're talking crazy."

"No. This all makes perfect sense. Stones is a nightmare bully, who is following us to camp. He's afraid of plants. They killed the bamboo because of him. We have to stand up for ourselves, and for the bamboo. We bring it back to life, scare the daylights out of him, and make it clear that it's here to protect us."

"And by 'bring it back to life' you mean make a puppet?"

"A life-sized one. At least as tall as he is. Something that we can control."

"Like with ropes," Ben said. An image flashed through his mind, "and pulleys."

"See, Ben, you're a genius at making things. You're just like Mom."

Ben felt very warm inside. "So, is this, like, the spine I'm holding?"

"It is if you say it is."

Ben was still worried about his sister. There was still something about her that seemed off-kilter. But what she'd been saying made sense, and he got her main idea. "He'll be so scared that he'll leave us alone at camp," Ben said.

"He'll be so scared he'll leave us alone for the rest of his life."

Ben stopped worrying. Jen was right. They had to do something about Stones, and it was obvious that Stones's father, the man who looked as if he were made of rocks and ate them for breakfast, wasn't the type to keep his son from being a bully.

Ben looked at the bamboo pole in his hand, then at Bonesy's arms, and began figuring out how to build this thing. Jen could see it in his eyes.

"We leave for camp in less than a week," Jen said, "so we have to get to him before then."

Ben had hoped to finish his *Gundam* robot model before leaving, but the idea of making a life-sized bamboo butt-kicker seemed like more fun. It would also keep him too busy to think about camp.

The next morning the kids were out of bed before their parents got up. They took Bonesy's arms and legs and the bamboo pole outside to a section of driveway that was never used. Their parents used the garage to store books, bolts of fabric, racks of clothes, and bins that contained everything you needed to make clothes. Most of the garage storage was for Sylvanna's work but there was also one wall for Dad's stuff that had a variety of ropes, climbing gear, and a workbench with tools on a panel and in drawers. Their father had given the kids permission to use any of the tools — they were all hand tools, nothing truly dangerous — and for years Mom had a couple of bins set aside with leftover fabric and other sewing items that the kids were free to use.

HANDMADE

Jen lifted the garage door open. Ben put the pole on the driveway, then placed Bonesy's arms off to either side of the pole, arms at the top, legs at the bottom.

"We need a pair of shoulders. I was thinking the bow," Ben said.

The bow had made it out with them when they escaped the assault on the bamboo. It was next to the stilts, which had also made it out. Jen brought the bow over and put it across the very top part of the pole, then Ben slid it down about six inches. "We'll need a little bit to stick out for the neck," he said. He moved the top of each arm closer to the ends of the bow.

"Ben! It already looks like it's going to work!" Jen grabbed Ben's arm and jumped up and down in a way she hadn't done since she was about seven.

"Yeah but the trick is going to be attaching everything," Ben said. This was a lesson Ben had picked up from talking to his mom. "When you draw something that you want to make," she'd said, "it's not that difficult because you're drawing. Everything fits because you can do anything you want with lines on a page. But when you place two pieces of fabric next to each other, that's when you have to face a much tougher problem. The hard part, the most difficult thing of all is to figure out how to stitch them together so that the two pieces become one thing, and that they move separately while staying together." Ben particularly remembered the part, "move separately while staying together," and felt that they were the most important words he would ever hear anyone say.

Ben had to figure out how to lash the bow to the pole and the arms to the bow, and keep those attachments flexible without falling apart, but also how to cover it all with bamboo in a way that looked.... He wasn't sure. He needed a picture. He liked instructions because following instructions was easy. But there were no instructions for building this thing.

Ben said, "I need to sketch a few ideas, make some drawings. Maybe you can go get some of the bamboo so I can mess around with it."

"OK," Jen said. Ben got a pencil and a pad of paper and began to sketch, filling pages until he had something that started to look like instructions, like the ones that came with the models he built. Close enough, anyway, to feel comfortable getting started.

It was still early, and a Sunday, so no one saw Jen pull stalks of bamboo from one of the bundles. It took a while because the bundle was bound up tightly. She had to yank hard to get the first couple of stalks out; she didn't want to hurt the bamboo any more than it already had been. After the first two they started to slip out more easily. She pulled five of them free and brought them back up the driveway.

"Should I do anything with these?" Jen asked.

"Yeah get the pruning clippers and cut all the small branches off until it's just a long pole."

Jen hadn't considered that they would need to wreck the bamboo even more in order to make this thing. The idea bothered her.

"You want me to cut it up?" she asked.

Ben saw that she looked upset. "Think of it like a haircut," he said to her. "Branches get trimmed all the time, it doesn't kill the plant. Not like, you know...." he trailed off, but Jen understood.

"I guess it's not the same as a chainsaw," she said.

Jen used the clippers on one stalk until she had a twelve-foot long pole. She held it from one end like a sword, or tried to. It was heavier than her wrist could support so she slid her hand along the pole until she found its balance point.

"I guess that's why they hold lances in the middle," Jen said. Thinking of warriors on horseback, she rotated the bamboo pole upright and rested its base on the grass next to the driveway, then wondered, if she pushed the bamboo back into the ground deep enough, would it just grow? But she knew it wouldn't.

She examined the trimmed branches and noticed that the branches themselves looked like smaller bamboo stalks, and that the twiggy branches that grew from those looked like even smaller bamboo stalks, as if maybe the bamboo would go on forever, but tinier and tinier.

She heard a crunching sound from across the street. She looked down the driveway and saw Stones jumping on the bundles of bamboo in his yard.

"I'm going across the street to start softening him up," she said.

Ben was so immersed in his drawing that he didn't look up. "What do you mean?"

"We have to make Stones think the bamboo is out to get him."

"That's a question I have," said Ben, concentrating on moving the pencil on the paper. "How can we make sure that it's us he's afraid of, and not just this, whatever-it-is thing we're making?"

Jen had thought about that. "Well," she said, "it's like this: The bamboo speaks to us, even now after they killed it, so we know that the bamboo isn't completely dead, and it's very, very, very mad. Like, murder mad. It wants our help to come back from the dead so it can live for revenge."

Ben looked up; Jen could see that he was blown away.

"Or something along those lines," Jen said.

"You sound crazy."

"Good." Jen marched down the driveway.

She stood on her sidewalk glaring across the street at Stones, who was stomping on a bamboo bundle in the front of his yard.

"You shouldn't have killed the bamboo," she said.

He looked at her briefly, sneered, hopped off the bamboo and started kicking it.

"It was our friend," Jen said.

Stones kept kicking it.

"We miss it," she said, "It talked to us. It soothed us. Like a mother."

Stones kicked the bamboo harder.

She raised her voice. "It still talks to us!"

Stones stopped kicking.

"It isn't actually dead." Jen said.

"You're crazy," he replied with a squint that made his nose look like a pig's.

"Last night," Jen said, her voice calmer, but deeper, "Last night the bamboo told me something strange."

"Liar." Stones gave the bamboo a swift kick.

Jen noticed that the middle of his forehead turned upward, the same look that flashed across his face yesterday. He was worried.

"The bamboo said," she made her voice sound as raspy as possible, "'We are hungry— we must return— we will return to eat the one responsible— guide us to him. Who killed us?'" She made every "s" hiss like a snake.

Stones stepped into the street and crossed over to Jen, his arms rigid at his sides, his fists clenched.

Jen stayed put as he approached.

"No they didn't!" Stones stopped about six inches away and leaned in until he was hovering over her. She riveted her gaze at his grey, colorless eyes. She didn't blink.

In her own whispering voice she said, "We haven't told them yet, because they sound so upset that we don't want them to think we had anything to do with it. We just need a little more time to make sure they trust us. We know what really happened. We know it was you."

One of Stones's eyes twitched.

She went on, "They make these ticking sounds when they talk. It's a little creepy. Behind their words there's like this..." she showed her teeth and clacked them fast and loud, *clack-clack-clack-clack*, and kept it up until Stones had to look away from her unblinking eyes.

Stones spat on the ground at her feet. "You're disturbed," he said, then turned around and walked back toward his house.

"And then they said something that sounded like, 'FEED ME!'" Jen shouted.

Stones scurried through his front door and slammed it shut.

Jen's heart was pounding so hard she could hear it in her ears.

* * *

They were out of bed early again the following day. Jen snatched five more bamboo stalks from across the street and began trimming them. Ben had got a lot done yesterday. He asked his father if he could have one of the coils of cord hanging on the wall in the garage, a cord one-eighth-inch thick, capable of stretching a little and very strong.

"No problem," his father had said. So Ben cut the cord into several lengths and used it to lash the bow to the central pole and the top of each arm to either end of the bow. His father had taught him how to wrap two sticks together in a figure-eight crisscross pattern. He called it, "sewing for trees". Mom, of course, taught Ben everything he knew about knots, which was quite a lot.

When he got to the problem of how to attach the legs he had a clever idea about making the hips. He took one of their old soccer balls, cut slits in it wide enough to slip it over the bottom of the pole and lashed it on. Without air in it, the ball was pinched where he attached it tightly to the pole.

"This is the pelvis," Ben told Jen. Both kids knew the names of the bones because their father taught anthropology at the community college and his specialty was bone structure. Ben understood that any pelvis had to handle weight and pressure, and, because it didn't seem possible to make a real spine with real flexibility, Ben knew he needed this pelvis to handle twisting and tilting. He had seen enough monster movies to know that twisting and tilting were essential to create scary movements.

Ben punctured two more holes in the soccer ball, one on each side, lashed the top of each leg to the pelvis threading through the holes. He used long lengths of cord so he could pull the cord ends through the bottom slit and continue to lash around the middle, where the ball was attached to the pole. It was a little complicated, but it worked.

He lifted up his skeleton by the spine-pole and rested Bonesy's feet on the ground. The whole thing stayed together as he moved the pole up and down and twisted it left and right. The knees bent, the arms waggled. Its shoulders stood a little taller than the tops of their heads. Of course, it didn't have a head of its own. Not yet.

"Wow," Jen said. "That is so cool. I love it!" then added, "Bonesy! You're back."

"Bonesy Two," Ben said. "But it's just the insides. No one will see this part. I'm going to start attaching bamboo to it today. We have to...." Ben hesitated. He leaned the spine-pole against the garage, and Bonesy Two was able to sit upright all by itself.

HANDMADE

Ben picked up his sketchbook and showed Jen the drawing he liked best. The arms, legs and chest were made of short lengths of bamboo bundles. Each bundle looked like a bunch of chopsticks held together.

"We need to use the poles that you cleaned up, but they're a little long, so..." Ben didn't want to upset her. He lowered his voice. "...so I have to cut them up. With a saw."

Jen didn't say anything for a moment. She sighed, "Not just a haircut."

"A little more than just a haircut."

Jen was surprised she wasn't that bothered. She felt that what they were doing was creating something, not destroying. The destroying had already happened, and now they were filling a hole that had been left behind.

She looked down the driveway, across the street at the emptiness, and said, "I understand what we have to do."

"I'll handle it," Ben said. Jen was grateful.

"Can I take some of the twig parts?" She asked.

"Yeah of course, all you want. What for?"

"I have an idea for what I want to show Stones next. Today's lesson," Jen said.

She took a few dozen thin bamboo branches each two or three feet long, grabbed some rubber bands from the garage, and went to the front yard.

Jen stuck bamboo branches into the soft ground in a square pattern about three feet on each side, leaving one side open, the side facing Stones' house. She had placed each branch about an inch apart from each other. As she looked at the shrine she created she realized that she had made a miniature version of the bamboo yard that was destroyed.

She bundled several branches together with the rubber bands and pushed four bundles into the ground close to one another in the very middle of the shrine, deep enough so that the bamboo bundle stood upright and splayed out like four trees that had a common trunk.

She got on her knees before the altar, sat back on her heels, rested her hands on each thigh, and bowed her head, practicing what she wanted Stones to see and hear. But her mind drifted for a moment and she found herself whispering, almost silently, "Please come back." Then she saw Stones looking at her through his open bedroom window, and she began to chant, loud enough so that he could hear.

Together.
We rise. Together.
As one. Together.
We all. Together.
Return. Together.
Together...

She heard the pounding and crashing of drums. Stones, playing his drums at 8:30 in the morning. She grasped the remaining bamboo branches, about three or four in each hand, stood up and raised the branches high, sweeping her arms in long arcs, bending at the waist, touching the ground with the bamboo, swinging it high again. Staring right at Stones seated in his room across the street. Willing him to watch her ritual against his will.

She caught his eye. It was working.

Two minutes later Stones was outside, slamming his front door behind him. He walked to the bamboo bundles on his front yard and began stomping on them again.

At the crunching sounds Jen became aware of her hands, the feeling of holding the bamboo in them. She felt the Xena wristband tighten, and then a twinge, a pain almost, that began at her hands and went past her wrists into her arms.

"I am the bamboo!" The words just came right out of her mouth. She wondered if it was even she who had said them.

* * *

The next day Jen spent about two hours at the shrine she had created in her front yard, and Stones blasted away on his drums, never coming outside while she was there. When she wasn't at the shrine she was up the driveway helping Ben bundle and strap bamboo onto Bonesy Two, who was starting to look very much like the sketch her brother had made, only green, and softer because Ben was adding twigs and branches to the bundles. The leaves, with their slightly curvy shapes made the creature seem friendly to her, even though it was still without a head.

She kept an eye open for Stones, but he never came outside.

The day after that, Stones played the drums a lot, hitting them especially hard whenever Jen was out front praying at her altar.

She went back up the driveway to check on Ben's progress.

Ben said, "If he's acting like he's scared to come out of his house maybe we don't have to worry about him anymore."

"I doubt it," said Jen, "and besides, even if he's scared he's probably just scared of me because I've been acting all weird out there. He could still think it's fine to mess with you."

Ben hadn't thought of that.

Jen said, "Are you worried that Bonesy Two isn't going to work?"

"Well, I'm sure it's going to work, you know, as a puppet thing."

"But you're not sure if it'll mess with his mind?"

"Is that what we're doing?" Ben said.

"Kind of." Jen didn't hesitate. "Actually, it definitely is, but it's for a good reason. Plus, it's not like we're actually hurting him."

But there was a part of Jen that did want to see Stones actually hurt. Maybe not bleeding-to-death hurt, but hurt nonetheless. Maybe a few broken bones so he knows what it feels like. His legs would do. The thought surprised her because, although Stones had said mean things many times in the past, and had embarrassed her horribly with the Jender-Bender episode, he hadn't physically caused her any harm. Then she became aware that broken bones is exactly what the bamboo experienced, and that she could feel it, almost as if the bones were hers.

"Jen!" Ben said loudly.

"Huh?"

"I asked you *how* are we going to make sure he thinks this thing is real?" Ben said as he got to his feet and lifted the creature, his hand in its back like a ventriloquist holding a dummy, only this dummy was taller and wider, and hid Ben completely. Jen leapt back.

"What the what! It looks like it's standing by itself!" Jen said with a small yelp.

"Check this out." Holding onto the spine from the back Ben rocked his wrist back and forth rapidly, which caused the arms to turn with the body and waggle. The wrists flapped and the fingers curled.

"Holy cow! Are you controlling its hands and fingers?"

"Nah. They just sort of do that on their own," Ben said, "When I move it, I mean."

"Well, don't worry. He'll think it's alive," Jen said. There was no question in her mind about that, and she wanted to reassure Ben.

"The only thing left to do is to really make sure that Stones thinks that it's with us, that we and it are..." She searched for the words.

"Working together?" said Ben, completing her thought, but Jen corrected him.

"*Living* together, is more what he needs to think. Like it really is our big sister—"

"Big brother." Ben said from behind Bonesy Two.

"We'll settle that later." Jen said. "The point is, it's here for us."

"I better get working on its head," Ben said.

"Yeah," Jen said. "I've got to go figure out a way to push Stones to the edge. He's getting close but isn't quite there."

Ben marveled at how much his sister seemed to understand how to push someone to the edge of... something. He wasn't exactly sure what that edge was, but he was glad it wasn't him being pushed toward it.

Jen returned to the shrine in the front yard, where she meditated and chanted until she fell into a trance so deep that she could no longer hear the constant battering of Stones, on his drums, doing his best to drown her out.

* * *

It was Thursday night. Jen lay in bed, fretful. Saturday they would leave for camp, so they had to spring their bamboo creature on Stones tomorrow night. Nighttime was key, of course, because it's scarier. She had certain plans in mind of how it would go. They would wait until Stones was asleep, walk it across the street, carry flashlights, appear in the window....

"Hey," she had a question for Ben, whose eyes were also wide open. "How are you going to control it?"

"I screwed some hooks into the stilts that I'll run ropes through, and they'll be tied to the wrists and a couple of other places. Basically I'm going to walk the stilts with it tied to the front. I'll be hidden behind it."

"So that's how it'll walk. That's good stuff. And the head?"

"Finishing it tomorrow."

Jen's eyes stayed on Ben.

"What?" He asked.

"You're a good brother to have," Jen said.

"Thanks," Ben said. "You too. I mean, sister."

"Tomorrow, the bamboo returns." Jen tried to sound dramatic, but the way she said it sounded dorky and they both laughed.

"This thing needs a name," Jen said, just before she closed her eyes.

* * *

Jen hopped out of bed later than she had the past few days. It was nine and Ben wasn't in the room. She figured he must be outside working on the head, so she threw on some clothes including the new waffle-soled, hiking boots because her dad had said it would be a good idea to break them in for a day or two.

Out on the driveway she noticed that Ben had used a saw to separate the old toy bongo drums that had been connected by a wooden bridge, and was tying several rows of thin bamboo twigs around the smaller bongo.

"That is so cool," Jen said, "and the right amount of creepy. I'm going out front to pray at that shrine like I'm going to raise the dead, and get that boy's attention."

She walked down the driveway, stepped onto the lawn and felt her stomach drop. The shrine had been destroyed, its outer posts yanked and snapped, all the leaves stripped off and thrown everywhere, and the four intertwined tree trunks ripped apart from one another, and stomped flat.

Heat shot up from Jen's knees to her eyeballs. She raced back up the driveway. "I'm taking some of these," she told Ben, not waiting for a response before grabbing a handful of the twiggy lengths of bamboo Ben was attaching to the head as hair.

As she marched to the street she slid bamboo twigs up each sleeve of her long sleeved T-shirt so it looked like bamboo grew from her arms. She unsnapped the Xena wristband and then put it back on over the twigs around her wrist. It was a tight fit but it stayed on.

She knew Nash wasn't at home because his truck was gone, but the way she felt, it didn't matter. BAM BAM BAM! She hit the door loud so that Stones could hear it over the clatter and bang of his drums.

The drums stopped, the door opened. Stones laughed as soon as he saw her then shut the door in her face, or tried to, but Jen was ready for it and wedged her foot between the door and the threshold. Her new shoes had soles so thick that her toes barely felt the pressure of Stones pushing the door into them. The gap was just wide enough for the two of them to glare at one another.

She pointed to where the shrine had stood in her yard. "You're too late," she said, her voice held steady by rage. "The bamboo has already spoken." She shook her fist, shrouded by a spray of bamboo sprigs held tight to her arm by the band, and pointed at him.

"It trusts us! It protects us!"

Stones's arm flung out like a switchblade, his fingers raked at her wristband, popped the top snap and was about to yank it completely away but Jen acted fast, withdrawing her foot and slamming the door shut on Stones's arm like a bear trap.

He let go of the wristband. Jen backed away fast, clutching the band to make sure it stayed on her wrist. She was at the sidewalk, keeping her eyes on Stones as he swung the door wide open, stepped onto his porch and looked as if he were about to come after her. Jen began marching back toward Stones, and pointed directly at him, this time with both hands.

"They know it was you!" Jen shouted, pointing, not stopping. "They're coming back!"

Stones retreated into his house and kicked the door shut.

"They're coming back FOR YOU!" she yelled at the door.

Jen returned to her side of the street. She re-did the top snap of the band. Her heart was pounding everywhere, in her chest, her ears, her hands.

Ben, who had heard the door slam, stood up and watched Jen carefully as she steamed her way back up the driveway.

"What were you doing over there?" he asked, worried.

"Poking a bear with a stick," she said.

* * *

Sylvanna had been holed up in her workshop working around the clock for days, forcing herself to ignore the occasional bursts of noise outside, telling herself, like most parents, unless she heard actual screams or cries for help, to just let kids work out their own difficulties. Ross had been working long hours, too, mostly not at home, grading papers and getting ready to teach his summer courses. The deal between the parents was: Sylvanna would get them packed, and Ross would drive them to camp. She had put off packing for as long as she could, so, late that afternoon Sylvanna emerged from the workshop, called the kids inside so they could at least see what they would be taking with them, went to their bedroom and began filling duffel bags.

HANDMADE

Sylvanna held up something that looked like a blanket with a hole in the middle.

"What's that?" asked Jen?

"It's a poncho, you wear it like this." Sylvanna put the hole over Jen's head. The material hung all around her.

"I know you like clothes that fit comfortably. And it'll keep you warm after the sun sets."

"I like it. It's kind of like armor," Jen said.

The sound of Stones's drumming began.

"I am so glad that kid is going to camp. That racket he makes is slowing me down. Also, the baby kicks more when he plays, it's a constant boom-boom-crash from inside and out."

Just then a screech, metal on metal, came from across the street. Nash was loading the huge gas grill into his truck. Its legs were removed so it looked exactly like a coffin as he shoved it into the truck bed.

Jen and Ben watched Nash through their window and sighed. They each felt their mother's hands on their heads.

"It'll be OK, sweeties, I promise. They'll be working in the kitchen and you'll probably never see them except at meal times."

"Meal times?" Ben said. "You expect us to eat that guy's food?"

Sylvanna returned to folding shirts and didn't respond. Neither Jen nor Ben knew how long they could last eating just bread and water, but they believed they could make it for a month if they had to.

"Can we go outside, Mom?" Jen asked.

"I'll finish packing, no problem," Sylvanna said, realizing that making the kids watch her pack is boring and useless. Jen would wear the same thing for as long as she could get away with and Ben would probably be the only kid at camp who would ask when the next laundry day would be.

Ben and Jen returned to the driveway to finish preparing for the night's raid.

ALIVE

Sylvanna and Ross had noticed that the kids were building a life-sized puppet using Bonesy's limbs, bamboo and old toys. They were happy that Jen and Ben were the kind of siblings who worked well together. They were also the kind of parents who let their kids do their own thing without asking questions as long as it didn't seem dangerous. They had lectured the children enough when they were younger, had learned to trust Jen and Ben's judgment, and knew when to stay out of the way, allowing the kids to figure things out for themselves.

Ben attached the head. Jen couldn't see any details of the bongo drum underneath. Bamboo sprigs were wrapped around the bongo and stuck into its drumhead creating a leafy green crown, its tips spraying upward in a lush fountain.

"Wow." Jen ran her fingers through the bristly wisps of bamboo hair, hitting a snag.

"Wooden tangles," she said. "Wait. Tanglewood. That's it!"

"What's what?"

"Its name is Tanglewood."

"I like it," Ben said. He didn't go into whether it was a girl's name or a boy's name.

Tanglewood, no longer headless, now lay face down on the ground. Ben had tied long lengths of rope around the wrists, ankles and waist. He threaded the ropes through a series of eyehooks he had screwed into three different places on each stilt.

"Control ropes," Ben said, as he hopped onto the stilts with three ropes in each hand. He leaned back against the garage wall for support and hoisted Tanglewood toward him.

Jen gasped. This thing was real.

Ben and the stilts were completely hidden.

"Oh my God, Ben! Move the arms!"

Ben raised Tanglewood's left arm, then its right, up high and a little fast.

Tanglewood's right hand fell off.

"Careful!" Jen yelped.

"Oops," Ben said. "Bonesy's joints were pretty loose. I can fix that."

He dismounted from the stilts and fixed the hand back to the arm tying in a few extra pieces of bamboo like a splint. He got back on the stilts and raised Tanglewood again.

He pulled on the wrist control ropes. "Is the hand OK?" he asked.

"I think so. Hold on a second. Lower the hand." Jen stood before Tanglewood, whose hand arced downward and brushed through her hair, which tickled. She held Tanglewood's hand in hers, unsnapped the Xena wristband and attached it to Tanglewood's wrist. It fit perfectly.

She looked up at Tanglewood, whose head tilted down as if looking directly at her.

"This helps," she whispered to Tanglewood, patting the wristband. "Trust me."

* * *

That night the moon was full. By the time they went to bed clouds filled the sky. The whole family went to bed early. Mom, exhausted from working hard, growing a baby, and packing for camp, Dad, wanting a full night's sleep before getting up early for the long drive into the mountains to drop the kids off and return in one day. The kids, of course, just went through the motions of bedtime and had no intention of going to sleep.

Shortly after midnight they snuck outside. Five minutes later they were across the street maneuvering to the side of the house where Stones's bedroom had another window, this one facing a tall hedge that belonged to a neighbor. Jen, a few feet ahead of Ben and Tanglewood, held a big flashlight and shined it briefly into Stones' room. She saw him in his bed sleeping restlessly, chewing on his pillow.

Sheet lightning lit up the sky for a few seconds. It wasn't raining but it felt like it was about to start. Jen shone the flashlight beam directly on Stones's face and rapped on the window with her knuckles.

Stones startled awake. Jen turned the light onto her own face and stuck her tongue out at him as he leapt out of bed, grabbed his drumsticks took two steps to the window and flung it open.

Jen quickly stepped to the side as Ben slackened the control ropes, leaning Tanglewood into a menacing pose.

"I'm gonna pound you!" Stones blurted as he vaulted out his window, his feet hitting the ground.

Jen crouched low, pointing the flashlight upward at Tanglewood. She wanted Stones to see his attacker lit from below, exactly like it would be in a scary movie.

"They're here for you," Jen said as creepy as possible.

Stones turned. A bamboo figure loomed over him, bent and reaching, encircling Stones with arms made of sticks and leaves. Its fingers curled.

Jolts of panic shot inward from his eyeballs.

"Don't eat me!" Stones flailed. His arms jabbed wildly with the drumsticks gripped tightly in his hands. He kicked the plant monster and connected. The force of his kick sent Ben toppling off the stilts backwards. Ben had to let go of the control ropes as he counterbalanced by thrusting his hands away from his body shoving Tanglewood directly at Stones. Stones watched in horror as the creature's arms swam at him, lunging inward to eat him alive.

Stones shot his arms forward to stop the man-eating plant, skewering its chest with the drumsticks. His hands made contact with the bamboo, which accelerated his fear that he would be sucked into this thing. His whole body contracted. With a desperate burst Stones uncoiled violently and heaved the creature up and away, over the hedge into the neighbor's yard.

Jen heard a splash. Lightning strobed. Stones disappeared through his window back into his room where he knocked over a cymbal with a loud CRASH.

"What the hell is going on in there?!?" The roar of Nash's voice penetrated Stones's closed bedroom door, traveled out the window and mixed with thunder from above.

Jen and Ben bolted across the street as the sky opened up and rain fell in sheets.

* * *

ALIVE

Nobody saw this part:

Stones had heaved with everything he had, and a boy as wired and wiry as Stones can throw very hard. The cords that tied Tanglewood's poles and leaves to his sticks and hinges strained. Tanglewood cleared the hedge then fell into a shallow concrete pond where he floated for a few seconds before sinking to its bottom. A koi fish swam up to whatever it was that had fallen into her world. She nibbled at some of the finer sprigs of Tanglewood's hair wondering if it might be food. The only part of Tanglewood above the surface of the water was his right arm, because as he fell into the pond the control rope of that arm had snagged on the ragged edge of a tall, pointy metal sculpture.

Lightning struck the sculpture. Jagged tendrils traced down the rope, coiled around the wrist, hopped from snap to snap on the Xena wristband then disappeared down Tanglewood's arm into the pond.

The koi fish recoiled when a buzz stung her lips. She swam away hard as the bamboo that had fallen into her pond began to shake, and then sat up.

* * *

Meanwhile, on the other side of the hedge not fifteen feet away Nash stood outside Stones' door, not wanting to open it. He didn't like to be bugged after dark.

"What the hell is going on in there?" Nash repeated, saying every word as if it were a separate sentence.

Stones, a wreck underneath his covers, was desperately convincing himself that he just woke from a nightmare. He bellowed toward his door, "Nothing!"

He listened as Nash stepped away from the door without saying anything more. There was so much noise in his head. No, it was raining, and the window was wide open.

"The window!" Stones leapt from his bed to close it, it must have flown open, the reason for his nightmare. His hand gripped the handle ready to pull it shut when a bolt of lightning flashed and blinded him. A cracking, a whoosh and a thud as a branch from the neighbor's tree fell from above, scraped his arm and hit the ground just outside his window.

"Haaaalp!" Stones blasted with the urgency of a siren as he threw his whole body backward onto his drum kit, his heels and elbows striking the batter heads and boom ba-boom-BOOM!! went the tom-toms and kick drum. He tried to do a backstroke off his drums but it wasn't working; a pajama pant leg and one sleeve were caught on the hardware so the boom ba-boom-BOOM!! repeated as he struggled. It sounded a lot better than his usual playing.

* * *

Just before he sat up in the pond, Tanglewood had felt a vibration that began in his wrist, a tingling he knew was supposed to be there. He felt another movement, a steady beat. It was also familiar but it was an outside vibration not an inside one. Rain going tappity-tappity-tap.

Unfamiliar vibrations came next. Deep waves that came from outside but didn't touch him like the rain. The waves moved into him, bounced around and seemed to trigger something that spread everywhere from a middle place.

He placed his arms and legs at angles that matched the vibrations, the ones that went boom ba-boom-BOOM, and began to dance. The koi fish kicked her fins to get away from the bamboo that kept stomping in her pond.

ALIVE

Tanglewood wanted to get closer to the sounds that came from outside and bounced around. They came from over the hedge, so he left the pond and walked into the bushes.

* * *

Nash burst through Stones's door. Clutching Stones by the scruff of his pajamas, he pulled him off the drum kit. As he stood upright Stones, unsure which problem to address first, saw the creature that attacked him standing outside his window.

"Dad! That thing! The window!" he yelped, jabbing his arm at it over and over.

Nash had been so mad about the drumming he ignored the window and everything else. He saw, now, that the window was wide open, and, even worse, branches and leaves stuck through the opening into the house. He recognized the tree it had come from. That tree next door, the one reason he considered not buying this place.

"I knew that oak was going to start a war!"

Stones didn't know what Nash was talking about. He felt his father let go of his pajamas, then watched him reach out the window and grab the thing, gripping several pieces of it in his hands then mangling it, biting through pieces that were too flexible to snap off.

"Kill it!" Stones cheered. But then he noticed that the branches his father twisted and bit into were not bamboo.

Nash's head reverberated with the crunching noises from his teeth as he ground through oak twigs and growled out curses. So he didn't hear or see a bamboo figure emerge from the hedge.

* * *

As Tanglewood came through the hedge he didn't hear the boom ba-boom-boom any more. Instead he saw what appeared to be a boulder devouring branches off a tree. Tanglewood ran away from it as fast as he could.

The rain fell heavy as Tanglewood skittered into the street where a blare came at him, bright and sharp.

The man in the car reflexively leaned on his horn when he saw Tanglewood appear in his headlights, but to him Tanglewood looked like foliage that the storm was bringing down and blowing in the wind, so he ignored the scraping sound when his front end clipped it, and continued on his way without stopping.

The impact grazed Tanglewood's hip and sent him spinning. He hit something hard, flipped backward, then was on his back, moving his arms this way and that until something round hooked onto his fingers. He clutched it and felt it swing open. A familiar smell wafted over him. He moved his head closer to the smell and noticed that the rain had stopped tapping his head, so he moved his whole body in and let go.

CLANG. The top of Nash's long steel grill slammed shut.

The noise frightened Tanglewood terribly, but it stopped right away, and wherever he was now it was dry, warmer, and a lot quieter, so he curled up as tight as he could and paid attention to the steady tingling vibration, the one that came from inside himself and seemed as if it were returning from someplace faraway and familiar. But too much was new.

NAKED

The rain had ceased. The sun wasn't up but Nash was. He threw a few towels on the truck bed to soak up water that hadn't drained. It looked to him as if the wind had blown open the cover of the grill so he strapped a couple of bungee cords over it to make sure it stayed shut during the ride. He loaded the rest of his gear onto the truck: two large plastic bins, two duffel bags, a couple of backpacks, and a dirt bike, covering it all with a canvas tarp that he lashed tightly to hooks which surrounded the truck bed.

"Security," he muttered to himself, and went inside the house. He lifted Stones out of bed and loaded him into the passenger seat.

"Nightmares aren't real but they are warnings of things to come," he had assured Stones the night before. And there was much to be wary of. This house had cost a bundle, and he had lost his job at the restaurant, which is why he had taken the position as a cook for the camp. Otherwise, there was no way he would have wanted to be around that many trees. Falling branches weren't accidents; they were deliberate acts of aggression. That's why he was bringing both his chainsaws with him.

Nash turned the ignition. A burst of blue-brown smoke belched out the back as the diesel engine roared to life. Nash rolled down his window and took a big sniff as the exhaust cloud wafted around the truck.

"I love that smell," Nash said. He had converted the truck to bio-diesel a few months before, and ever since then Nash, who had always loved driving his truck, felt even happier knowing that every time he put his foot on the accelerator plants burned inside the machine.

When the engine had warmed up and settled into a steady pocketa-pocketa rhythm, Nash threw the truck in gear and stomped on the pedal.

* * *

Ross woke to the sound of Nash's truck pulling away. Neither he nor Sylvanna had expected that the head cook at the camp would be a dedicated vegetarian. They weren't sure if that meant vegetables would be the only food at the camp but they decided not to pursue it, trusting that the kids would make the best of it. After all, it would still be good food. The dinner Nash had prepared them was one of the tastiest he and Sylvanna had eaten in a long time. And it was obviously going to be good for the kids to learn to eat vegetables.

Jen and Ben deserved to have their favorite breakfast on the day they went to camp.

"Bacon and sausage and eggs on toast in fifteen minutes," Ross said, poking his head into their room about an hour later. He noticed that the blinds on the window were down. "Since when did you kids start closing the blinds?" he wondered aloud, expecting no answer from the sleepy heads.

NAKED

Actually, Jen was already awake and keeping her eyes closed in the way that you do when you don't want to get out of bed.

"You up?" she asked Ben.

"For like the past three hours," he groaned.

Jen was pretty sure that last night's mission worked. If she were Stones, she thought, she would have believed Tanglewood was real. She, herself, wanted to believe Tanglewood was real. She wanted to stay in bed and hold on to that thought. She let out a sigh.

Ben let out a sigh of his own, but for a different reason, an emptiness he felt whenever he had completed a project. If he had finished the *Gundam* model he would have felt it, but this emptiness was vaster than usual. Maybe because Tanglewood was the biggest thing he had ever built, or the most fun, or the most real.

He also felt dread.

"Camp," he said. "I guess nothing happened to make it go away."

A cold spasm roused Jen fully awake. She clasped her left hand over her right wrist.

"My wristband." She said.

In thirty seconds Jen was dressed and running across the street. She looked everywhere around the side of Stones' house for the wristband, then all around the yard, breathing deep with worry that she would see Tanglewood chopped into little pieces. But there was no evidence of Tanglewood at all. In fact, the bamboo bundles that had lain on the ground were gone, along with their scooped-up roots. She had been so preoccupied these past two days that she hadn't noticed they had been hauled away.

The yard was empty. She was surprised that the sight of no bamboo at all was even worse than the sight of the bamboo just lying there, dead in the dirt.

The nothingness felt like a hole in her chest.

She went back to the side of the house by Stones's window and forced herself to think through last night's events. It was difficult. Everything had happened fast. She closed her eyes to see her memory better, and replayed the key moments.

Stones leaps out his window.

She shines the flashlight on Tanglewood.

Stones's body becomes rigid with fear.

Stones kicks Ben off the stilts.

Tanglewood tumbles onto Stones.

Nash's voice booms.

She and Ben speed across the street back home.

But there was something else. Before Nash's voice sent them running, Tanglewood had flown into the air. Stones had thrown him.

Jen opened her eyes.

"The hedge," she said. She snaked her body through the hedge into the neighbor's yard, a place she had never been. She saw a pond with a fish in it. She wasn't sure if the metal thing by the pond was supposed to be art because it looked like junk but it sat on a small pedestal, like a sculpture. On the ground, next to the pedestal she saw a short length of rope a few inches long that had specks of color the same as the cord Ben had used to control Tanglewood, but mostly it looked burnt. She tried not to think about fire.

Jen's eyes darted around the yard, beyond the pond. Lots of plants, a big oak tree, but nothing that looked like bamboo.

Agitated, she went to the front door of the house and knocked, waited about ten seconds, then rang the doorbell.

An old man opened the door.

"You're lucky I get up early," he said, smiling.

"Sorry. I'm Jen from across the street. My brother and I we made a, like kind of a big kid out of bamboo but I don't know where it went and it's gone and I think it went over your hedge." She stopped herself from talking for a second, to breath and not sound so crazy. "Have you seen any bamboo in your yard?" she asked.

The old man said, "That oak dropped a bunch of branches but I already cleaned those up. Didn't see any bamboo, not since they chopped it all down next door. I was sorry to see it go."

* * *

Ben stood on their front porch looking for Jen. He saw her at Stones's house looking into its windows.

Ben trotted across the street to her.

"What are you doing? Dad's got breakfast waiting."

"My wristband. I think Stones must have found it and taken it."

As they walked back to their house Ben noticed that Jen's right forearm had a band of pale white skin several inches wide and all the way around in the exact shape of the Xena wristband.

"Is that your real color?" he said, pointing where the wristband used to be.

Jen covered her wrist. She felt naked.

PART TWO
WOODS

PASSAGE

A wave of exhaustion melted Ben from the inside as he sat in the back seat. His mind flickered, fragments from this morning in no particular order.

When they had pulled away from the house Jen had pointed out that all the bamboo had been hauled away. The yard across the street had been stripped bare, and he hadn't noticed until that moment. It was strange, he thought, when you don't actually see a thing disappear you can forget if it ever existed in the first place. His eyes grew heavy then popped open when he flashed on the image of saying good-bye to Mom. It wasn't easy. Neither Ben nor Jen had been away from home long enough that saying good-bye needed ten hugs, not that Ben minded hugs. The difficult part was the sound of Mom sniffing as a tear from her eye spread a pool of warmth into his cheek as she squeezed. Then he felt the baby kick, and that caused her to laugh a little. Ben knew Mom was going to miss him and Jen, but his only thought at that moment was whether he was going to be jealous of the baby.

"We're gonna be OK, Mom. You just get to work on those dresses. Make better clothes. And a baby," Ben had told her as he got in the car.

The next thing he knew Jen was jostling him saying, "You're drooling." Ben opened his eyes. He was in the back seat of the car, next to Jen.

"I think you were dreaming," Jen said.

"Yeah I guess so. Hey Dad," Ben said, "are we there yet?"

"Ask me again in about three and a half hours and I'll answer 'Yes'." Ross smiled at Ben in the rear-view mirror. Then Ben noticed that the stretch of highway they were on was very familiar. They had left home only ten minutes ago.

"Why do brains do that?" Ben said.

"Do what?" Jen said.

"Trick you. Like you forget what's really going on."

Jen mumbled. Ben saw that she was staring out her window at nothing in particular. Then he noticed that her left hand was wrapped around the white skin of her right wrist, squeezing it rhythmically.

"They probably have leather crafts at camp," Ben said. "I bet I could make you a new wristband no problem." He had watched his mom make a jacket out of leather. He knew that leather required a little extra patience and strength.

Jen said, "I want mine back."

Ben understood. He knew how much his sister got attached to things.

Jen, still staring in the distance out the window, unclasped her wrist, reached over to Ben, stuck her fingers into his hair and gave his scalp a gentle skritch, a feeling he had always loved. So did she. It was calming.

"Hey kids, mind if I turn the music up?" Dad said from the front.

"Sure," the kids answered. Dad's taste in music was a little weird but it made him happy, and because he was usually in a good mood anyway, music pushed him into a kind of goofiness that Jen and Ben found both funny and embarrassing. The car was a safe place for Dad to listen to his music.

"Check this out," Ben said to Jen as he reached into the backpack at his feet. Jen saw him pull out bamboo tied in small bundles, a doll about eight inches tall, a miniature Tanglewood.

"I call it Mini-T. I made it in case Stones needed a reminder.

Jen smiled. "Seeing that would definitely freak me out after what we put him through." She ran her fingers along the length of Mini-T. Her lips pursed together as she made a face that was both happy and sad.

"I didn't see Tanglewood anywhere when I went looking for my wristband. Or any part of him."

"Well, he's somewhere," Ben said. "Things don't just vanish. He's probably stuck on the top of that hedge."

Jen hadn't thought of that. Maybe, when they returned home, the hedge will have been replaced by bamboo. Maybe it would use the hedge to grow back and then it would spread and fill the yard, and then grow into Nash's house.

* * *

The entrance to Triple-Bar was dry and dusty, as was the drop-off area. Their car tires raised a dirt cloud that needed to drift past before Jen and Ben could see the cause of all the noise they heard when they got out of the car. The sound wasn't laughter, and it wasn't screaming, but some strange mix of the two. Just beyond a group of trees at the edge of the drop-off area was a field and on the field were dozens of kids, maybe hundreds, some younger some older, some hopping up and down, some running wildly in zig-zags. Jen noticed a few kids hiding behind trees, not hide-and-go-seek hiding, just plain hiding. Ben didn't see any grown-ups on the field, but a handful of teenagers were at the edge of the drop-off lot. None of them looked like they were having any fun. They all wore the same yellow T-shirts, and were either staring at a clipboard or plugging up one ear while using a walkie-talkie, their eyes squinting.

Ben saw a man emerge from the driver side of a car that had been in front of them on the entrance road. The man stomped around the front of the car and yanked open the rear passenger door. A boy inside the car stayed inside, immediately grabbed the handle and pulled the door shut. Then the father and boy began yelling at one another through the closed window.

Another car pulled into a space several yards away. Before it had come to a complete stop its rear door swung open and a girl hopped out then sprinted to the field shouting a bunch of names over and over, her arms waving like a windmill. The girl's mother stepped out of the car and laughed.

"Whew! Finally! All year long all I hear is 'When do I go to camp? When do I go to camp?' Hallelujah the day has come! Peace and quiet for a whole month. Am I right?" The woman said it to Ross, who smiled politely, and said, "It's our first time."

The woman looked at Jen and Ben, and blurted, "Well lucky you!" By that time she had pulled a duffel bag from the back seat and dropped it onto the dirt next to the car. Then she got back into her car and began to drive off.

"Whoa, wait!" Ross shouted at the woman. "You shouldn't leave the bag there and then just leave."

"That's what they prefer, here." The woman said, happily, "It creates less of a scene. There are tags on the duffel bags, they always sort it out. Have fun!" She drove away, disappearing into a cloud of dust.

After an awkward silence Dad stretched his arms and said, "Wow! These trees are beautiful, aren't they, kids?"

"Nice try, Dad," Jen said.

Ross opened the trunk, removed the duffel bags then crouched down to be at eye-level with Jen and Ben, who gave one another a look that said, "Uh oh, Dad's going to say something."

And he did. "Listen you two, I know I look on the bright side to the point where you think I'm just a goofball but everything is going to be OK. However uncomfortable you are now, it won't last long. I'm sure that woman is right, they've got everything here under control, and even if they don't all the time I have complete confidence in each of you. You're both really careful and you've always been great about watching out for each other."

Jen and Ben rushed in to give their Dad a big hug, partially because they loved him but also to get him to stop talking.

Then, in a whisper, their father said, "Mom and I have a small present for you." He pulled two blue plastic grocery bags from the trunk. He held them open just a bit so the kids could see that inside each was a jumbo package of beef jerky, the three-pounder.

"Keep this on the down-low, OK, kids. I have a feeling meat has a very short life span around here if anyone finds out about it."

The three of them hugged tightly.

* * *

The camp's kitchen lived off the dining hall, which was its own building — Triple-Bar's largest because it had to hold everyone at once. Most of the dining hall was a giant room filled with picnic tables, the kind that had benches attached on either side. The cafeteria line was off to one side and behind that lay the kitchen itself.

When Nash first entered the kitchen he was happy to see it had lots of counter space available for chopping. He went from machine to machine hitting buttons to make sure that they worked. The camp had a couple hundred kids in each session so cooking for that many required industrial-sized equipment. There was a mixer so big that it sat on the floor, and its bowl was large enough for two kids to curl up inside. A food processor the size of a laundry basket sat on one of the prep tables. Two large ovens were installed in a wall; next to these, two stove tops — one with gas burners and another whose top was one, long griddle. Everything was stainless steel, including the drawers. Nash pulled them all open to check out their contents. When he found the knife drawers — there were three — he removed all the knives to inspect each one. As he expected they all needed sharpening. Nash liked to sharpen knives.

Nash then opened the ovens, ran his finger along the sides and sniffed the blackened gunk. It smelled like burnt beef and chicken. He had brought his own grill with him because he wasn't sure if the ovens would be usable even after a good scrubbing, which would be Stones's first task.

"Stones!" Nash called out. "Time to get to work."

After a minute Stones entered the kitchen through the side door.

"Where were you?" Nash asked.

"Just outside, pulling the canvas off the truck bed like you told me."

* * *

Tanglewood was in the truck bed. Actually, inside the grill that was on the truck bed. He had been curled up in it ever since he had climbed in to escape, well, many things that he wasn't sure of. But they were bad. During the hours he had been inside the grill he had put himself into a kind of trance that felt better because of its stillness. But now that he was fully alert it felt uncomfortable to stay in one place.

He also felt something was missing, something he had always needed, a thing that was yellow and bright. This place was black, which was good for a while but no longer felt OK. He extended his arms, his hands touched a lid at the top of the blackness and his fingers felt warmth radiating through it, so he kept extending his arms. A crack opened up and light poured in.

Tanglewood hopped out of the grill. Whatever he had landed on was pleasantly soft. He scrunched his toes into the surface and remembered dirt. Then he felt something caress him all over, another softness he knew well — the breeze. He turned into it, and moved toward where it seemed to come from, and very soon he was next to a thing that was like him, but not. He touched it. It was big, it didn't move, but it had a nice vibration going through it, just a small one, so he pressed his body close to feel it better, which felt good, but he wished it could press back into him. Why couldn't it?

If anyone had seen this — and no one did — they might have said, "Is that a bamboo boy hugging a tree?" although the idea of such a thing was so ridiculous they would have said it as a joke, thinking that their eyes were playing tricks on them.

* * *

The afternoon was awkward. The counselors working check-in, distracted and busy, simply told Jen and Ben which cabins they were assigned to. To their surprise they were in different cabins, a fact that seemed obvious afterwards because everything was separated along boy-girl lines. But Jen and Ben had always shared a bedroom so this was the first time that they wouldn't, and it bothered both of them. Each had assumed they would be in the same cabin even if they were sharing it with kids they didn't know.

"We didn't think that through," Ben said.

"Yeah, well, nobody told us," Jen said.

The girls' and boys' cabins were on opposite sides of the camp, a distance that seemed like a long way. In his mind Ben tried to guess how far apart they would be based on distances he understood. Was it like down the street, or one block away, or two blocks? Looking at it he couldn't tell because all he could see were dirt paths and trees.

When they separated, each hiding a grocery bag of secret beef jerky under a jacket, both Jen and Ben were hit by waves of loneliness.

Jen arrived at her cabin. It looked more like a tent in the shape of cabin instead of what she expected from the word "cabin," which was supposed to be made of wood or logs. The walls of this cabin were canvas, and instead of a door there was a slit, like where curtains meet in the middle. She pushed her way through the opening and immediately noticed that it was very dark inside. She stumbled into something, swore, and said, "Hello?" No one answered. She parted the cabin's entrance slit to let some light in, peered around and saw several cots. Each had a duffel bag on it. Hers was on a cot in the middle. She memorized the path to the cot before letting the slit shut, took three steps forward, two to the left, let the grocery bag with the beef jerky drop from the bottom of her jacket onto her bed. She groped at the bag in the darkness and tore open the top. She needed something comforting and a piece of beef jerky would have to do. She stuffed a slice of jerky into her mouth, crammed the open package back in the grocery bag, rolled it up, shoved it under her duffel then got out of there because the cabin creeped her out. Maybe it wouldn't be so bad with people in it, or with a light on, or a window open, if it even had a window.

She had no success starting a conversation with a group of girls as she wandered back to the central area, which was annoying because as she approached them she forced herself to gulp down the wad of jerky before sucking out all its flavor.

She saw a counselor whose eyes stayed fixated on her cell phone as Jen walked up. Jen yanked the counselor's yellow T-shirt.

"Who's in charge?" Jen asked.

"Ha ha ha," the counselor laughed. It wasn't a mean laugh, and Jen wasn't sure what was funny, so she pretended she got whatever the joke was by laughing, too. But it sounded forced.

"What's so funny, kid?" the counselor said, her eyes still glued to the phone.

"Nothing," Jen said. "What am I supposed to do?"

"Just hang out on the field for now," the counselor pointed. Her walkie-talkie squawked, the voice on the other end — a teen-aged boy's — sounded stressed out. The counselor marched away muttering something about needing a break.

Jen went to the field, which was even more chaotic close up than it seemed from the drop-off lot. She had to block a soccer ball from hitting her in the head. A frisbee landed nearby so she trotted to it but another kid swooped in, grabbed it, flung it to someone on another part of the field, then ran away.

A lot of kids were in groups talking rapidly, as if they already knew each other, which Jen figured they probably did. She tried saying "Hey," to a couple of kids who were by themselves but every one avoided eye contact and walked away like they had no idea what to say back, or, worse, didn't want to talk to her.

Jen leaned against a tree, watching the goings on around her without participating in any of it. For the first time ever she felt like nobody knew her. In her experience Ben was always there, or soon would be. Something about this situation made it feel as if he wasn't close by. She worried if Ben would forget about her. "What's wrong with me?" Jen thought to herself. Then she felt needles and pins in her fingers, and realized that she was squeezing her right wrist so tight that her hand had gone numb.

"This sucks," Jen said out loud.

SECRET

Clanging pierced the air, metal against metal but much harsher than a bell. It made Jen cringe.

A voice descended from the tree she leaned against. "Everyone into the dining commons! First camp meeting!" The voice, a woman's and a little too cheery, squawked from a loudspeaker mounted on the tree, ten feet above Jen's head.

She followed a throng of kids along the edge of the field toward a building that she hadn't seen yet. It was much bigger than the multi-purpose building at her school but made of wood. It had windows, which Jen took as a good sign. Off to the side, near the back, was a porch where Nash stood hitting a rusty iron triangle with a hammer, the source of the clanging.

Once inside the building kids streamed to different tables, most of them rushing as if they knew where to go. This room had more tables than Jen had ever seen in one place. She had no idea where to sit.

"Take your seats quickly, everyone. Your cabin number is your table number," the too-cheerful voice said, now amplified by a speaker not as grating as the one strapped to the tree, but still, too loud.

Jen slithered through the sea of kids until she found a table with a placard on it that said "16". She sat. All the chatter and bustling in the room collected and bounced, creating a noise that sounded like a truckload of marbles falling on concrete. More than ever Jen wanted to be alone in a quiet place.

She did her best to tune out the sound by concentrating on what she could see, scanning the room looking for Ben.

Somebody was tugging at her jacket.

"My name is Froggy," a weird voice said. It sounded like it came from a cat Jen had seen in a cartoon.

Jen turned to her right and saw a girl with eyes the size of teacups.

Froggy, who had seen the look on Jen's face on the faces of others many times before, said what she usually did. "I was four years old before they knew I couldn't see that good. These glasses work."

They sure do, Jen thought, but didn't say anything. She really wanted to keep searching for Ben. The girl who called herself Froggy smiled at her. She had no front teeth. The huge gap in her mouth hit Jen with the same impact as her magnified eyes. And it explained why she spoke with a very obvious lisp.

Before Jen could figure out what to say the cheerful sounding woman's voice took over the room.

"Welcome everybody to Camp Triple-Bar — Whee-Hoo!"

The woman stood at a lectern clutching a microphone. The fist holding the mike shot into the air. As she brought the microphone back to her mouth it generated a high-pitched screech that lasted for a few seconds. Whether intended or not the screeching silenced the roomful of kids.

"I'm your camp director, Ginger Berger and WOW — I am so excited! We'll have day hikes and night hikes, soccer and swimming, arts and crafts, and after we pass a safety inspection in about a week or so we'll officially reopen our archery range. We'll spend our evenings sitting around roaring camp fires telling scary ghost stories..."

Jen thought of Stones. None of the stories told at this place could possibly scare him as much as she and Ben had the night before.

Ginger Berger kept talking but Jen tuned out her words as she noticed how odd the woman looked. The way she dressed....

At another table Ben was having the same thought. He smiled, imagining the comments his Mom would make if she were sitting next to him right now. "What in the world was she thinking when she bought *that*?" A comment that would have made Ben giggle because he would have known what she was getting at. Ginger Berger wasn't fat but she was, well, round in a lot of places. She wore a tracksuit top and bottom that were a little too small. Ben heard his mother's voice in his head, "Whatever you're wearing you never want to bulge. And what is going on with those colors?" Ginger Berger's running suit was a very dark red with white stripes running up and down the sides. Her bulges pushed the stripes into S-shaped curves. Ginger Berger looked exactly like a giant slice of bacon.

"As many of you remember," Ginger's speech continued, "last summer we had a little bit of a problem with the food so after many conversations with some of your parents we decided that this year we are going to have a much healthier kitchen."

Back at her table Jen heard a loud, lisping whisper in her ear, "It was food poisoning. I think it was the chicken, but it happened twice, once with some kind of meat, but not to me. I don't eat animals."

Jen didn't want to be totally rude and ignore the bug-eyed Froggy girl entirely, so she gave her a quick, polite smile, but she could tell by the way her face felt that it was probably more of a sneer.

Ginger kept talking. "So let me introduce the newest addition to our family, our new cook — honey, what is your name?"

"Nash, but call me 'Chef' in front of them," Nash said.

"Well come up and say a little bit about what's cooking, Chef!"

Jen and Ben knew exactly what would be cooking.

Nash took the microphone from Ginger, peered into the crowd of kids and began talking very seriously, almost scolding. His voice boomed.

"Cows are slow. Pigs are filthy. Fish are slippery and chickens are chicken! You are what you eat. At this camp you will become powerful because vegetables— are—" Nash pounded his fist onto the lectern, "POWER."

Ginger began fanning herself rapidly with one hand.

The room became so quiet that a meek voice could be heard asking the question that was probably on everyone's mind. "What about hot dogs?"

"No meat in my house! This entire camp is MY HOUSE. If anyone is harboring meat NOW is the time to confess. I've already done a random search through several cabins and sniffed out this."

Nash held up a jumbo bag of beef jerky. Jen's heart stopped. Across the room Ben's heart stopped. Then he looked around quickly, his eyes darting from table to table. He knew the bag Nash held must be Jen's because he could see that it was open, and he hadn't opened his yet. There she was, about six tables away. They made eye contact.

Jen, wide-eyed, saw Ben shaking his head "no" as he pointed at himself, then he pointed at her. Jen nodded, very slowly.

"Unless you love peeling potatoes and scraping dishes so much that you want a whole week of kitchen duty for yourself AND your cabin mates I better not find any more," Nash said. Then he added, "And speaking of kitchen duty, Cabin One is up first. Report back here in one hour."

The placard at Ben's table had the number "1" on it.

Nash's face cracked into the mean smile that Jen and Ben had already experienced up-close, which made its ugliness that much easier to sense from a distance. Nash pulled a big carrot out of a pocket and stuck it between his back teeth.

"Now who here loves carrots?" he said, crunching down.

Ginger Berger raised her hand and blurted, "Ooh. Me!"

TREES

The dining hall was dismissed. Jen didn't stick around to meet her cabin mates or find out if there was a specific counselor she needed to report to. She leapt up from her seat and moved as quickly as possible to Ben, who was doing the same thing, working his way toward her. They met in the middle and then headed to an unused door in a dark corner of the dining hall.

Once outside Ben sped up, pulling Jen toward a nearby dirt road. They stopped when they were behind some trees.

"So was that yours, that bag?" Ben said.

"I'm pretty sure. That guy is all kinds of wacko."

"I better get mine out of my cabin, and get rid of it, like now."

"Well don't throw it away!"

"Then what should we do with it?"

"Hide it."

"Where?"

"Not anywhere around here." Jen stomped her foot into the dirt. "This is stupid! We could probably disappear right now and no one would notice, but a bag of beef jerky gets tracked down like it's a bomb."

She took a deep breath and exhaled slowly through her nose.

"There. We have to hide it in there," Jen said.

"That's into the woods," Ben said.

Jen nodded. "They probably won't look that far."

* * *

Jen stayed with Ben as he made his way back to his cabin. They walked just behind the trees that ran along the edge of the dirt road.

"I'm pretty sure this road circles the entire camp," Ben told her as they walked.

"How do you know that?" Jen asked.

"I wandered along a bunch of paths trying to figure this place out."

"Well I sure couldn't get anyone to explain anything to me about what's going on here."

"Me neither. That's why I started wandering around," Ben said.

They arrived at the edge of Boys Town, which is what Ben had heard a counselor call the cluster of cabins where the boys lived. Jen stayed behind a tree while Ben sped into the cabin marked number one. He returned a minute later with the grocery bag hidden under his jacket.

"No one saw me."

"Let's go this way," Jen began walking.

"Why that way?"

"We passed a place where the woods sloped up. If we go up it will be easier to find our way back. All we'll have to do is go down, which is simple to remember," Jen said.

Ben, who felt complete confidence working within the space his hands could reach, was glad that Jen had the same confidence moving through larger spaces, even ones she hadn't seen yet. Ben knew that if there hadn't been paths to follow around the camp he wouldn't have explored at all. He admired his sister because she didn't seem to need a path. As the up slope became steeper Ben bent forward, stretching his hands to be closer to the ground.

Jen said, "Here, hand me the bag," which Ben did right away. He was glad to have both hands free to grip rocks or branches. The steep slope gave him a queasy sense that he could slide or tip over backwards at any moment.

Up the slope they trudged. Ben looked behind him from time to time to make sure he could still see or hear the camp below, and to reassure himself that they wouldn't lose track of the way back. Worst case, he kept telling himself, is that we scoot on our butts and let gravity guide us.

After a while the ground continued uphill but leveled out enough that Ben felt comfortable walking fully upright.

"How dumb is it that we have to hide a bag of meat in the woods?" Jen said.

"Maybe it would be easier if we just ate the vegetables," Ben said.

Jen turned to face Ben but continued to march up the slope, only backwards. "Look," she said, "at some point in our lives we'll have to eat vegetables because it seems like that's just the way things are. I don't know about you but I'm just not ready."

Ben nodded. He didn't feel ready either.

"Do you think we should bury the bag?" Ben said.

"Ugh," Jen said, "we don't want bugs to eat it."

"I mean there are animals out here, right? Like what about raccoons?" Ben said. "We could stash the bag under a rock. Do you think raccoons can lift up rocks?"

Jen hadn't gotten to these details yet, which made her think about all the things she didn't know. She came to a halt.

"God, I hate not knowing the rules," she sounded angry.

"Rule number one is: No Meat," Ben said.

"Not those kinds of made up rules! I mean the real rules, like the rules of all this." She swept her arm at the woods surrounding them.

Ben didn't think that trees had any rules at all.

The trees seemed to go on forever, as if the two of them had reached the edge of where people lived and if they kept going beyond this point they would never see another human being ever again, only trees and whatever lived with trees, or on them. Or, in them. Ben forced himself to think about something else because he could feel his imagination conjuring up weird and scary things.

He moved to the trunk of a nearby tree and poked it. "This is just a tree," Ben said, intending to sound reassuring, but his voice came out flat and distant. Jen watched the trees, scanning them for.... She did not know what, but she felt uncomfortable. There were a lot of trees.

"They're like a bunch of teeth sticking out of the ground," Jen said, "like the earth has teeth."

Ben reacted immediately. "Can we NOT explore your imagination right now?"

A breeze rustled the tops of the trees. An eagle's screech, somewhere up in the sky, caused Ben to twitch. Then something howled in the distance.

Jen scooted closer to Ben as he stood silently next to the tree trunk he had poked. Then something grabbed her hair.

"Aaaccckkk! Giant spiders!" Jen yelped.

TREES

Ben didn't have a chance to see what was going on because Jen was flailing her arms in a whipping, wheeling motion and hit Ben square in the face with the grocery bag.

Ben, stunned, fell to the ground. Jen was pulling at her own hair when a weight fell onto her back. She crumpled face-first into the dirt.

Ben, laid out flat, lifted his head against the tilt of the slope. Through his squinting eyes it looked like a branch had fallen on his sister. He rolled to his side, pushed himself to his feet and rushed to help her.

The branch stood up and took a step toward him. His vision was still blurred from the hit on the head so he knew what he saw was impossible, not just because the branch seemed to stand up but also because it looked like it had a head, and, even more impossible, the head looked like the one he'd made for Tanglewood. Ben forced his mind to get a grip and his eyes to focus.

It *was* Tanglewood.

Tanglewood reached a hand toward Ben's cheek. Ben was frozen in place. His lips were moving, but the only sound coming out of him was *"nagoggin-nagoggin-nagoggin."*

Meanwhile, Jen pushed herself up from the ground spitting leaves from her mouth while rubbing dirt from her eyes so she could open them. Everything was hard to make out but she was pretty sure it was Ben standing just a few feet in front of her, but there was also someone else next to him. That someone was reaching an arm toward Ben when a ray of sunlight bounced off an arm — two glints of light that she knew, she KNEW because she had seen those two glints many times reflecting off the two snaps on her Xena wristband.

"Damn you, Stones!" Jen yelled, and lunged at her wristband to claim it back from this horrible pig of a boy who was determined to keep haunting her and her brother and would not leave them alone.

As she reached to grab at the snaps another arm swung up and fingers seemed to stretch toward her face but did not actually touch her. She blinked several times, which cleared away most of the dirt that was left in her eyes. She saw a hand, made of bamboo, as was its arm, and both belonged to Tanglewood.

Jen stared, her body in the same frozen pose as Ben.

"Err-rrm. Buh," were the only sounds she could make, as Tanglewood reached his arm carefully to her, gently inserted his fingers into her hair, and skritched her scalp.

Seconds seemed to last much longer, minutes, at least, and during whatever time actually passed the ideas pulsing through Jen's and Ben's minds were impossible to pin down. But they shared this one thought: "Now is the time to wake up." But they didn't because they were already wide awake, and each spent what felt like an hour facing up to that fact, although it was only about ten seconds.

And during those same ten seconds, Tanglewood experienced both a sad memory and an excited feeling. He had emerged from the dark place (the grill on the truck) and then found the tall, stuck-into-the-ground beings (the trees) and they felt familiar because of some vibration that went through them. He pressed himself to one tree after another hoping to trade vibrations, but it never happened. It made him feel like something was missing, like he was too much all alone, which he did not like. After giving up on hugging the trees he pulled himself up onto a branch and focused on the sensations within him until he stopped feeling too much all alone. Then, they came toward him, two somebodies, and, whatever they were, they were definitely special because Tanglewood felt the back-and-forth feeling he had wanted from the trees but did not receive. Not only that, the two somebodies moved from place to place on their very own, just like he could. As they got closer he became more excited and was filled by a feeling that was the opposite of loneliness. They were like him, one just a bit more so than the other. So he reached out to that one, and when his hand made contact, the vibrations inside him turned into something entirely new, but not new. Something lost but now found.

The three beings stood, watching one another.

"Ben, what did you do?" Jen spoke.

"Whaddya mean what'd I do?"

"It moves by itself! How is it alive? How is it here?"

"I don't know!" Ben cried.

"You made it!"

"It was your idea to make it!"

During all this shouting Jen began gesturing wildly and moving her legs in a herky-jerky motion, hopping, sort of, but much less coordinated.

Tanglewood imitated Jen's movements. Tanglewood was having fun.

Jen yelped, "It's freaking me out!"

CLANG-a-LANG-a-LANG-a-LANG! The harsh sound pierced the air. The iron triangle by the kitchen, hit hard and repeatedly. Tanglewood felt like something was cutting into him.

"Kitchen duty! Prep team report! Cabin One, this means you!" Nash's booming voice was unmistakable to Jen and Ben.

Tanglewood felt all the goodness of the moment leave his body. The cutting clang and that voice, the same sound as the boulder he had felt rolling toward him the night before. He backed away, up the slope.

"We got potatoes to peel and squash to scoop out. Cabin One, let's go!" Nash belted out.

Tanglewood didn't want to leave, but his body forced him to run from that boulder sound. Up the slope and deeper into the woods he fled.

"Hey!" Jen shouted at Tanglewood as he disappeared behind the trees.

"I'm in Cabin One," Ben said, "That's me. I gotta go."

"I think— I think she was having fun. Do you think she was playing with us just now?" Jen said.

"She?"

"Tanglewood."

"She's a boy!"

"How do you know?"

"I—" Ben hit a wall inside his own head. Too many other questions pushed him into it, questions that seemed more unanswerable than whether Tanglewood was a boy or a girl.

The iron triangle clanged again.

"We have to go," Ben said, "We don't want them to think we're missing."

"You've got to go, I don't," Jen said, as she began walking swiftly toward the trees where Tanglewood had disappeared.

Ben grabbed her sleeve.

"You can't go up in there!" Ben wanted to sound stern, but his voice sounded more like pleading.

"Ben," Jen said, looking her brother in the eye, "She's got my wristband. Cover for me until I get back."

Jen took off up the slope. Before she disappeared behind the trees she turned to shout, "Don't forget our bag of meat!"

Ben picked up the grocery bag, and hurried down the slope, unsure whether he let Jen go because he trusted her, or because he was too afraid, either of the woods, or of what would happen if he didn't show up for kitchen duty, or both.

SUSPICION

Nash re-entered his kitchen after clanging and calling for kitchen duty. He plunked a head of cabbage on a cutting board that sat on a stainless steel prep table, and glared at it.

Something about the head of cabbage caused Nash to think, an activity he didn't like because it always led to an uncomfortable tightness in his chest. It was the shape of the cabbage that bothered him, a roundness that made it look like a real head, which made him think about brains. It was bad enough to be surrounded by people with thoughts and feelings of their own; how horrible it would be if a plant also had thoughts and feelings. In fact, Nash already believed that they did, and that the only strategic disadvantage plants had was that they had to be stuck into one place in the ground. If they could move around, Nash thought, that would be the end of everything.

The cabbage seemed to be judging him. Nash opened a drawer, took one of the long-bladed knives he had just sharpened and chopped the head of cabbage in half. No brains inside, Nash reassured himself, just leaves.

"Stupid cabbage," he muttered, then shouted, "Stones, prep the grill."

* * *

Stones was staring up at the tree tops on the back porch of the kitchen when he heard his father bark the order. He wore an apron that was ridiculously long. It looked like a maxi-skirt even when tied at the waist. Grabbing a wire brush, he popped open the grill and began scraping off burnt residue from the last time it was used. Back and forth, Stones stretched his arm to reach into the full depths of the grill, the cover tilted at an angle above his head when a twig that was snagged onto bolts inside the cover stuck into his hair. When he felt it jab, he shoved his fingers into his hair, spitting reflexively, thinking it was a bug, but it was a stick. No, it was bamboo.

Stones yelped, tossed the bamboo twig into the grill, slammed the cover shut and turned all the burners to "Ignite." All six of them ticked on, then BOOMF! The lid hopped as the enclosed gas inside lit up. Stones ran into the kitchen.

"Scraped clean and burning hot?" Nash asked Stones without looking up as the screen door slammed.

Stones said, "Yeah it's heating up," but nothing else.

Ben came stumbling out of the woods not far from the kitchen's back porch where the iron triangle hung and a stainless steel grill stood not far from a pickup truck, both of which he recognized. They made him think of home, a thought that Ben shut down as soon as he had it, because nothing about Nash and Stones should feel like home.

He walked directly to the porch, and when he was about twenty feet away he heard Nash's voice come through the screen door.

SUSPICION

"Dammit, Stones, you left the igniters on!" Nash said.

His voice shook Ben to full physical alert. On the way down the slope his mind had been racing so fast and in so many directions that he had lost all awareness of simple, obvious things, like the fact that he still held the grocery bag with beef jerky inside it. It was too late to put the bag somewhere specific, so he flung it away somewhere off to the side and behind him. He didn't watch where the bag went. The beef jerky landed in an open backpack inside an open bin on Nash's truck bed.

The kitchen's screen door swung open. Ben's eyes met Nash's. Ben felt like a character in a western movie, standing on a dirt road about to have a shoot-out with the bad guy. Only, he had no gun. Nash held a knife. He put the knife down on a wooden table next to the screen door.

"Ready to slice and dice, uh, it's Jen, right?"

Ben had no energy to comment so he said, simply, "I'm Ben."

"Well, get inside and help Stones with the peeling," Nash said. "Wear this." Nash took an apron off a hook that was just inside the screen door and handed it to Ben as he entered the kitchen.

* * *

Stones sat on an overturned bucket peeling turnips. Ben approached, said nothing, but cleared his throat a little. Stones glanced up, vaguely pointed to one of the prep tables and said, "Get a peeler. First drawer."

Ben got the peeler, sat on another upturned bucket across the pile of turnips.

The two boys sat there, in silence for the moment, glowering at the turnips in their own hands rather than at one another, scraping the woody outer layers off. Neither one of them liked the smell that filled the air.

The silence made Ben squirm, but it was broken soon enough. The unmistakable voice of Ginger Berger approached from somewhere outside the screen door. "Yoo Hoo, Mister Man, I think we need your help." She was talking to Nash who was fussing with the grill.

"How are you at chopping wood?" Ginger added before Nash had said anything.

The screen door creaked open, Nash poked his head into the kitchen. "Got an important job to do. Stones is in charge 'til I get back." Nash slammed his way out.

Ben and Stones continued to peel in turnip-smelly silence. Ben, more and more awkward with the silence, began having a conversation with himself, in his head. Part of Ben wanted to apologize to Stones, but he wasn't sure whether it was because he and Jen had scared him so badly, or whether the crazy thing Stones thought he saw may have not been so crazy. At least, the part about Tanglewood being alive wasn't crazy. But the idea of Tanglewood eating anybody, that was crazy. Wait a minute. If the "being alive" part wasn't crazy, what made him so sure that "Tanglewood eating somebody" was still crazy? Maybe that part is true, too.

Ben's thought was interrupted as he noticed a bamboo leaf stuck under a layer of Stones's hair. He reached over and snatched the leaf.

"Where did this come from?" Ben demanded as he held the leaf just inches from Stones's face.

Stones, stunned by the bamboo leaf more than by Ben's hand reaching into his hair, knocked the leaf away and pointed the vegetable peeler at Ben.

Ben suddenly remembered that he had Mini-T in his back pocket, keeping it on him just in case Stones ever needed a reminder of their awesome power. And now the look on Stones's face, an awful mixture of terror and anger, caused Ben to reach into his back pocket like a cowboy going for his pistol at the first sign of trouble — the action he imagined when Nash confronted him just minutes ago.

The effect on Stones was immediate. The miniature version of Tanglewood caused Stones to sink to his knees and cover his eyes like a vampire at dawn as daylight streams through his window.

"Please!" Stones yelped. "I didn't think it would still be alive! It wasn't my idea to cut it down, I didn't know they could come back! I don't want it to eat me!"

Ben felt a jolt go through him at the idea of Tanglewood eating a person, an image he had been pushing away just a minute ago. The image stayed with him this time.

"What?" Ben said.

"The bamboo was going to eat me, I don't want it to eat me!"

Ben needed to reassure himself. "That's not how plants behave!" But as soon as he said it, he realized that he wasn't sure anymore how plants behave. Not at all.

A moment later, Stones risked looking through his fingers to see if Ben was about to summon up something horrible with that miniature bamboo monster, but Ben was gone. The screen door slammed.

Ben bolted out the kitchen back into the woods. His long apron flapped against his legs as he pumped up the slope. He clutched the Mini-T in one hand and a vegetable peeler in the other. "Jen!" he cried out. "Jennnn!!"

ATTACHMENT

Jen huffed and puffed, wondering what on earth she was doing running blindly into the woods after a creature made of sticks. Although she was exerting herself, at the same time she was able to concentrate on complex thoughts, a weird detail about how her mind worked that she had noticed only recently. The tetherball game against Stones was the first time she had become aware of it. As the ball had whizzed by, whipping around the post first one way then the other, she wondered, "How can I keep track of where the ball is, and where I am, and then figure out where the ball will be and then move my arm that way and hit it?" Then she thought, "And how can I wonder about how I am doing it while I am actually doing it?" In the middle of all that brain activity she had won the game.

Now, as she drove herself uphill following glimpses of green, spiky bamboo that flashed in the gaps between tree trunks, dangling branches, and their countless leaves, Jen wondered if she was really going after Tanglewood just to recover her Xena wristband. She dodged around a fallen tree. No, that isn't the only reason, she decided, even though all day she'd felt that adjusting to camp would be a lot easier if only she had her wristband back on her arm. She didn't like feeling powerless. The whole day up to this point had made Jen feel invisible and irrelevant. Until she saw Tanglewood, alive, actually alive! It was if it were possible for her thoughts to become real just because she had them. Nothing could be more powerful than that.

The ground leveled out. She needed to catch her breath. She stopped to look around and saw that she was at the top. If she went too far in any direction other than exactly where she had come from, she could easily get lost. Getting lost in the woods was completely unacceptable. She was standing by a tree with a very wide trunk, wider than she was tall, and noted that the branch above her pointed back the way she had come. She memorized its shape and position.

"Tangle-wooood!" She called out, in frustration. "Come here!"

Silence, except for her own breathing. She gasped and turned as she felt a tap on her shoulder. Tanglewood's head was poking out from the other side of the big tree trunk, its fingers opening-closing the way really small children wave bye-bye. Jen lunged to grab Tanglewood's arm but Tanglewood snapped back and disappeared around the tree trunk. Jen darted the other way around the trunk to catch Tanglewood, but as soon as she was two feet away Tanglewood turned and ran the other way round the tree.

First left, then right, halfway around the tree then back again. It was annoying.

"Tanglewood, stop! STOP!" Jen's voice began to take on the pleading tone of a six-year-old being teased. "Quit it, Tanglewood!" she begged after the eighth time going left, or right. She had lost track.

"Dang, dang DANG." Jen gave up trying to catch Tanglewood; she slumped against the tree trunk, and slid to the ground.

"I just want to talk," she groaned, feeling defeated. She heard a light, scraping sound to her left. Tanglewood sidled, slid his backside down the tree trunk and sat in the dirt next to Jen.

"Are you a girl?" Jen asked. "Because I think you're a girl, or I want you to be a girl, but you sure act more like a boy, so maybe Ben is right about that."

Tanglewood cocked his head to one side and extended his fingers toward Jen's hair. Jen recoiled, putting her hand up but spoke gently. "OK— but just be careful. Your fingers are pokey like a porcupine."

Tanglewood's attention suddenly shifted to Jen's forearm, now that it extended out of her jacket sleeve. Tanglewood placed his wrist alongside hers, lining up his wristband with the white skin on hers, then traced around both with his finger.

"I—" Jen hesitated. She was about to say, "I want that back," but a horrible thought stopped her. What if the wristband was keeping Tanglewood alive? She thought of the moment when, in their driveway, Tanglewood's hand had popped off. When the hand had fallen on the concrete she had that same queasy feeling as when she had broken her arm when she was five, which was scary. She had bled and thought she was going to die. Kind of silly because it was just a broken bone, but broken bones seemed like they would be lethal to Tanglewood. Now that Tanglewood was alive the last thing she wanted was for Tanglewood to not be alive.

"Never mind," Jen said. Then she had an overwhelming desire to run her fingers through Tanglewood's wispy bamboo hair. She slowly put her hand near Tanglewood's hair, then into it. The wispy tickles between her fingers made her feel as if she were in the back yard across the street, playing, with Ben, safe like birds inside their bamboo nest. The memory was happy and sad.

"You can touch my hair if you like," Jen said, and Tanglewood did just that. He put his fingers into Jen's hair, slowly, just as she had done with his, and wriggled them.

Jen giggled. "Your fingers feel just like lice check, at school, when they run a pencil through your hair looking for lice, which are these little bugs that live in— Hey!" Jen drew back. "You aren't covered with bugs and spiders are you?"

She put her hands on her head feeling around to make sure there weren't bugs crawling from Tanglewood into her hair, and then her fingers got entwined with Tanglewood's. Seconds later Jen's hair and Tanglewood's fingers were in a giant knot.

"Ow!" Jen yelled. He yanked his hand back. During the short while he had been with Jen he felt, for the first time, comfortable and at home. He did not want to leave that feeling. "Ow!" Jen yelled again, pushing against him. Tanglewood began to panic.

"Stop it, Tanglewood!" she sounded upset, which made Tanglewood yank harder, so Jen had to clasp Tanglewood's wrist to stop him from yanking and her fingers accidentally popped open the snaps on the wristband.

Tanglewood's arm pulled away, free, only without the hand, which was still in Jen's hair and dangled in front of her face.

* * *

Ben heard screams. At first he thought his ears might be ringing, his head throbbed from breathing so hard. He stopped to listen carefully. It was screaming, and it was Jen's voice. His sister was at the mercy of a man-eating plant!

"Jen! I'm coming! Fight for your life, Jen!"

Fortunately he had already reached the plateau so he sprinted. In less than a minute he saw his sister, or the part of her from the knees down. Her feet kicked into the dirt while the rest remained hidden by the trunk of a really big tree.

Jen didn't hear Ben's call, or his foot beats. She was busy talking to herself as she nervously stuck Tanglewood's hand into his arm, her own hands shaking as she snapped the wristband to hold it all together.

"OK," Jen quavered, "you're a plant, right? Plants fix themselves all the time, right? I mean, getting a part lopped off here and there is not a big deal to a plant, right? As long as you're still in the ground, right?" Jen hated where her logic was leading. She looked at Tanglewood's legs and feet; they were definitely not still in the ground.

She was pulled to her feet with a sudden jerk.

"Mon-sterrrr!" Ben roared as he shoved Jen off to one side and jabbed at the air in front of Tanglewood with the Mini-T. He had intended to jab with the vegetable peeler but forgot which hand held which.

Tanglewood was thrilled when he saw The Mini-T! It was obviously just like him, only smaller. On Ben's third jab Tanglewood reached out for it. Ben, startled by Tanglewood's swift movement, let go of both the Mini-T and the vegetable peeler, and trembled all over.

"Ben!" Jen was shaking him. "Ben, stop! It's OK!"

Ben gawped at the life-sized bamboo puppet he had built on his driveway only to have it magically appear in these woods. And when he had seen Tanglewood earlier it still moved like a puppet, all herky-jerky. But now, Tanglewood's movements had the subtlety of a real, living thing. He held the Mini-T as if it were a doll, cradling and caressing it. As if it were not just a doll.

Tanglewood sat on the ground between the tree and Jen's legs, then mushed the Mini-T against his own cheek, rocking back and forth at his waist.

"How—" Ben began to speak, slowly. "How old is he?"

"He acts like he's, I don't know, maybe three, or four?"

"That's weird," said Ben. "All the time I was building Tanglewood, I was thinking of him as a teenager."

Jen watched Tanglewood as he sat on the ground holding and hugging the Mini-T as if it were his own baby. And she stopped caring whether Tanglewood was a boy or a girl. She just wanted him to be happy. And safe.

* * *

After reassuring himself there was nothing about Tanglewood that suggested he was a flesh-eating monster, Ben began to wonder what Tanglewood was capable of doing.

"Did you, uh, talk to him?" Ben asked Jen.

"I don't think he talks."

That made sense, Ben thought. To save time he had skipped giving Tanglewood a mouth.

"Well did you see him do anything besides run?" he asked Jen.

"He played hide and seek around that tree for a while — that was irritating — then he sat next to me and he wanted to touch my hair so I let him, then his hand fell off after it got stuck in my hair and I accidentally unsnapped the wristband."

"What about peek-a-boo?" Ben said.

"Huh?" Jen had no idea what Ben was talking about.

"Can he play peek-a-boo?"

Jen sat and faced Tanglewood. She poked his shoulder to get his attention, covered her eyes with her hands, waited two seconds.

"Peek a boo," Jen said, in the soft, sing-song way that everyone says "peek a boo".

The only sound that Tanglewood could make was rustling, his leaves and sticks rubbing against one another as he moved, and Tanglewood rustled vigorously after Jen uncovered her eyes to say, "peek a boo." His shoulders and butt wiggled in exactly the way that children do when they giggle.

Jen was thrilled. "OK, now you do it." She pantomimed covering her eyes then pointed at Tanglewood, who took her hand and put it on his face.

"No, silly. Cover your face with your own hands." She tapped but did not grab the wristband.

Tanglewood covered his face, and just kept his hands there.

"You have to open them up," Jen said. "Like this." She gently pulled at Tanglewood's fingers.

"Like this," Jen demonstrated on herself, putting her hands on her face then springing them open, saying "peek a boo" a little more exaggerated and goofy than before. Tanglewood giggled, then imitated her movement perfectly.

Ben wondered if he should have taken the time to make Tanglewood a mouth, and if the bamboo leaves he had woven onto his head to look like eyes actually functioned as eyes. Whatever was going on, Tanglewood may be mute but he was clearly not blind.

"Alright, that's enough," Ben said. "Peek-a-boo is for babies, anyway," Ben said. "He's got to be older than that. Let me try something."

Ben sat down and scooted into Jen. As he shoved her over so that he could face Tanglewood, Tanglewood grabbed Ben's shoulder to stop him.

"Shh shh-shh-shh," Jen said, putting her hand on Tanglewood's arm reassuringly. "It's just Ben, Tanglewood. See," Jen mushed her cheek against Ben's so that their faces were side-by-side. "See. Ben's just like me."

Tanglewood let go of Ben's shoulder, tilted his head one way, then the other. Then he gently scraped some of the dirt from Jen's cheek and smeared it onto Ben's.

"That's right, baby. See everything's fine," Jen said.

Ben looked at her, one eye cocked. "Baby?" he said.

Then he faced Tanglewood. "Let's try patty-cake."

After several trials of awkward half-slaps and missed claps Ben and Tanglewood hit a stride and found a good pace. CLAP double-slap, clap-slap clap-slap, CLAP double-slap...

"Look at him go!" Ben was excited.

A few minutes later the excitement wore off for Ben. "I forgot how quickly patty-cake gets boring. Is there another part to it?"

"Only the words," Jen said.

A series of whistle bursts came from down the slope followed by an announcement over the outdoor loudspeakers. The squawking voice reached their ears, disrupting Jen's and Ben's fantasy that the three of them could go on playing without disruption from the outside world.

"Mid-afternoon activities in five minutes. Uh— Everybody report to your counselors or be on the field in, like, five minutes. Or now. Everybody?"

It was a teenaged girl's voice, and, with the microphone still on, she added, "Eww, my voice sounds gross over this thing."

Ben stood up, his mind peppered with details, and worries.

"Has anyone in charge seen you yet?" he asked Jen.

"It was kinda hard to tell if anyone was paying attention. There was no one in my cabin, if that's what you mean, and then in the dining hall all I met was this one weird kid. Really weird."

"What about a counselor?"

"No, not really," Jen said.

Ben looked over to Tanglewood, who was still playing patty-cake by himself, his shoulders and butt shaking.

"We have to stay out of trouble. You need to show up to some stuff. I mean, sooner or later they'll wonder where you are."

"Did you see your counselor?" Jen said.

"Yes, in my cabin. We didn't really talk or anything but he definitely checked my name off a list."

Jen didn't want to go back down but where else was she going to go? She stood and had taken only one step when Tanglewood shot to his feet, lunged and latched both his hands to her whitened wrist.

"Tanglewood, you have to stay. I'll be back, OK? Don't let anyone see you. Just stay right here. Ow, not so hard! That scratches!"

She began to pry Tanglewood's fingers from her wrist but then he threw both arms around her waist as she took a step back.

The loudspeaker below squealed as it came on again, a boy's voice this time: "Uh OK. It's time for everyone to be on the field. Heh-heh. Hey, this thing is kinda cool it makes my voice super loud."

"Jen, we gotta go," Ben said.

"Well, what am I gonna do about this?" It seemed cruel to pull away from Tanglewood when he was clamping onto her like his life depended on it.

Ben sighed. "Let's just take Tanglewood with us, get him as close as we can to camp and then, I don't know, we'll have to figure something out after that."

So the three of them walked down the slope as quickly as they could, holding hands, which Tanglewood enjoyed immensely.

LAYERS

The field at Triple-Bar was the camp's largest open space. Between two posts at one end of the field stretched a long cord that was used for air-drying bed sheets. This was part of Triple-Bar's green campaign to use less energy and save money instead of running an industrial-sized electric drier for several hours a day. "The sun is free," Ginger Berger had pointed out during a budget meeting.

Sheets hung along the cord's entire length to build up a stock of fresh ones before the kids began ruining them with dirt, the occasional bed wetting, and vomit, which happened at least once a day at camp even when there wasn't a stomach flu going around.

Jen, Ben, and Tanglewood neared the edge of the field as they descended the last bit of slope. Ben saw the sheets. "Let's go there," he said.

Jen hung back with Tanglewood, making sure he stayed completely hidden behind some trees, while Ben moved to the sheets and peered through a crack between two of them to see if the coast was clear.

The area surrounding the sheets was empty enough, but the rest of the field was in the same chaos they had seen when they first drove up, only this time there were more objects flying through the air. Frisbees, volleyballs, badminton shuttlecocks, all shooting up and coming down like popcorn above an undulating sea of dust in the middle distance.

Ben returned to Jen and Tanglewood. "It's crazy in there but maybe that will help. You've got to check in with somebody and at least get your name crossed off a list. Where is your cabin?"

Before Jen could respond an arrow pierced one of the sheets and stuck into a tree trunk with a *thwockita-sproing* only four feet away from her and Tanglewood.

"Wally!" a counselor shouted from somewhere in the chaos. "There's no archery allowed yet, Wally!!"

"Then why was the equipment closet with all the cool stuff in it left unlocked?!?" the kid named Wally yelled back.

Back behind the sheets Jen and Ben watched the arrow vibrate until it came to a full rest.

"Maybe it's better if nobody knows I'm here," Jen said.

"That's insane, Jen! When you're nowhere to be found they'll call Mom and Dad. Then everyone will ask *me* what's going on. You know how terrible I am at lying!"

As great as Ben was at making things he was truly bad at making things up.

"I wasn't being that serious!" Jen said. Then she turned to Tanglewood, patted his cheek, and gesticulated as she explained. "OK. Tanglewood, you have to stay here for just a bit, you just stay with Ben. Ben will take care of you. I'll be right back, there's just some work I have to do but then you'll see me again, soon, all right?"

Jen convinced herself that Tanglewood understood and accepted what she just said, so she turned to go, but Tanglewood threw himself at her, same as before. He just would not let her out of his sight, it seemed.

"Here you go, Tanglewood. Over here. C'mon, boy. That's a good boy," Ben beckoned with a sappy voice as he patted the front of his thighs.

"Oh for heck's sake, he's not a dog, Ben!" Jen said.

She spoke to Tanglewood with a bit more firmness. "Tanglewood, you are going to be fine without me for five minutes," she said, as if talking to a two-year-old. But Tanglewood, now clutching her leg and sitting on her feet, shook his head vigorously.

"Hey, he understands how to say 'no'." Ben was genuinely impressed now that he thought of Tanglewood as a toddler.

Jen sighed. "We need another plan."

"Maybe we can dress him, disguise him like he's just another kid, really cover him up and no one will notice, not for a little while, anyway. You have that poncho thingie that Mom gave you. It has a hood, right?"

Maybe because his idea to hide Tanglewood under some clothes was as close to a complete lie as Ben had ever thought up, Jen was impressed. So impressed that she overlooked all its obvious flaws, except for one.

"Problem: You'll have to go get the poncho. Plus get some bandanas. They're all still in my duffel."

"I can't just walk into a girl's cabin!"

"You can if you're me," Jen said, as she began taking her shoes off.

"What are you doing?" Ben said.

"We're switching clothes. Put your hair up with this." She pulled her elastic ponytail band off and handed it to Ben, along with several strands of her hair that were knotted in it.

"Ick," Ben said, taking it with two fingers.

A minute later Jen was in Ben's clothes and Ben in Jen's. Jen now had the apron on her and she liked the way it cinched in the middle then flared underneath. She didn't think of the apron as a dress, which is how Ben had thought of it when he had first put it on back in the kitchen, feeling ridiculous wearing it. To Jen the flaring shape reminded her of Xena's outfit, except this was white. Well, not as white as it used to be, having gone up and down a heavily wooded slope. Plus all the sitting on the ground playing patty-cake. The dirt on the apron reminded her of an important detail.

"There's one last touch before you can convince everyone that you're me," Jen said, picking up a small handful of dirt from the ground. "Close your eyes."

Ben, who never mistrusted his sister because she never did anything mean to him, closed his eyes and then felt a bunch of dirt cascade through his hair.

"Hey!" He yelped.

"Your hair's too shiny to be me."

"But you said nobody saw you."

"Nobody that I saw, saw me," Jen clarified.

"Yuck. I hate dirt!"

"Don't think of it as dirt, think of it as makeup."

Ben turned to head down the perimeter road in the direction of the girls' cabins.

"Don't forget to check me in!" Jen said.

Ben had almost forgotten that was the problem they had started with. Now there was more than just that one.

He marched down the road, not feeling like a girl at all, except for the ponytail, which not only tugged uncomfortably as if someone behind him had grabbed his hair, but also prevented him from covering up his face. He felt exposed.

LAYERS

Jen watched Ben walk away while Tanglewood stared at the arrow stuck in the nearby tree trunk. He thought, it didn't belong there but at the same time it did. The arrow captivated him almost as much as the Mini-T, which was now tucked into the shoots of his chest. He reached out to grasp the arrow but Jen beat him to it and yanked it from the tree.

"That's too sharp to play with," Jen said, "it isn't safe." Now that she thought about it, was it safe to stay behind these sheets? She liked the idea of having a wall that stopped others from seeing them, but sheets obviously would not stop arrows. Hopefully that wouldn't happen again.

She picked up a stick — a fallen branch — and handed it to Tanglewood. "Play with this. It's safer."

Tanglewood held the stick and removed the Mini-T from his chest. Then he stuck the pointy end of the stick into the Mini-T.

"Hey, don't hurt it!" Jen said.

Tanglewood understood the word hurt, or rather, he understood that Jen didn't want him to put the stick into the little-little one, which is how Tanglewood thought of Mini-T. He was confused because the stick and the little-little one seemed like they were supposed to be together, just as the arrow had been with the tree. But he did not want to upset Jen, so he stopped pushing the stick into the little-little one and sat down in the dirt.

He began tapping the stick on the ground, not thinking about what he was doing as he tilted the stick upward and let it drop with a plunk. With each tap vibrations moved through the stick and up Tanglewood's arm. He stopped, holding the stick up in front of him to feel what would happen. No more vibrations in the stick. Tanglewood began tapping again, steadily. Tap. Tap. Tap. Then stopped once more, this time keeping the tip in contact with the ground. The vibrations got softer, but they were still there. He touched the ground with his fingers and felt a faint murmur that continued even after he removed his hand from the dirt. Was this vibration new? Or was it the one he had felt inside himself? He held the stick directly onto his chest and felt a magnified vibration move up the stick and into his arm.

The stick was important, and the ground, too. There appeared to be something living underneath.

* * *

Ben stood at the edge of the girls' cabins, happy to not be the only kid milling about the area so he wouldn't stick out. He wanted to avoid eye contact but he thought staring at the ground might appear suspicious so he smiled directly at one girl, then another, and they both ignored him completely. He felt cast down, but under the circumstances being ignored was better than getting attention.

He saw Jen's cabin, number 16, parted the canvas enclosure slowly, heard nothing, scooted inside, let the canvas close. A partially rolled-up window opening let in a shaft of light, enough to make out which duffel was Jen's.

He unzipped the duffel and rifled through her things.

"Is that stuff yours?" A strange voice asked.

Ben jolted — his insides experienced a thorough rattling that was becoming a regular event, like the hourly gong of an ominous clock. He turned and saw— he wasn't certain what, some kind of creature.

"Gaaack! Those eyes! So huge!" Ben blurted.

"I was four years old before they knew I couldn't see that good."

It took Ben a second to figure out that the eyes were large because of eyeglasses that were more like magnifying glasses than eyeglasses, and that the creature was just another kid. And just as he was starting to calm down the canvas slit entryway popped open and a counselor appeared.

"Anybody in here I haven't met yet?" the teenaged girl said without looking in, her eyes glued to a clipboard.

"Yes," said Froggy.

"I already checked off your name, Froggy."

"Um, she means me," Ben said. "I mean, my name is Jen."

"Uh huh. Jen. Got it." She scratched across the clipboard with a pen. "I'm Erin. You can call me Erin." Still not looking away from the clipboard. Then another counselor interrupted from just outside the cabin and Erin stepped out.

"Hey Erin, girl. So how's your day?"

"Oh my God, gross. Too many kids."

"I know. They really packed them in this year. Ten to a cabin? Forget it. I can't keep track. Anyway, I just needed to remind you that you guys are up first tonight."

"Uch. Fine," the counselor named Erin said, then she squinted into the cabin. "So, Jen, you like stories?" She sounded cheery all of a sudden.

Ben said, "Um, yeah, sure," wanting to keep it simple so he wouldn't have to say much.

"Great! We're responsible for the ghost story at the campfire tonight and you get to tell it."

Ben didn't want to say "OK," or anything at all but Erin didn't wait for him to respond. "Make it scary, not stupid, Jen. I gotta go," Erin said, and she was gone.

Ben grabbed what he needed from Jen's duffel, stuffed it into a wad under his — Jen's — jacket and dashed out of the cabin. He was retracing his steps back to the perimeter road when he heard the unmistakable, heavy lisp of the bug-eyed girl from Jen's cabin.

"My name is Froggy. Where are you going?"

Ben kept up his pace. Froggy was now alongside him.

"Do you know a lot of scary stories?" she asked Ben.

Ben halted. "Froggy? Your name is really Froggy?" He wasn't really asking, so he kept talking. "Froggy, I just don't have time to talk right now."

"Right, OK. Let's keep walking and we can talk later."

Froggy's enthusiasm was undeniable, and as he continued on his way it became clear that she was also unshakeable so Ben made a quick decision. Instead of heading to the out-of-the-way perimeter road he took off, instead, for the dust cloud raised by the chaos of afternoon activities on the field, darting this way and that to lose Froggy in the midst of the mess, believing that anyone seeing him would ignore just one more kid zigging and zagging because dozens were doing just that.

He emerged from the cloud on the other side and looked behind him, saw no Froggy or anyone else following. The sheets lay straight ahead but he veered sharply to the left so he could approach the clothesline from an angle where no one could see that's where he was headed.

* * *

Jen stared at the arrow in her hand, glanced at her wristband — now Tanglewood's wristband — and began fussing with the material of the apron, wrapping and tying it, trying to imagine how a quiver is made so that she could carry the arrow in it, slung on her back, if possible.

Ben flew in from the side and dumped the clothes he held against his belly onto the ground.

"Let's hurry. This place is unpredictable," Ben said as he shook out the poncho, looking for its head hole.

LAYERS

Jen went to Tanglewood who was sitting and whacking the ground with the stick now, not just tapping gently. "Tanglewood, you have to stop that for a minute. We need to cover you up."

Tanglewood was hard to distract. Jen and Ben moved in swiftly and began putting the clothes on him. Fortunately, a poncho doesn't have arm holes so all they had to do was get it around Tanglewood's head but that wasn't easy, not just because the poncho kept getting snagged by bits of bamboo that stuck out everywhere, but also because Tanglewood began to squirm.

Jen managed to tie a bandana around Tanglewood's head to cover his face — some of it, anyway.

"Tanglewood will you hold still for just one second," Ben said while stuffing Tanglewood's hair twigs under the poncho's hood, which was pretty large but the hair twigs were long and there were a lot of them.

"Don't break any hair twigs," Jen felt she had to say to Ben. He refused to respond because he was already concentrating really hard so that he wouldn't break any hair twigs. That should have been obvious to Jen, Ben thought to himself.

"Mmph. Come on, Tanglewood you've got to stand up now," Jen said as she hoisted him.

Tanglewood stood, his head now hidden by the poncho's large hood, the cloak of the poncho draped over his shoulders and down. There was just enough material to cover his arms completely as long as he kept his arms close to his body. He rested the stick on the ground, gripping it like a staff.

"He looks like that death guy. The one with the hooked blade," Jen said. She felt uneasy.

"It's called a scythe," Ben said, "And Death doesn't have green legs that stick out beneath his cloak." He hoped to use the apron as a wrap around Tanglewood's waist, covering up the lower part of his legs, but the elaborate knots Jen had used to affix the apron to herself were taking too long to untie. "Take Tanglewood and hide behind that tree," he told Jen. He went to the sheet at one end of the clothesline, and yanked it down. Then he realized he should have checked the other side more carefully.

"Hey there you are!" Froggy called out as she trotted toward him from the dust cloud that enshrouded the afternoon activities.

Ben dashed back to Tanglewood with the sheet. "Hurry!" he implored Jen. "Help me put this on him, there's a kid coming!" She hoisted the poncho; Ben pushed one edge of the sheet on Tanglewood's waist then ran around Tanglewood with the sheet and quickly tied and tucked the ends.

Tanglewood's legs were now completely hidden by the sheet, a bright, white maxi-skirt that made him look a little less like Death. And just in time.

"Is this a special activity?" Froggy said as she arrived. Jen had tried to stuff herself and Tanglewood behind a tree when she heard footsteps approaching but she didn't have time. She turned to face Froggy, trying to think up some really big lies.

Froggy shifted her blue, magnified eyes from Ben to Jen to Tanglewood, several times.

"Hey are you two guys twins? You look like twins. I always wanted to be a twin. Who's that?" She pointed to Tanglewood.

"Um..." Ben stalled.

"That's Tangie, she's our cousin," Jen jumped in, her voice lowered to a conspiratorial whisper. "She's not supposed to be here."

"Definitely not supposed to be here." Ben unexpectedly found himself wanting to help fabricate the cover-up story. "It's a secret, and if you tell anyone—" he stopped because all he could think of to say next were threats, and threats didn't seem like they would work as well as a good lie. His mind drew a blank.

LAYERS

Jen jumped in once again, lowering her whisper even further. "It's just that Tangie has a skin problem. Like that weird disease where the sun is really bad for you. She begged to go to camp but her doctor wouldn't let her so we snuck her in. Please don't tell anyone."

Froggy's eyes floated across the wide arc of the lenses mounted in front of them. She said nothing.

The pause unsettled Jen and Ben and gave them a chance to notice just how strangely built Froggy was. She was skinny but not bony, and muscular but not bulky. As if she were made from strands of twisted wire, or cables like the kind used to hold up bridges.

"I know what it's like to be invisible," Froggy said, eventually.

Jen and Ben had no idea what Froggy was talking about, each of them wondering if maybe this girl was as odd on the inside as she looked on the outside.

Froggy's eyes landed on Tanglewood, who was bent forward resting his hooded head on the upright stick. "People always say I'm too weird and then pretend I'm not there," Froggy continued.

Ben and Jen felt queasy.

"I don't like it when people treat me like that," Froggy said, "because it makes me feel dumb, but I'm not, I just need big glasses so I can see things better. I wish that my glasses could be a secret, but they have to live on my face in front of the rest of me. I guess that's why people focus on them too much."

Although she was light-headed and crabby from hunger, Jen instantly understood what Froggy was trying to say. She put her hand on Froggy's shoulder. "We won't ignore you, Froggy, we promise. Right, Ben?"

Ben gave a halfway nod, but only halfway. He didn't mind the idea of being nice to Froggy, but he was wondering if his opinion counted. Jen didn't really ask for his agreement just now, as much as she demanded it. Jen was a pusher. She pushed and pushed. This whole afternoon had been one complication pushed on top of another, the layers piling up too fast to stay on top of what was going on, and how to keep the whole stack from toppling over.

Ben closed his eyes and took a deep breath.

"Wanna see something?" Froggy said. Ben opened his eyes.

Froggy smiled at him and darted her tongue in and out of the wide gap between her missing two front teeth.

"These grow in for most kids by the time they're seven but I'm a late bloomer," Froggy said while flicking her tongue.

Ben desperately needed a normal moment, so he asked a normal question hoping that it would start a normal conversation with normal information passed along in a normal way. "How old are you, Froggy?"

"Ten and three-quarters next week on Friday, but not until three in the morning because that's when I was born, which happened in the elevator of my parents' apartment building." Then she asked Ben, "How old are you, Jen? I remember your name is Jen because I heard you tell the counselor back in our cabin, where we met." Froggy began tugging the real Jen's sleeve, "But I don't know your name yet," You're Jen's brother, I'll bet. Say, a brother and sister can still be twins, right?"

"I'm his sister. He's my brother," Jen said. Ben felt Jen had tossed out this revelation too carelessly, like she didn't worry at all what would happen when her actions and stories began to conflict and left holes everywhere for the lies to leak all over the place making one, big mess.

"Froggy," Ben spoke with an edge, "there's another secret you have to keep. My name is Ben. That one is Jen." He poked at his sister in a peevish sort of way, which Jen reacted to immediately.

LAYERS

"That one?" said Jen. "Did you just call me *that one*?"

"Yeah. What about it?" Ben tried not to be defensive.

"You sounded snotty."

"I was just explaining an important detail. Yet another one."

"What do you mean by 'yet another one'? What is with the way you're talking to me all of a sudden?"

"There's just a lot of stuff to clean up."

"What kind of 'stuff'?" Jen's eyes had become intense.

Ben didn't trust himself to reply to Jen's questions fearing that he might answer with too much truth. Maybe he did sound snotty but he wanted her to know that he felt like a mule, doing all the hard work required to travel every path Jen decided to go down, even where there was no real path. He had admired her earlier for blazing a trail up the slope, but now he saw Jen as a bushwhacker, hacking away without thinking things through, or picturing what may lay ahead, which could be a thicket of thorns. Or a cliff. Ben was convinced they were heading toward both. Where would they be without him covering up all their tracks? is what he wanted to say, and he wanted to say it like he was mad. Only he had never, ever told Jen when he got mad at her, or had let on when he was. It didn't happen often, but when it did, he always wound up feeling like it would become a showdown where he wasn't allowed to show up, so he would just keep quiet until his aggravation had passed. And this time he struggled harder than ever to say nothing. Why did he let her convince him to build Tanglewood in the first place? Now, within just hours after arriving at a strange camp where he didn't want to be, where he knew no one, where he had to eat stinky, mushy food — here he was dressed in his sister's clothes and covered with dirt, and — AND! And on top of ALL that, it appeared they would have to spend every ounce of energy hiding a bamboo boy that had come to life like Frankenstein's monster, only it was he, Ben, who had made it. Jen had turned him into Doctor Frankenstein.

Ben stopped his mind from going any further. He had to shut it all down before he completely lost his mind.

He clenched his jaw, glowering at Jen as best he could. "I. Don't. Think. We should have this discussion. Right now."

Jen watched Ben as he stoically said nothing further, her lips pressed tight. She breathed through her nose.

Froggy broke the silence.

"Sometimes when my parents fight I'll squeeze my eyes really tight and hum like this, kind of high pitched," Froggy said, and then demonstrated with a *Weee-Oooo Weee-Oooo.* "It really works," said Froggy, "It sounds just like a siren and you don't hear anything else around you."

"We better switch back into our own clothes," Jen said. "But I'm keeping the apron."

Ben didn't care about the stupid apron. "Fine," he said, handing Jen her elastic ponytail hair band, wishing he could also return the dirt that she had dumped on his head. His scalp itched like crazy.

When Ben was back in his own clothes he looked over to Tanglewood and rolled his eyes because he now had to remember to call Tanglewood "Tangie," and that to Froggy, Tangie was a girl.

Too many layers in too tall a stack, thought Ben, to himself.

HUNGER

Nash was enjoying his afternoon. He had followed Ginger Berger to the woodpile where hundreds of logs were piled up. Near the wall of logs stood several mounds of branches. Sycamore, pine, oak, maple — all drooped and drying out.

And there was a long-handled axe.

"Tell you what," Nash said. "I'll cut up all the wood for every campfire as long as I get to set it ablaze each night."

That was fine with Ginger Berger, who spent the next hour watching Nash splitting log after log, first in halves, then into quarters, then splintering some of those into kindling.

"I get to burn those dried up branches, too, right?" Nash said, pointing at a pile off to the side.

"Oh, absolutely," said Ginger Berger.

Now, after that satisfying workout, and looking forward to starting a big fire later in the evening, Nash stood in his kitchen feeling great. Green peppers sputtered on the grill outside while on the stove pots of turnips and cabbage bubbled, occasionally sending off a splatter to hiss as it hit the stovetop. Beautiful sounds.

Then he saw Stones sitting in a corner looking glum.

"What's wrong with you?" Nash said.

Stones gave a small shrug and shook his head a couple times.

"Well, I feel great," Nash said.

"Well, I don't," Stones said.

Nash didn't want to deal with Stones's negativity. "If you feel like you have a boo-boo or want to boo-hoo at someone then go see the nurse."

Stones listened carefully for some kind of sympathy in his father's words, not finding much, or any. Maybe the nurse was a good idea. He got up and left the kitchen.

"Great," Nash said under his breath as he watched Stones slam the screen door behind him. Then he shouted, "You better be back by the time we have to serve dinner — you got one hour, mister."

* * *

Stones opened the door to the infirmary. Its hinges creaked the same horrid way as the kitchen's screen door. Then he became unsure what he would say to the nurse if he actually went in to talk to her. He was about to turn and leave when a husky, but relaxed voice said, "Well, it had to start sooner or later. Come on in." So he did.

Stones didn't see any one, just an empty waiting area and a corridor. An arm extended into the corridor and beckoned him.

"I'm in this room," the woman said. "Over here."

The lighting in the infirmary entry and waiting area was dim. Stones moved cautiously. He entered a room lit almost too white. The woman was seated at a desk, writing on some kind of form and holding a chocolate bar with the wrapper halfway torn off.

"I'm Nurse Ripperton. Call me Rip. Have a seat. What's the problem? Go ahead, just start talking, I'm listening, I promise," Rip said, continuing to fill out the form.

Stones felt heaviness in his chest as he came up with a way to say what he wanted. "Plants," he began, "Plants and animals. I— I can't tell the difference."

Rip put down her pen and pivoted in her seat toward Stones. She pointed at him with the chocolate bar.

"That's one you don't hear every day," she said. "Did anything bite you?"

"Um, no," Stones said. "Not yet."

"Are you bleeding?"

"No."

Rip put a thermometer in Stones's mouth.

"Are you homesick?"

"My dad is the cook here," Stones said with the thermometer in his mouth.

"Well that explains why you look like you need to eat more steak." The thermometer beeped. "No fever."

The feeling in Stones's chest tightened. "How do you know if you're crazy?" Stones said.

"Is this about the plants and animals?"

"Maybe."

"Kid, you're fine," Rip said. These woods can get to you sometimes. I see branches moving in the wind out there and it creeps me out, too. Give me a beach any day."

"I think I saw a plant with arms and legs," Stones said. "And a head. It acted like," Stones tried to think up a not-so-crazy way to describe it. "Like it was hungry."

"That happens sometimes. It's always a prank by the older kids. They can be really mean. Don't fall for it." Rip opened a drawer on her desk and reached in. "Here, have a Snickers Bar. It'll help."

* * *

Stones still had time left after leaving the infirmary so he walked around the perimeter road, thinking. He had been a wreck since last night, and after talking to Rip he wondered what he had seen, really. It was dark when Jender and Bender came to visit him with that bamboo thing, and like Rip had said, it must have been a prank. And then Ben had spooked him again, just a few hours ago — with a doll! Stones felt ashamed. Then he started to get mad at everything. He was mad that he had to move to a new house, mad that he was confined to a summer of crappy kitchen work, and very, very mad at himself for being spooked so badly by Jender and Bender. They had gotten to him at a time of weakness. Just before he moved to the new house he had been convincing himself that his father was telling him lies all these years about plants. The only proof Nash had ever shown him was by forcing him to watch all the horrible things plants did in those movies. Why had he never seen anything like that in real life? That's what had begun to nag at Stones. Until he moved across the street from Jender and Bender. It was almost as if his father had hired Jender and Bender to scare him, as if Nash had seen that Stones was about to rebel and purposely moved him near the twins from hell so they could work against him, and wear him down.

That must be it, Stones thought. His father could tell that he was about to realize the truth. That the whole idea of plants being alive, with an ability to move by themselves and attack people, it was obviously an insane idea. And Stones had almost believed that he was the insane one. It was Nash who was crazy, not himself, although his father being insane was its own, big, problem. But it was better than being unable to trust his own mind.

Stones had wandered to the side of camp opposite the dining hall. He looked around to make sure no one could see. He unwrapped the Snickers Bar. His mouth watered. Candy was as unacceptable as meat to Nash. A couple of years ago Stones had pointed out that candy was made from plants, but Nash said that it didn't count because they took all the fiber out, and that it would just make him weak. Since then Stones snuck candy whenever he could, and he always felt guilty about it. He took a big bite of Snickers Bar. It was sweet and warm as it melted. Rip was right, the candy helped.

Stones decided to never listen to his father again.

But the warmth lasted only a few minutes before an emptiness took its place, which he thought was caused by knowing he had to return to that stupid kitchen. But as he sorted through his mind he found himself pushing away a sadness he hadn't let himself feel in a while because he wasn't a little kid anymore. If only he had a mom.

* * *

Jen, Ben, Tanglewood, and Froggy had meandered through the woods around the camp keeping just far enough from the perimeter road so that no one could see them behind the trees. They weren't talking much, Froggy noticed, and after Jen and Ben had given her a series of short, unsatisfying replies to her questions and comments, she turned to Tangie.

"Where are you from, Tangie?"

"Tangie can't speak," Jen said.

"Oh," Froggy said, "poor Tangie." Ben almost had a heart attack as Froggy reached to take Tanglewood's hand. Tanglewood responded by taking hers.

"Wow, Tangie," Froggy gasped, "your hands are really rough. Oops! I'm sorry, Tangie, I forgot you have that skin thing! My skin is kind of dry, too, so I have this lotion you can try. It works really good. Maybe it can help you."

Fortunately, the poncho covered both their hands and Froggy didn't see what Tanglewood's hand really looked like.

Ben could hear his thoughts becoming louder and louder. In his mind he was shouting at Jen. "Just how long is this going to last before it all falls apart?" But he also hoped Jen was getting the next raft of lies ready. They would need a lot, he figured, like fifty a day, which didn't seem possible.

The dinner bell clanged.

"Dinner time!" Froggy let go of Tanglewood's hand so she could clap excitedly. "I'm so hungry. My mom said the food is going to be really good this year."

Jen and Ben gave each other a look and had to force themselves to not laugh. In that instant Ben was happy because it proved that he and Jen were still connecting. Maybe we can make this work, he heard his inner voice say. Then he calmly accepted that they were up against the next problem.

Ben reminded Froggy, "No one must know that Tangie is here." They all turned to Tanglewood, who was back to tapping the stick on the ground.

"OK," Froggy said, "I can sneak out some food for you, Tangie." Ben was glad that Froggy found and filled that hole in this section of their half-baked plan.

He looked over at Jen. She was slumped, her expression was flat, her eyes were heavy. Seeing Jen that way upset him; he needed her to be alert and engaged. Then he realized that Jen's main problem, right now, was simply hunger. When Jen was hungry, she lost her patience first, and then all her energy. Ben felt his own hunger, but he didn't fall apart as fast as Jen when the gap between meals became too long.

"Jen," Ben said, "I think we should take turns eating. You go first, with Froggy."

"Whether I go at all is up to—" she pointed vaguely at Tanglewood.

"Froggy, would you go on ahead and wait outside the dining hall?" Ben said. "We just have to talk over some stuff with Tangie. She's kind of shy."

"Yeah, OK. But you'll be there?"

"One of us will be there. I promise," Ben said, and Froggy left the trees.

"I think he's pretty busy with that stick," Ben said to Jen. "You need to eat, otherwise you'll—" He trailed off.

"Otherwise, I'll what?" Jen said.

"Otherwise, you'll bite someone's head off."

Jen didn't have it in her to argue. "Yeah but that food..."

"You can't not eat, Jen. They've gotta have something relatively normal like apples and carrots."

"Apples and carrots, bleh." Jen pouted.

"Just walk a few steps toward the camp. Let's see what happens."

She did. Ben said, "Wait."

Jen knew this wouldn't work. Tanglewood needed her.

"You shouldn't take the apron and that arrow with you," Ben said.

"Oh. Yeah. You're probably right." She didn't bother untying anything, she just pushed the knotted-up apron past her hips and left it on the ground.

Tanglewood didn't freak out as Jen took a few more cautious steps and then kept walking away. I guess he's comfortable with Ben, now, Jen thought. She looked back over her shoulder to make sure that Tanglewood was all right, saw him happily absorbed by the stick and the ground, and felt good at that sight. She wasn't sure if she felt good because Tanglewood seemed happy, or because she preferred that it was the stick, not Ben, that made him able to be without her. Either way, she definitely needed some alone time.

* * *

Jen and Froggy stood on the cafeteria line — not the alone time that Jen had wanted.

"So, do you guys dress as each other a lot?" Froggy asked.

"No. Not anymore," Jen gave short, true answers because they required minimal mental energy.

"Why is one of your wrists white like that?"

"Something used to be there, but it's gone."

"What—"

"Froggy," Jen said, almost begging, "no more questions until after dinner."

Then they were served their food. A metal soup ladle plunked onto Jen's plate and dumped a mound of white glop with pale leaves jumbled within it. Then metal tongs unloaded black-and-green, slimy, tongue-like ribbons next to the white stuff. The glop and slime flattened and merged into one another.

"Isn't there anything else?" Jen had to ask. She looked up to see Nash and Stones side by side on the other side of the serving counter. Nash had the ladle.

"Of course," Nash said, using the ladle to scoop half the food off her plate, "let me just make some room," He paused. "For Hunger." And then that crooked smile.

"This smells yummy," Froggy said. "What's for dessert?"

"Okra pudding," Nash said, "but only if you come back for seconds. Or thirds, for Jen here."

"How does he know your name already?" Froggy asked Jen as they headed toward their table.

"He doesn't," Jen said. Froggy let it go.

They sat. Jen forced herself to eat. She held her nose.

"Here let me show you a trick," Froggy reached to the center of the table, grabbed some pats of butter and the salt and put both on Jen's food. "Try it now."

It was still terrible, but Jen could eat it.

"Thanks, Froggy," Jen said.

There were other girls at the table, all talking with one other while completely ignoring Jen and Froggy, which was fine as far as Jen was concerned because at this point she believed the best situation would be for no one else to know anything about her, or that she existed.

Erin, the counselor, arrived at the table. "Now which one of you did I say has to tell the ghost story tonight?"

"You told Ben," Froggy said. "I mean, you told Jen. Her." She tapped Jen's shoulder.

"Ghost story? What?" Jen muttered.

"Oh, yeah," Erin said, "you're the one." She leaned on the table and looked Jen right in the eye. "You can tell any story you want, but no axe murderers, no suicides. Got it?" Erin said to Jen.

"When is this?" Jen could feel her mind beginning to work again, even though she had no idea what was going on.

"Tonight. Campfire. Tell me you understand the rules," Erin said.

"No axe murderers. No suicides," Jen echoed.

"Awesome. You're my witness, Froggy," Erin winked, and then left.

"Last year there was an axe murder and they had to send a kid home," Froggy said with food in her mouth. "I mean someone told a story about one, and it freaked a kid out."

Jen knew what Froggy had meant. She forced herself to eat more because she was obviously going need all the energy she could get. “Pass the salt,” Jen said.

* * *

Ben was getting antsy. The sun was below the ridge above camp when Jen and Froggy had left to eat, and the sky now began to turn a darker blue, meaning the sun had set. He felt the air getting cooler, then felt a shiver. Then he really needed to pee.

“Um, Tanglewood?” Ben felt a little silly talking to Tanglewood but he felt he should say something. “I’m going just behind that tree over there to uh— to pee,” and because Ben wasn’t sure if Tanglewood had any idea what ‘to pee’ meant, he gestured with his thumb in front of his crotch, as if spraying the ground.

Tanglewood responded by extending his arm that held the stick, and pointing at the woods.

Maybe Tanglewood understood. Ben said, “I’ll be right back.” Then he went behind a tree about ten yards away and peed. He had been holding it in for a while so it took longer than usual. When he returned Tanglewood was gone.

Ben spun in a circle; his eyes darted everywhere. “Tanglewood!” He looked behind this tree and that, then went to the next layer of trees in the woods, where he found the poncho and sheet lying on the ground. He picked them up hoping that Tanglewood would be underneath.

“Oh, no,” Ben said.

“Ben?” It was Jen’s voice. “Ben, where are you?”

“Oh, no,” Ben repeated to himself. Then he answered, “Don’t come over here,” and immediately thought, why did I say that?

Jen saw Ben trying to hide the empty clothes behind his body. “What did you do?” she asked. “Where’s Tanglewood?”

"I needed to pee!" Ben said.

"Tanglewood!" Jen called out while running deeper into the woods, leaving Ben to deal with Froggy's next question.

"Who's Tanglewood?" Froggy asked Ben.

"Uh, OK. That's what Tangie's nickname is," Ben said.

"Aren't nicknames supposed to be shorter?"

"Yeah, that's what I meant. I meant Tanglewood is her real name." Ben felt good that he remembered to call Tanglewood 'her'.

"Tanglewood seems like a strange name for a girl," Froggy said.

Jen returned, out of breath. "It's getting dark in there. We need to get the flashlights."

"You can get *your* flashlight," Ben said. "I'm not going in there again, not in that kind of dark, with or without a flashlight."

"Ben!" Jen sounded mad, "This is *your* fault. You had one job!"

"You're not the boss of me!" Ben felt like he was six-years-old.

"All you had to do was watch Tanglewood for twenty minutes," Jen fired back. "I mean Tangie. All you had to do was watch Tangie."

"Ben told me that Tangie's real name is Tanglewood," Froggy said.

Jen narrowed her eyes at Ben.

"You said it first," Ben said, steadily. "Twice!"

Froggy spoke. "I can go to the cabin and get my flashlight while you guys keep looking. And I can get yours, too, Jen, if you have one."

Jen kept her stare-down with her brother going as she answered Froggy. "Thanks, Froggy. It's somewhere in my duffel bag."

"I'll leave the food I snuck right here in case Tangie gets back before I do," Froggy said as she scooted off.

Ben was hungry. He broke off the stare-down with Jen to pick up the napkin of food Froggy put on the ground. He took a scoop of whatever it was and stuffed it in his mouth.

"This is awful," Ben said. But he ate it.

HEARTBEATS

The dining hall was now empty except for Nash and Stones in the kitchen.

"If you get all those pots washed in time you can go to the campfire. But not until then."

"I don't care." Stones sulked at the deep sink, his arms sunk in the gray water, scrubbing under the surface.

"I get to start the blaze."

"Big whoop," Stones said under his breath as he blasted a pot with the sink sprayer.

Ginger Berger rolled in. "Coodle-Coo! Ready to light my fire?"

Grown-ups can be so gross, Stones thought.

Nash flexed his biceps, the one with the tattoo of the burning tree. "Like that?" he said.

Ginger Berger made a sound — something like a squeaky hinge or a nail pulled across a chalkboard.

"Is Junior coming along?"

"When he finishes his work," Nash said.

"Well, work fast, honey," Ginger said to Stones. "You don't want to miss a scary story."

Stones watched them leave the kitchen, and stuck his tongue out at their backs. He had no intention of going to a stupid campfire to hear stupid stories, so he cut off the water, dried off his arms, and planned to take his time.

He looked up at one of the large pots on the rack that hung from the ceiling, picked up a wooden spatula and struck the pot with it — a pleasing sound, like a gong, which gave him an idea.

Five minutes later Stones was at the back service entry to the kitchen. He sat on an overturned milk crate. In front of him were five drums — two upside-down pots and three upside-down, empty plastic buckets, different sizes but all big. Drumming had always been a stress-reliever for Stones when he was mad, and he had been very mad as he was setting up this improvised drum kit. But now, sitting there, he felt calm and relaxed as he prepared to play, which was new to him. He decided to close his eyes and take a deep breath. Then something else entirely new happened: he heard what he wanted to play before he played it. Whether the music he heard came from somewhere in the woods or came from inside his own head, he couldn't tell. All he knew was that he had to play it. He opened his eyes and began tapping on the kitchen drum kit, using two wooden spatulas as sticks. Stones had never played this carefully and deliberately before. He usually bounced and jabbed when he played drums; now he swayed, feeling the rhythm rise within in his body as it made its way to his arms.

* * *

Tanglewood, before he left Ben, had felt that same rhythm. He had sensed it in bits and pieces ever since Jen had handed him that stick. The beats had come through the ground into the stick.

Then they started to come through the air. He needed to find where the beats were coming from, and he needed to get out of whatever Jen and Ben had used to cover him because it prevented him from moving freely, and also made him itch. So Tanglewood had ditched the clothes and walked into the trees, touching the ground with the stick from time to time, and sometimes touching the trees. As long as the beats felt strong, Tanglewood pursued their direction and didn't feel alone, but then they faded, and now they had stopped. Suddenly he didn't know where he was, felt completely alone, and a coldness spread through him. He couldn't feel the vibration of Jen's presence, or Ben's, or the other one they had found, the frog girl with warm hands. He felt a vast nothing, and was about to curl up into a ball when he felt the rhythm begin anew, a little different than before, sharper, and closer, and behind him, where he had come from. So Tanglewood turned around. His body swayed as he trotted toward the sound.

* * *

While Froggy went for the flashlights Jen reluctantly waited, and obeyed Ben's warning to not blindly lunge into the woods as they were getting dark. She dissipated her nervous energy by putting the quiver-apron back on, fussing with it until she had formed a deep pocket to hold the arrow; then she threw on the poncho. A horse would be a good thing to have right about now, she thought.

"Ben, she'll be scared out there by herself," Jen fretted.

"You mean he'll be scared," Ben said. "You've got to keep your all your stories straight. And *he's* the one who decided to go in there; maybe that's what he wants."

"I'm not so sure," Jen said. "He's just a baby."

"How do you know what Tanglewood is?" Ben said.

"Because I remember what he was before he was born."

"That's crazy."

"No it's not," Jen said. "I was there. Me and Xena."

Jen, cloaked in the poncho, standing in the growing darkness saying weird things made Ben wary. He reassured himself by thinking he was lucky to be her brother, because having Jen as an enemy would be scary. Ben felt the temperature around him drop. He zipped up his jacket.

Then a powerful beam flashed the trees and shone right on Jen and Ben.

"Froggy?" Jen said.

"Froggy's at the campfire, where you two need to be right now." It was Erin, the counselor.

* * *

The fire roared in the pit, which was about the same size as Jen and Ben's bedroom and surrounded by rocks you could sit on when they didn't have flames licking them. Orange light hit all the crags in Nash's face. His eyes gleamed at the inferno, dried leaves crackling, small twigs practically melting before his eyes. Nash was proud of the fire he created. It was big.

Erin led Jen to a large, round podium — a two-foot high section of tree trunk. "Hop up, Storyteller," the counselor prompted, and there Jen stood, facing a restless crowd, most of them ignoring her.

They sure make a big deal out of telling ghost stories at this place, Jen thought to herself as she listened to Ginger Berger talk excitedly about bedtimes and breakfast, plus a bunch of other announcements that Jen wasn't able to pay attention to. The fire behind her pushed at her back like a hot wall. The campfire pit rested at the bottom of an embankment where semi-circular rows of kids on wooden bleachers settled down, and began staring at her.

Or maybe they were staring at the fire. In either case, all their faces had an identical look: We Are Totally Bored. How many kids were at this camp? Jen wondered. She had never seen a stack of faces like this before, from this angle. Was this what it was like to be a rock star on stage? With that thought Jen got nervous. Her mind had been elsewhere, on Tanglewood, but now, it suddenly dawned on her that, not only did she need to come up with a scary story right away, but it mattered that people liked it.

"Jen, is it? It's Jen, right?" Ginger Berger was talking directly to her.

"Yes, ma'am."

"Aren't you polite? Are you ready to tell your story?" Everything a question. Ginger Berger was one of those adults who talked to all children as if they were still four.

Jen began, "Once upon a time..."

The first heckler chimed in, "Once upon a time is for babies!" The whole crowd laughed and there were several other snide re-marks, all directed at Jen.

Jen felt her cheeks flush, then go numb as her mind went cold and crystal clear.

"Shut uuuuuup!!!!" Jen's arms shot outward to her sides from under the poncho. "You want a scary story? I'll tell you a scary story! Your minds will *burn* from fright!" Jen lowered her voice and launched right into it. "There was a young woman who made clothes in her garage and she was pregnant — with TWINS."

The crowd was completely silent now.

"Two little seeds grew inside her, but the woman was small and there wasn't enough room so as the seeds grew into little eggs and the eggs grew into babies they began to fight inside her. And one of them was stronger, *much* stronger than the other one, and hungrier, *much* hungrier, so she began to bite the other twin and she bit and bit and chewed and chewed until there was nothing left of her brother but bones. And then she fell asleep, and waited to be born."

Ben, on a bleacher about halfway up the embankment, sat with his mouth dangling open. He had never seen Jen like this. The poncho enveloped her like a shroud that hid forces only she could control. Her fingers curled, her hair flew around her, unkempt and wild, covering half her face. Her voice, like gravel, harrowing. She held her limbs at strange angles. Frightened and alarmed, Ben gulped. Froggy, next to him, said, "She's like a witch."

"And on the day they were born," Jen continued, "they had a funeral for Brother Bones whose body had fueled his sister so well that she came out twice as strong, twice as smart as a regular baby. And the mother cried and wished that she could knit a skin for Brother Bones and bring him back to life but all she could do was bury him so her husband dug a grave in the back yard, and they covered Brother Bones with dirt."

Every kid hung on every word. Jen felt the silence of the crowd, and the tension, and she paused to see how long that feeling would last. They needed her to finish the story. She had them, and it felt good, as good as it felt to scare Stones with Tanglewood. Somewhere in the crowd, Jen thought, Stones must be feeling her power once again.

But Stones wasn't in the crowd — he was playing drums on the kitchen porch, peacefully. But at that very moment he did, in fact, feel Jen's power once again, because Tanglewood, lured in by the drumming, popped out from the nearby trees and began to dance around Stones. Only to Stones it didn't look like dancing. It looked like a bamboo monster was about cut his head off with the axe he held — Stones couldn't see that it was just a plain stick.

But that detail wouldn't have changed his reaction. Stones ran and screamed, and his scream echoed throughout the camp.

Jen felt the crowd jump at the distant scream, a perfect cue for her to burst into the rest of her story.

"Brother Bones lay in the ground!" She amped up the drama, her voice and body stronger than they'd ever felt. "The sky thundered, BOOM! It rained and rained and rained until the ground was soaked and the back yard became a thick pool of mud. Brother Bones's skeleton floated up through the mud until he was back on top of the ground. The sky shook again, BOOM!" The crowd gasped, and Jen began acting out the story as she was telling it, "Lightning struck, sending a jolt into the earth that spread into nearby plants which began to grow and grow. They grew TOWARD the skeleton of Brother Bones, they grew INTO the skeleton of Brother Bones, filling his bones, wrapping his bones and then BOOM! another jolt of lightning hit Brother Bones but he didn't burn, no, he did not burn at all. HE ROSE UP FROM THE MUD AND WALKED! YES HE DID!! He limped to the house, dragging his heavy feet as he entered the house, to the baby's room where his stronger, hungrier sister slept peacefully, and there he stood, over her. His mouth opened, his jaw loose and wide like a snake's, drool pouring down the sticks that had become his teeth. CHOMP! Hunger! CHOMP CHOMP! Meat! He longed for the taste of meat! CHOMP CHOMP CHOMP! He wanted more!"

"Oh, my God," Ben said aloud.

"More!!" Jen roared. "MORE!!!"

Just then Stones bolted into the campfire circle, and streaked across the path near the fire, right in front of Jen.

"Ahhhhhhh!!!" Stones screamed. "It's gonna eat me!" He ran past the fire pit and into the darkness that lay beyond. And right after him came Tanglewood, also running fast because he needed to catch up to that boy who knew how the rhythm went. That boy is just like me, Tanglewood thought as he ran after Stones. He knows what it feels like to be me!

The throng of spectators screamed as Tanglewood streaked across their view.

Froggy elbowed Ben in the ribs, "Hey, look! There's Tangie!"

The entire camp erupted into applause. "That girl is awesome!" someone shouted. "How'd she do that?" another one asked. But Jen didn't take the time to enjoy the thrill of all the cheering and clapping, all of it for her.

"Tanglewood! Wait!" Jen shouted, and immediately took off after him.

In the pandemonium, as counselors scrambled to keep the kids from tearing up the seats and rushing the field from all their excitement, Ben grabbed the flashlights that Froggy had brought with her, and ran into the woods after his sister. Miraculously, no one else followed.

POSSESSED

Stones backed against a tree, frozen. When he ran from the creature he didn't think about where he should or could run, he just ran, wishing he could break out of his skin and leave himself behind. He had stuck to the camp's pathways but there was too much light. He headed toward the fire because there were people there, but he heard footsteps closing in behind him and then everyone at the fire screamed which multiplied his fear. His legs wouldn't have stopped even if he'd wanted them to. He picked up speed, into the trees. Maybe he could hide, find a place where there was no light, where nothing and no one could see him, and take him. A metal box. A hole. Anything. As the ground sloped upward more severely he drove himself harder and harder until he couldn't breathe anymore, then hid behind a large tree trunk. The light of the moon pierced through the tree canopy here and there. He wished it were darker. He needed to stay still, he needed to be quiet, but his lungs heaved and his mind screeched in all directions. In his entire life he had never felt as abandoned as he did right now. He had to face cold facts. The creature existed. He had seen it, fully, all its details highlighted by the bare bulbs hanging above the kitchen's service entry.

The thing approached him out of nowhere, the bamboo he had cut down, that his father — damn him! — had made him cut down. Bamboo that had taken the shape of a person as big as he was, or bigger, and it moved in a crazy way, unpredictable and frighteningly happy, a victory celebration before devouring its next meal. Stones was horrified, thinking of himself as a meal.

Stones felt the tree trunk behind him press into his back as hard as he pressed against it. If only he could become that tree. If only he could just disappear into it, to merge with something hard and impenetrable. If only he could feel nothing.

There was nothing left but to accept that his father was right. Plants were alive and out for blood, his blood. He tried to think of alternative explanations but none worked. This felt too real to be a dream. In a last-ditch effort he thought maybe his father truly was insane and had passed that insanity on to him, which would mean that none of this was really happening, and that would be good. But it would also mean that he was crazy, which was bad. Was all hope reduced to these two, lousy possibilities — to be hunted by plants or to be insane?

Stones heard a twig snap; he turned to look — he couldn't stop himself. A ray of moonlight shone on Tanglewood, who peeked out from behind the tree trunk, cocked his head to one side as he held out the little-little one, the Mini-T bamboo doll that Stones recognized from when Ben had wielded it in the kitchen. But this was much worse: The Creature had its own mini-creature, who, for all Stones knew, might itself have yet another, more miniature creature, and on and on — an infinite army of monsters able to ingest Stones at every level down to the individual molecules that used to be him. Stones's knees buckled as he fainted into a crumpled heap on the ground.

Tanglewood was confused because crumpling to a heap on the ground seemed like a strange way to respond to a gift.

"Tanglewood!" Jen ran up to Tanglewood and grasped him by the arm. "You have to listen to me! No more running away!"

A flashlight beam bobbed and flickered just behind Jen. It was Ben, who had been sweeping the beam everywhere to keep from running into a tree.

"God, it's creepy up here." He said through heaving breaths.

"Then why did you come?" Jen said.

"Have you lost your mind?" Ben said. "We can't be with Tanglewood all summer!"

"I can," Jen said. "I will."

"Tanglewood doesn't belong to us."

"Tanglewood belongs to me."

"It's going to have to learn to be by itself. It can't be with you forever!"

"Don't call Tanglewood 'it'."

"Why not? It's a plant!"

"No she isn't."

"See! You can't even tell if it's a boy or a girl. That makes it an 'it'."

Ben startled when the ground near his feet began to groan. He shone the light and there was Stones.

Jen pulled Stones up to his feet and shook him. "What do you know?" she demanded of him, her eyes ablaze.

"What?" Stones's voice was weak.

"Tell me what you know!" Jen said again.

"None of this is really happening," his head lolled.

Tanglewood gave Stones a big hug, lifting him off the ground by an inch or two.

Stones didn't even struggle. "Nothing is real," Stones kept his eyes shut.

"Tanglewood, don't hug him," Jen said. "He's a bad guy."

"He isn't acting like a bad guy right now," Ben said. "I think we should leave him alone."

"No," Jen said, "he knows too much."

"What does that mean?"

"It means," Jen had to catch up to herself. "Gimme your flashlight," she commanded Ben. He had two, so he gave her the one he had stuffed in his back pocket.

"Keep holding him, Tanglewood," Jen said. Tanglewood continued to hug Stones, who began to repeat, "There's no place like home. There's no place like home...."

Jen pulled off the apron-quiver from beneath the poncho, bit into its main knot until it loosened then used it to tie Stones's wrists together behind his back.

"You're taking prisoners?!?" Ben would liked to have laughed but there was nothing funny about this.

Jen didn't respond. She held the arrow in her right hand and shone the flashlight at the tree trunk.

"I know this tree. This is our tree, Tanglewood. Remember? We'll stay here," Jen said.

"Stay?" Ben said. "Here?"

She took the stick from Tanglewood and lay it on the ground. "Lie down right here, Tanglewood," Jen commanded. And Tanglewood complied. He felt tired, so the idea of putting as much of himself as possible on both the stick and the ground seemed very appealing.

"Help me tie Stones to that tree," Jen pulled Stones by the apron and began knotting its loose ends around a smaller tree a few feet from the big one.

"No," Ben said. "No. No. I am not going to do that."

"Fine!" Jen pulled her awkwardly bulky knot as tight as she could. Stones was able to slide down the tree and rested his butt on the ground. Tanglewood still had the bandana on, but it had come to rest around his neck. Jen removed it, and tied it around Stones's mouth, like a gag, but not too tight.

"Can you breathe?" she asked Stones.

Stones nodded. All he wanted was to close his eyes and sleep forever, so he let himself faint.

Ben was trapped between his fear of Jen and his fear of what Jen was doing. "I'm not going to be any part of this."

"Suit yourself," Jen took off the poncho, lay next to Tanglewood, and covered them both. The poncho was big enough to be a blanket, as long as she stayed curled up.

"What do you expect me to do, Jen?"

"I don't care as long as you don't tell anyone that we're here."

"We're at camp! Someone will notice!"

"Ha! No one down there notices anything!"

"They noticed your story," Ben said. "You sure made an impression with that one. I don't think they're going to forget you. In fact, they're probably all down there now looking for you, to get your autograph."

Jen hadn't thought about it that way.

"If you love me, you'll cover for me."

"What?"

"Just be me," Jen said. "You know how to do it. You used to do it all the time, remember?"

"I was five!"

"You were eight the last time you pretended to be me to fool other people," Jen said. "Until today, and it obviously worked!"

"There's supposed to be two of us! You have to come back!"

"Maybe," Jen said from underneath the covers. "Eventually, I guess."

Ben knew his sister was stubborn, but she was breaking all previous records.

"Then I'm taking Stones back with me. They'll come looking for him."

Jen leapt up and put her face in Ben's.

"He'll tell. You know he will! And if he does, no one will believe him, except Nash, and do you want Nash finding out that there's a Tanglewood?" She lowered her voice. "He already destroyed the bamboo once."

Ben did not want anything bad to happen to Tanglewood. And, although he was mad at Jen for being so stubborn, he was also afraid, not only afraid of her but also afraid for her. How far would she go? Ben did not want to find out.

"How are you going to eat?"

"That's a 'tomorrow' problem," Jen said as she got back under the covers.

Tanglewood was glad that she did because it was warmer when she was next to him. He could feel a jangling type of vibration going back and forth between Jen and Ben, but he didn't care because there were so many other pleasing vibrations to focus on. One came from Jen. One came from the stick. One from the ground. And one from the new boy, the one who knew about rhythm and could make it himself. He was glad that Jen wanted to keep the new boy. Maybe he could play other beats that Tanglewood could dance to. Tanglewood could tell that there were other beats to play. Many of them. He felt them, or the idea of them, faintly. They came from somewhere. The ground, maybe, or the trees, or.... Tanglewood drifted off as he turned inward, and found sleep.

* * *

Ben descended the slope, thinking no matter what he did, he would get caught. They would all get caught. And who knew what that would look like. But he didn't panic, which surprised him. He thought of his father, and one of the few times it was just the two of them — no Mom, no Jen. He couldn't remember why it was just the two of them but he remembered Dad saying, "Ben, most problems aren't as bad as you think they are at first. The key to conquering any problem is, you have to own it," his father had said, "and you have to focus on what you do have that might solve the problem; there's no point thinking about what you don't have."

It was only now, alone on the dark slope with the weirdest day of his life still piling on top of him, that he understood what his father meant about owning a problem. It meant acting like only he could solve it. "OK," Ben said to himself. "Problem, I own you." On the other hand, maybe the problem owned him. He chased that thought away, but found himself dwelling on things he wished were available right now, like a giant robot. He silenced all his wishes, and began to mentally sift through how to keep this situation from exploding using only what he had available. Or: who he had.

Ben picked up his pace down the slope to the camp. He needed to talk to Froggy as soon as possible.

PART THREE
SPIRIT OF THE WOODS

SPLIT

It had been a long day for Senpai, and he was restless. First days were always the hardest work and the least fun for everyone working at or arriving at his camp, which he had named "Spirit of the Woods". Senpai, whose given name was Coyote Lee-Baumgartner, took time to talk with each parent at drop-off, answering last-minute questions, helping them say good-bye to their children for the month and then getting each child outfitted and settled in before introducing them all to the instruments.

Senpai's camp was not a typical music camp. According to the advertising brochure, its exclusive focus was "immersion into the culture and practice of Taiko drumming for students who seek the rhythmic power that lives in nature." Coyote had written those words himself and he really meant it. Before printing the brochure he had asked his friend Anka for her opinion; when Anka said, "Do you really mean to say, '...who seek the power of music *in a natural setting*'?" Coyote replied, "No. The main thing is that nature is attached to music in the same way that people are attached to music, so music is the common language." Coyote's answer caused Anka to fall in love with him because it was such a beautiful idea, even though most people would think of it as nutty. But not Anka, and not the parents who sent their kids to Spirit of the Woods.

Coyote himself was raised in a woodsy suburb by parents who were very open-minded. He grew up believing that the things he wanted to be true might really be true. "If you could live long enough," his father told him once, "everything you can think of winds up being true. But don't expect other people to believe that."

Coyote saw his first Taiko drum concert when he was nine on a trip to Japan with his Japanese grandmother to visit her relatives. She had married a man from Taiwan whose last name was Lee and their son became Coyote's father. Coyote's mother was the "Baumgartner" in his last name, Lee-Baumgartner. His mom told him that her relatives had come from so many different countries that when people asked where she originally came from she would reply, "I'm from planet Earth." His parents were a little eccentric but they weren't unusual for the town where he grew up. The town itself was unusual, though, compared to where most people come from.

After Coyote had returned from his trip to Japan, all he talked about was the Taiko drum concert, how he could still feel the rapid ticking and waves of boom-boom-boom that filled the concert hall, and how he wished he could hear those sounds all the time. "I want to live inside a Taiko drum," he said. So his father built him one, not big enough to live in, but perfect for pounding on. Ever since then Coyote played the Taiko drums every day. He became very good over the years, so skilled that he had earned the right to be called "Senpai" by all who learned from him. He could have told the kids at his camp to call him Sensei instead of Senpai, which is what he would be called in Japan because of his mastery of the art, but he felt that he didn't deserve that name just yet. "Sensei is a name only for people who know all there is to know and I still have too much to learn," he had told Anka.

"Like what?" Anka had said.

"Like what the trees are feeling," he told her, "and how to talk to them."

Coyote believed that there was a deep connection between animals and plants. He believed that music was the key and that Taiko drums, in particular, were the best instrument to find the connection. Taiko drums were both animal and plant: its barrel-shaped body came from trees and its head, the part you hit, was the skin of an animal. Their sound came from working together, and that's what Coyote wanted more than anything — to bring plants and animals back together.

He saved his money. And one day he had enough to buy a piece of property that was about to be claimed by a company that wanted to cut down its trees for lumber. Coyote spent everything he had to buy the place before they did. He began living in the woods year-round, and created the camp because he believed that the only way to keep learning is to teach. Also, he needed to bring in enough money to keep it all going.

"Call me Senpai," Coyote said to this first group of the season on their first night. He stood on low platform in the center of the drum circle at Spirit of the Woods. "This summer you and I will play our music with the trees, and learn how to talk with them."

* * *

Jen woke up. It was still dark. She didn't want to be awake but a dream had shaken her sleepiness away. She couldn't remember anything about the dream, but she wasn't groggy or in a fog. She was wide awake and fully aware of every detail that led her to sleeping on the ground under a poncho next to this tree in these woods.

Her only weird thought was that nothing felt weird, as if she was supposed to be right here, right now, the same feeling she had every morning waking up in her own room.

The moon was gone from the sky so it was darker now than when she had shut her eyes. She looked to her side and couldn't really see Tanglewood, but he was there; she could feel the bamboo leaves brushing against her skin, plus there was an odd smell coming from under the poncho-blanket. It wasn't intolerable, but it definitely wasn't pleasant, and no smell like it had ever emanated from her own body, so it had to come from him. He smelled kind of like a wet dog.

Jen noticed that she thought of Tanglewood as "he" and "him" now. She still wanted Tanglewood to be a girl, but it no longer made sense. Maybe it was the smell.

She could tell she wasn't going to fall asleep again and began to feel boredom set in. It was too cold to leave the warmth under the blanket so she decided to wake up Tanglewood.

She jostled his shoulder. "Tanglewood, wake up," she said, but Tanglewood kept perfectly still even after the jostling.

Perfectly still, and that seemed wrong. Someone who is sleeping shouldn't be perfectly still because they should be breathing. Jen put her face close to Tanglewood's head and her hand on his chest but she felt no breath and detected no movement. She thought, maybe Tanglewood doesn't breathe normally because he didn't appear to have a mouth. He had never said a word or had made any sound other than the rustling of his leaves. But that observation didn't stop the terrible question bursting forth in her mind. Was Tanglewood no longer alive?

She rolled him over, rested her ear on his chest, and held her own breath so she could listen carefully — she definitely heard a beat, and just as she was wondering how to be sure that the beat came from Tanglewood and not from her own heart, Tanglewood raised his arms, stretched, then curled up again, his arms now embracing Jen, engulfing her with same type of bear hug she had used when sleeping with her favorite stuffed animal, Smokey.

"Pee-yew," Jen said, her face now smushed into Tanglewood's armpit.

After a couple minutes of squirming she managed to slip out from Tanglewood's grasp, and none of her pushing and twisting had woken him up.

"Brother," Jen said, "you sleep like a log."

"Sn-ucch." The snoring came from Stones. The bandana had slipped off his mouth during the night. Stones's long, bony neck slung forward almost at a right angle from his body; his chin rested on his chest.

The stars faded as the sky became a deep blue, and silhouettes began to emerge from the uniform blackness of the nighttime woods.

Jen hated being the only one awake. She picked up some pebbles and began tossing them one by one at Stones. They were small and she didn't throw them that hard.

"Wake up," Jen said with each pebble she tossed. After about fifteen of them Stones stirred.

"Lee mee 'lone," he said.

Jen kept tossing pebbles.

"Quit it." His speech was less slurred.

"No," said Jen.

"Please," said Stones.

"Wow," Jen said, "you actually know that word?"

Stones lifted his neck and opened his eyes.

"Why?" he said.

"Why what?" Jen said.

SPLIT

"Why aren't I dead yet?"

Stones's question raised mixed feelings for Jen. The whole point of last week, before coming to camp, was to convince Stones that he could be dead if she wanted him dead, but now, hearing him sound so worried she felt a little sorry for him. She didn't want to let any sympathy show, but she was curious how, exactly, Stones understood this whole situation, given that she didn't understand it herself.

"Why would you be dead?" Jen asked.

"Because I'm plant food. I don't want to be plant food. But I'm plant food."

"That's a stupid idea," Jen said. "Why would you even believe that it's possible to be eaten by a plant?" She genuinely wanted to know. "Is it just because of those movies you watch? You're too old to believe movies are real."

"My dad was right."

"Right about what?"

"The plants, they're alive — and they want us dead."

"What the hell?"

"My dad said it, he's always said it. And you! You said it, too. The bamboo was coming to eat me! And you showed that thing who I was, and now it's here because it followed me here! It's like The Terminator!"

Jen's mind fought against itself. Part of her wanted to keep Stones thinking this way because having Stones be this kind of afraid was the plan and Jen didn't change plans easily. But another part of her felt insulted, and offended.

"How could you think that Tanglewood would come here because of you?"

"Who?"

"Tanglewood!"

"It has a name?"

"Don't call him 'it'. He doesn't care about you. He wouldn't come here for you. He came here because I'm the one who's important to him!"

Jen sidled out from under the covers, stood up and addressed Tanglewood.

"You came here because of me, right, Tanglewood?"

Stones startled as Jen stood up suddenly, and talked at a heap under her blanket.

"You came here because of me, right, Tanglewood?" Jen said, but he didn't budge, so she yanked the poncho up and away revealing Tanglewood, still in a fetal position.

Stones fixated on the now-exposed creature coiled on the ground.

"Get UP you sleepyhead!" Jen commanded. Stones believed Jen was orchestrating his final moments.

Birds chirped.

The light blue dawn spread across the sky, casting just enough light for details to be misinterpreted. Stones saw small versions of the creature crawl out from its insides. He clamped his eyes shut and began to sob, quietly. Jen, because she was closer to Tanglewood and not freaking out, saw, instead, three baby blue jays sticking their heads up from within the wisps of Tanglewood's hair. She also saw two squirrels squeeze their faces out from between Tanglewood's ankles and a raccoon on the ground behind Tanglewood's legs, nuzzled into the crook between his knees and his butt.

"Please untie me," Stones pleaded. "At least let me run and try to live. Give me a chance!"

"You're going to be fine," Jen said, calmly. "Look at him. He's like Bambi with all the forest critters."

And then she said, "Awwww."

SPLIT

The way Jen said "Awww" caused Stones to open his eyes — it sounded so friendly and sweet. He saw a young deer silently approach and begin nibbling at a cluster of Tanglewood's leaves.

"Hey quit doing that! He isn't food!" Jen hollered at the deer. The deer kept nibbling.

Tanglewood suddenly sat up, turned toward the deer and skritched it behind the ears. Then he twisted his torso the other direction and saw the boy. The one who played the songs!

Tanglewood hopped over to Stones, crouched in front of him, wiggled his hips and began slapping the ground.

Stones stopped breathing altogether, part of him glad that the end was finally here so he wouldn't have to think about it anymore.

Tanglewood grabbed the stick. He had almost forgotten about the stick. Then he stood before Stones and pointed it at him.

"Tanglewood, ignore him!" Jen cried.

Her words gave Stones a dim hope that Jen would call the creature off. He could no longer close his eyes because constant anxiety forced them open. Tanglewood stood above him holding a long stick like a warrior with his sword drawn, pointing it right at Stones's chest, slowly moving the stick-sword toward his chest, closer, closer.

Being stabbed by a sword would be better than being eaten, Stones thought, just as Tanglewood began tapping the stick onto Stones's chest. Not stabbing, just tapping, right over where his heart was.

"What is he doing that for?" Stones said.

"Tanglewood, what are you doing that for?" Jen asked, only because she wanted Tanglewood to stop paying attention to Stones instead of her.

Tanglewood kept tapping Stones with the stick.

Jen moved herself between Stones and Tanglewood. "Hey!" Jen said, "You're supposed to listen to me."

And Tanglewood stopped tapping.

She turned to Stones. "See. He listens to *me*."

Because Jen seemed to want the creature to stop paying attention to him, Stones now counted on it listening to her.

Jen noticed Stones's eyes shift away from her gaze to focus on whatever was going on behind her. She turned and saw Tanglewood pivot away from her while lowering himself into a half-crouch. He extended the stick outward once again, but this time bobbing it in the air toward a stand of trees that grew on the other side of a clearing. The sight of Tanglewood wielding the sword-stick with his wrist-banded arm made Jen believe, for a moment, that she was looking at herself.

"Tanglewood, what the heck are you doing?" Jen couldn't stop asking Tanglewood questions even though he couldn't answer in any form she might understand. Tanglewood suddenly stood up from his crouch and began moving swiftly across the clearing — the opposite direction from where they had come the night before.

"Where are you going? Hey, stop!"

Tanglewood sped up as he approached the trees growing beyond the clearing. Jen began to run after Tanglewood.

"Hey!!! You can't leave me tied up!" Stones yelped.

He was right. The thought of Ben knowing that she had done such a thing....

Then she remembered the dream that had woken her up. She had dreamt that Ben had never been born.

She stuffed that thought back down, and frantically untied Stones. As soon as his wrists were apart she pulled them together again, away from the tree trunk and re-wound the apron string around his wrists, then around his waist and quickly tied a knot that still left plenty of apron material for her to hold onto, as a leash. Stones's arms and legs had become too cramped to stop her.

"You're coming with me," she said. She pulled Stones by the apron-leash, grabbed her arrow from the ground where it had lain next to her during the night and began poking Stones in the back so that he would keep moving in front of her as fast as she wanted to go. They head across the clearing, and entered the trees, picking up speed.

Stones spent all his energy keeping his balance as trees popped up everywhere and the ground began to tilt, getting steeper. He felt at the edge of his ability to react and control his own body.

But his ears were still under his control. He heard drumbeats, the same rhythm that had drifted toward and through him when he had sat at the plastic bucket drum set outside the kitchen. That rhythm had soothed him until the creature jumped out from the darkness. Then it became the last sound he thought he would ever hear. But now the beat was back, and he was alive to hear it. Even as he careened down the slope the rhythm sent a wave through him that he wanted to join — it was a feeling he couldn't resist.

"That sound!" he said. "You hear it?"

"What about it?" Jen said.

"Go there." Stones said.

"What for?"

Stones twisted his body sideways to avoid smacking into a tree. "Because that's where he's going," he said.

Jen didn't want to listen to Stones, but she had completely lost sight of Tanglewood and had no other ideas. So she veered left where the drumbeats seemed to come from, and entered a stand of trees that grew even closer together.

* * *

Ben woke up after a lousy sleep. His mattress was only an inch thick and he could feel each and every bedspring. Somehow the springs managed to both poke upward into the mattress and sag downward toward the floor. His back hurt.

The night before, when he had returned to the camp after leaving Jen in the woods, the first thing he noticed was that the camp, at night, was the same as it was during the day — kids running around everywhere, only in darkness illuminated by spotlights, each making a cone of light swarming with bugs.

At the edge of one of the lights he saw Froggy. Froggy didn't ask questions as Ben opened the conversation, "We have to make it look like Jen is down here even though she's really up there." He pointed at the darkness and trees.

"I can pile up her stuff on her bed to make it look like she's asleep under her blanket," Froggy had said. Froggy was the most willing and helpful person Ben had ever met.

Ben didn't think the chances of Froggy's idea working were high but he didn't have a better plan for hiding Jen's absence that night. If he went back to pretending he was Jen, then he would be missing, and he had no equivalent of Froggy in his cabin to close up that hole.

"That's a good idea," Ben had told Froggy. "When's bedtime, anyway? Isn't everyone tired by now?"

"Last year I heard one of the counselors say that the more we're worn out the faster we'll fall asleep, and that falling asleep fast was important so they could all get started on the meetings they have at night to plan the next day's activities."

Ben had thought to himself there was no way these counselors seemed to spend any time planning anything at this camp, which might be helpful because he was frantically making up his own plans out of thin air.

"I need you to get me some of Jen's stuff before people go to sleep," Ben said to Froggy.

When Froggy returned and handed Ben the clothes, she asked, "Are you going to bring these to Jen and Tangie so they can have clean clothes in the morning, wherever they're secretly staying?"

"That's exactly right," Ben said, just so he didn't have to explain further. The truth was that he wanted to have some of Jen's clothes handy so that he could dress up as her if he needed to. Who knew what crazy problems tomorrow would bring?

Later, as he fell asleep he remembered, suddenly and horribly, that Jen wasn't the only one who could be discovered missing. Stones was up there with her! His mind spun. It seemed like all he could do was to hope that no one would notice, an absurd idea but then, he thought, it might be possible. Stones was at camp to work so he probably wasn't in a regular cabin. The only one who was keeping track of him was Nash, and Nash, he could tell, wasn't the kind of parent who paid a lot of attention to his kid. If they were staying in the same room, wherever that might be, that would be bad. But Ben couldn't do anything about it until morning. He was about to give up worrying when he thought, "What the heck will I do about it in the morning?" So he stayed awake for hours, half of him listening for Nash to raise an alarm during the night, while the other half struggled to come up with a plan. The next thing he knew, he opened his eyes and tomorrow had become today.

The light was dim. No one else in his cabin was awake.

His counselor's bed was empty, and it looked like it hadn't been slept in. Ben wasn't sure what that meant. It occurred to him that maybe all the counselors had stayed up all night looking for Jen and Stones after noticing they were missing. He had told Froggy to come get him if she noticed anything that suggested her counselor or anyone else knew that Jen was not actually in her bed. If Froggy's plan had worked — and it appeared it had because she didn't show up during the night — that still left Stones to worry about.

Ben got out of bed slowly, not just because his body hurt but to make as little noise as possible. Outside, the sun wasn't up and the camp grounds were empty. He had the worst taste in his mouth but didn't want to risk going back into the cabin to get his toothbrush. He felt a pit in his stomach, its emptiness filled with dread. There was no way to avoid confronting the situation, so he made his way to the kitchen to carry out the plan he devised while falling asleep.

Of course Nash was up. Nash would be. And he would also be happy about being up at this awful hour. There he was, whistling, standing at a prep table dumping what looked like sawdust into a large, metal mixing bowl.

Ben cleared his throat. Nash stopped whistling and looked over to him.

"Um, OK, so I'm here instead of Stones," Ben said.

"Why?" Nash said.

"Well he and I had a bet and I lost and I told him that if I lost I would work in the kitchen for him for, like, today, or part of it..." It took effort to prevent himself from talking too fast or saying too much. "We haven't worked out exactly for how long but I'm here instead of Stones." Ben finished. "For now," he added.

"Huh. What was the bet about?"

"It was more like a race and I lost. He won." Ben began to bite his tongue.

Nash seemed proud, and he chuckled. "Lots of grit and tooth in that boy, just like his old man. Where is he now?"

"Sleeping in, I guess. I mean, he said he was going to sleep until at least lunchtime."

"Fine by me, loser. Here, stir this."

SPLIT

Nash slid the mixing bowl toward Ben. It contained a thick paste with pebbly chunks.

"What is this?" Ben said.

"Pancake batter," Nash said.

"Is that tree bark in it?"

"Chaff! Whole grain or no grain! Stir it even but leave it lumpy."

Ben left it lumpy because the lumps weren't going anywhere. He watched over the pancakes as they bubbled on the griddle. He never would have believed that the sight of pancakes would wreck his appetite but these did as he watched the lumps pop open to reveal nuts or seeds or whatever it was floating in the batter. On the griddle the pancakes turned from pasty gray to a flecked brown that was unlike any pancake Ben had ever seen, or wanted to.

He kept an eye on the dining room on the other side of the serving area. As soon as he noticed kids at his cabin's table he told Nash, "I'll be right back. I have to go to the bathroom."

He went up to his counselor who stood near his table talking to another counselor.

"Hey, Troy," Ben said, "I'm working in the kitchen today. All day."

"We did kitchen duty last night." Troy said.

"Well, I volunteered to do more. I like to cook." Ben said.

"That's weird, but OK." Troy waved Ben off and returned to his conversation.

Ben saw Froggy and motioned for her to come to him. He led her to a darkened corner of the dining room, near the bathrooms.

"How's it going?" he whispered, his eyes scanning for anyone who might be close enough to listen.

"Really good," Froggy said, "I came up with a great idea because I wasn't sure how long Jen will be gone today, so I got up early and put away everything that was Jen under the covers and then when my counselor woke up I told her that Jen felt sick and went to the infirmary."

"What?" Ben tried to keep his voice down to a whisper. "That's a terrible idea. The infirmary is a specific place!"

"Why are you so upset because it's a specific place?"

Froggy had used so many *ess* sounds in a row that Ben became fixated on her tongue as it darted in and out the gap between her teeth, turning all the *ess*'s into *th*'s.

"Seriously," Froggy continued, "the infirmary is a great idea. Kids get forgotten when they go to the infirmary. Sometimes for a whole day. It happened to me once. I looked inside it last night before I went to bed and the infirmary already had six kids waiting, and that was before bedtime. Well this morning when I checked again some of those kids were still there — some kids wind up spending the night especially if it's homesickness. So this morning there were even more, like ten new ones, all sitting there." She paused, and then smiled. "So I put Jen's name on the list."

"What list?"

"The waiting list to see the nurse. It'll be hours. If Jen gets back sooner we can just scratch her name off the list and that's that."

Ben wanted to believe everything Froggy said, but he struggled.

"Froggy, just to be sure, I think I may have to spend some of today dressed up as Jen, kind of like when we first met. We don't want anyone to go looking for her. So if you think you see Jen, remember, it could just be me, and don't talk to me until you know for sure who I am."

"Don't you just stay you, no matter what?" Froggy said with a completely sincere look on her face.

"I mean until you know who I'm pretending to be."

"Oh, I see. Because you might still be pretending to be yourself. That's confusing, but I understand. When is she coming back do you think? Jen, I mean." Froggy said.

Ben didn't know. It had been twelve hours since he had last seen Jen, and it felt like forever. They had never been apart for this long before.

TRAVERSAL

Jen continued rushing downhill. The drum sounds stopped. Then she stopped, pulling the apron-leash taut, as if it were a bridle and Stones her horse.

"Shhh!" she said to Stones, "stop breathing so loud." She listened carefully but heard only the silence of the woods. "Where'd they go?" she said.

"I don't know," Stones said. "Can you untie me now?"

"No."

"Why not?"

"Because I don't trust you. Why did you say Tanglewood is going toward the drums? Why would you help me find Tanglewood after, you know, everything that's happened?"

"I'm not sure, I'm all confused. My dad always said—"

"Forget about what your dad said. You're dad is nuts!"

"I know! I mean, that's what I'm starting to think. But if Tanglewood is real then my dad isn't wrong about plants being alive like that."

Jen didn't like the idea of Nash being right about anything. "Well he's wrong about other stuff, like plants eating people."

"It happened to my mom."

"What?"

"She was eaten by plants."

"How do you know?"

"My dad said."

"You know, for a bully you sure listen to your dad a lot. I thought bullies didn't listen to their parents."

"My dad is hard to ignore."

"Well, your mom wasn't eaten by a plant."

"How do you know?"

"Because it makes no sense! Plants don't eat people! They can't even move that fast."

"What about Tanglewood?"

"Tanglewood is different."

"Why?"

"Because," Jen hesitated. "Well, for one thing he doesn't even have a mouth."

"That probably means he's hungry all the time, which will drive you crazy."

Stones's head drooped, in defeat, Jen thought. She started to feel sorry for him again. If anyone she had ever met looked hungry all the time, it was Stones. Her stomach felt so empty right now that she could imagine how awful constant hunger would be. She imagined....

Wait a minute. Jen sniffed the air. The last thing she needed was for her own mind to start playing cruel tricks on her, thinking about hunger this way, craving food in a place where there was none. She sniffed again, more deeply and there it was again: the smell of bacon. Her imagination couldn't possibly be that good. The scent grew stronger, and with it, her belief that it came from the real thing.

"This way," Jen yanked the apron and marched, following her nose.

"I don't hear any drums from there," Stones said.

"This way!" Jen began to run.

* * *

Coyote began each camp day early with a drumming session before breakfast. As a payoff, breakfast at his camp was always a huge and satisfying meal. He understood that the early morning wasn't everyone's favorite time, but in his approach to teaching Taiko, Coyote emphasized that it wasn't just about hitting things hard. There are soft beats, tired beats, high-energy beats, smooth beats and ratchety ones, and it was important for his students to become aware of what their bodies felt like at different times of day. "Drumming sounds are created by our bodies but rhythm has a deeper source," he had told his students the morning of the first day. "Rhythm comes from our hearts and our minds, and from deeper still, from the center where all vibrations live, some good and some bad, some tight and some loose, but all of them wanting to get out into the world where they can meet others like themselves and create life. If we do our work and do it well, we might see the Spirit of the Woods dance as the vibrations meet one another."

Anka had told him, after the first time she heard him give that speech, "You know, Coyote, the kids probably think you're just a dork when you say goofy stuff like that."

"That's OK," Coyote had said back to Anka. "I kind of am a dork; and sometimes the truth is goofy."

BOOM. BOOM-BA-BOOM. BOOM-PA-PA-PA-BOOM.

Coyote had taught the kids the first of his Sun rhythms. The students, standing at their drums in a big circle, were going at it. They were doing a pretty good job, most of them staying together but a few lagged and a few others rushed the beat. But that was all right because eventually he would teach them about syncopation, where some beats fit between others to create sounds that fight against one another and work together all at the same time. The lagging and rushing drummers created an accidental syncopation. The complex result made Coyote smile.

It also got Tanglewood's attention. He felt its direction, and ran toward the sound.

Coyote, conducting from a low podium in the center of the drum circle, flowed with the sound, his eyes closed as he moved his arms while listening intently. Suddenly, one kid shouted, "Senpai, I see it! I see it coming!"

Coyote's eyes popped open as the rest of the kids gasped and the rhythm started to fall apart. A tree creature burst through the dense woods that surrounded the drum circle and began dancing wildly.

"Holy crap!" Coyote was stunned into using words that he would never say as "Senpai". Although he had spent his life watching for evidence that the trees could speak with him he hadn't pictured how that moment would actually look. For a split second he wondered if this dancing thing was just someone dressed in a tree costume — but it would have to be a miraculous costume worn by a bare skeleton because its limbs were too skinny for a person to be inside it. And it wasn't made of "tree" — it was made of bamboo. Did bamboo even live in these woods? He had never see any up here before, and he had hiked these woods for years, both on and off the trails.

"Is it real?" said one kid.

"It moves weird," said another.

Tanglewood stopped moving because the boom-pa-pa-pa-boom had stopped completely. He slowly lifted up the stick and pointed it around him, turning in a circle.

"Does that mean it's turning back into a tree, Senpai?"

Coyote snapped out of his trance fearful that the creature would disappear because of the silence. "Children!" Coyote called out, "Children! Keep playing! *Motomoto!*" He had already explained to the students that *motomoto* meant, "move fast, now." The drummers responded and the drums boomed, which made Tanglewood very happy.

* * *

"The drums! They're back!" Stones shouted at Jen as he dodged one tree after another even as the slope leveled off. "They're coming from over there!"

The drums thumped away somewhere to the right of where Jen was heading; she kept to the direction her nose led.

"There it is!" Jen pointed at a narrow gap in the trees. "I can see it!"

"See what?" Stones said. "What can you see?"

"Bacon."

Jen snuck in closer and there, placed across a long outdoor grill were at least a dozen pans of sizzling bacon. A woman stood next to the grill.

"Anka!" a man's voice shouted, "Come here! Quickly!"

The woman at the grill turned the burners down. "Justin," she said to someone nearby, "Senpai needs me, keep an eye on the grill." She trotted off, but the grill stayed unattended.

"Here's our chance!" Jen said, and pulled Stones with her as she popped out from the trees, ran at the grill, and grabbed one of the pans by its handle.

"H-Hot! Ow!" Jen dropped the pan and immediately reached around Stones to grab the flared-out part of the apron and use it as a pot-holder. "Get closer to me!" Jen said to Stones while tugging the apron, and him along with it, twisting him around so that the only way for him to "get closer" was to stumble backwards toward the grill.

Jen wrapped the flared end of apron around her hand, grabbed a pan, as Stones, watching over his shoulder, writhed to avoid getting splattered by its sloshing hot grease. He ducked, causing his elbow to knock one of the burners all the way up, which neither he nor Jen noticed. All Stones noticed, now, was that he had hit his funny bone. His arm lit up with pain as Jen returned to the trees, extending the bacon-pan-holding end of the apron in front of her with one hand and grasping the Stones-hauling end with the other. Stones did his best to avoid the tree trunks as he lurched and wobbled against his will. He scraped a cheek and clocked a knee before Jen finally came to a halt by a rock.

Jen dumped the contents of the pan onto the rock, got on her knees to blow on the greasy pile, picked up a strip of bacon, waggled it in the air and stuffed it in her mouth.

"Oh my God so good. So so good," Jen said, grabbing, cooling, and devouring another. "Here." She grabbed a third strip and held it out to Stones. "Eat."

"That's meat."

"Not just meat. BACON."

"Can't eat it."

"Because of religion?"

"My dad says it'll kill me."

"Your dad is wrong about everything! Do you understand? It's food! You need to eat. That's your whole problem. Eat it. Now!"

Stones had given up so many times in the past few days there was no fight left in him. He was hungry, it was true, so hungry that he felt like his insides were nothing but an empty stomach that stretched down into his legs, sideways into his arms and upward into his head. And, although he had wavered about whether or not to believe his father about anything any more, it was only at this very moment that he became sure it was the right decision. Maybe the soothing rhythmic pulse of the nearby drums had something to do with his certainty, and if all he ever heard again were these drums it would be fine with him. For the first time in his life he felt it was possible to stop being afraid all the time, which didn't exactly make sense because, right now, he was a prisoner with his hands tied behind his back as his captor stood before him, a fierce look on her face, her hair flying in every direction, the whole of her shrouded in a dirty poncho — a destroyer of worlds if ever there was one. This moment, Stones knew, was definitely the end of something, and he was ready for his world to be destroyed so he could enter a new one.

"Eat or be eaten," the destroyer said.

"Fine," Stones said. "Feed me."

Jen blew on the bacon slice once more to make sure it was cool, then held it where Stones could easily take a bite.

"Careful," the destroyer said. "It may still be a little hot."

He took it in, and the beating of the drums seemed to get both louder and softer at the same time. Something inside him — happened. If bacon killed you it did it in a very nice way, Stones thought as he chewed then swallowed. His mouth felt — happy? That's ridiculous, he told himself, mouths don't feel happy. But what about smiling? Smiling is a happy mouth. The happy feeling moved its way down, and he no longer felt empty. He mumbled, a huge grin on his face.

"What did you just say?" Jen's words seem to come at him through a pink fog.

"Sm-smile. Smile smiling is a happy happy. Mouth. Not empty," Stones babbled. "Not empty."

"You're an idiot," Jen said.

Stones passed out.

"Stones! Get up. This isn't sleeping time! Stones! Stones?"

Jen's mind raced. If you've never eaten bacon before and then you do, does it kill you? That can't be true, otherwise the first time you eat bacon you would die. She had heard her parents say that too much bacon was bad, but not just one bite, or even hundreds of bites, which is probably what she'd eaten over her life so far.

She knelt next to Stones and could see that he was breathing. Jen hadn't felt so relieved in a long time, but she couldn't wake him, just as she couldn't wake Tanglewood earlier. Stones just lay on the ground with a big smile on his face, breathing steadily.

FOOMF! The grill, just twenty yards away, burst into flames.

"Anka!" a man's voice yelled. "A grease fire! Come help!" Jen could see a young man standing not far from the grill but not going near it, his face reflecting orange from the crackle and spit of flames that licked upward from the grill. The woman who had been standing by the grill earlier came rushing back. She ducked from the heat as she circled to the back of the grill, then gave the lid a shove. It swung down heavily and the flame disappeared.

"Turn the knobs off!" The woman shouted. "Why didn't you keep an eye on it?" She asked as she fanned away smoke with a dish towel.

"Because I was standing over there watching," the man said. "I couldn't believe it. I saw it! The tree spirit that Senpai always talked about. It's true! It's here."

"Apparently," the woman said.

Jen knew what they had seen. She dropped the apron strings and was about to dash toward the drums, but then stopped. What to do about Stones? She could leave him lying there unconscious and alive. But tied up — that seemed like taking things too far. What if he started choking and needed his hands free? It was essential to get to that spirit the man and woman had mentioned, so she had to risk dealing with Stones later.

She untied Stones's wrists and double-checked to make sure he was still breathing, then ran to where the drums were loudest, keeping back far enough to stay hidden in the trees until she saw people — strangely dressed, short people banging away on big drums.

Jen stayed in a crouch as she snuck in to get a closer look. Keeping low, she stuck her head through a gap between tree trunks. These weren't short people — they were kids playing the drums. But the way they moved and the way they dressed wasn't like any kids she knew. And the drums were unlike any she had ever seen. They looked like big barrels. Some stood upright but others were on their sides held up by stands shaped like ladders. The drummers wore shirts with cloth belts strapped around them, or maybe they were short jackets. Their pants were too long to be shorts and too short to be regular pants, and they were loose, billowing out almost like a skirt. The sticks they used to beat their drums were fat and looked heavy, but the kids could move the sticks fast. And every kid wore wristbands on both wrists. A diet that included bacon was reason enough to be envious of these kids but the sight of the wristbands took Jen beyond the cravings of hunger, into the fear of loss. Tanglewood was hers. Why was he here?

Jen felt a wave of jealousy. A man shouted *"Kyuu-Shifu!"* or something that sounded like a sneeze, and everyone stopped playing.

"Spirit," the man said, "we welcome you. You honor us."

Jen scooted around a tree and poked her head through another gap to get a look at who was talking — some grown up guy wearing a long coat or robe; he bowed low, and he was bowing at Tanglewood.

Tanglewood wiggled his hips, scratched the guy's head with his fingers, and then turned to the biggest drum of all, a sideways drum on a tall stand. Tanglewood held up his stick — the one she had given him— and gave the drum a whap. KON-DON, went the sound, a deep, low vibration. The drumhead was so wide Jen could see it vibrate.

"Spirit," the man said, "may I give you these *bachi* — a gift."

He held out two of the thick, heavy-looking drumsticks to Tanglewood. Tanglewood dropped his stick and took them, one in each hand.

Jen had seen enough. She marched into the drum circle.

The kid who had called out to Senpai earlier said, "Senpai! Look! Another spirit from the woods is here!"

"Hey!" Jen said as she shoved her way between Senpai and Tanglewood, looking directly up at Tanglewood. "I gave you that stick! You gonna just drop it and forget it like it doesn't exist anymore?"

Coyote stepped back, startled by the presence of this new spirit, who looked remarkably similar to an ordinary girl. But no girl in his memory had such a wild look or was so encrusted with dirt and dressed in a shawl of what looked like the bark taken from some exotic tree. Coyote could tell right away that she came from an untamed world that lay beyond the everyday woods.

"C'mon," Jen took Tanglewood by the wrist. "We've got to get back."

"Stop! Please!" Coyote said. "I have been calling to this spirit and waiting for an answer for a very long time. Now he comes to me, finally, and he comes freely. Who are you to take him away?"

Jen let go of Tanglewood to pull out her arrow, which she had poked in and out through the poncho material several times, like her mother did with pins through fabric. She yanked it out and pointed it at the dude in the long coat.

"I am Xena. Back off."

A minute ago, when Jen had showed up, Tanglewood was happy — so many good things had all come together and were with him now in one place! But the happy feeling melted as all the good things now seemed to be pushing against each other, and as they pushed he felt as if they were also pulling him in different directions. The sensation was uncomfortable. Tanglewood escaped it by turning inward until he discovered a feeling of comfort that seemed to come from his hands. The *bachi* — the sticks the man had given him — felt like part of his own body, as if he and they had come from the same place and found their way back to each other. Holding the *bachi* reminded him of what it felt like to hold onto the little-little one.

But where was the little-little one now? Tanglewood reached for his chest and into the space where he had tucked it away but it wasn't there. Where was the little-little one? Images flickered through Tanglewood's memory as he tried to recall where he had last seen it but instead of a picture of a smaller version of himself lying on the ground somewhere he saw something much bigger than just himself. Something that was both below the ground and above the ground. Something that had been taken apart.

What am I? The question reverberated through Tanglewood, and then it became, Who am I? Then, Why am I here?

Coyote, meanwhile, pursued his concern about whether Xena was friend or foe. "Who are you, Xena," Coyote said to Jen, "and why do you take this *kodama* away from where he chooses to go?"

Jen thought it was strange, the way this guy in the long coat was talking to her — not at all as if she were a child, but as though she were his age or maybe even older. That was new. And he used odd words as if he expected her to know them even though she had no idea what they meant. But there was no way she was going to let him know that.

"This *kodama* is mine," Jen said, her voice steady as a rock.

Coyote had put a lot of time into his belief that it was possible for trees to manifest their spirit to him in a form he could interact with. Now that it had really happened, instead of feeling triumphant and satisfied, Coyote became aware of how much he didn't understand the workings of the spirit world. This Xena, for example, was totally unexpected. And she seemed very aggressive. Was she taking the spirit as her prisoner? Coyote became very uneasy. Was Xena a manifestation of the tree-spirit's mortal enemy — a dark spirit known as The Woodcutter, who laid waste to the trees to satisfy his greed.

"Are you The Woodcutter, Xena?" Coyote said, carefully.

"What did you call me?" The name itself wounded and insulted her.

Coyote breathed slowly, deliberately. He could see that Xena was upset by his question. But he decided to press ahead; he hadn't waited all these years to have his dream of contacting the spirit world turn into a missed opportunity to save a spirit of the woods from destruction.

"I called you, 'The Woodcutter'. Are you here to cut this spirit down, Xena? Or the trees that made him?"

Jen's jaw clenched. She picked up the stick Tanglewood had dropped and faced Coyote, pointing the arrow and the stick, one in each hand, the stick twice as long as the arrow, and hefty. It felt good to hold a sword again, even if it was just a stick, even without her wristband and the surge that would have come as she tightened her grip. She leaned forward just far enough for the stick's tip to rest against Coyote's chest, over his heart.

"Don't you ever call me that." Jen's anger at his accusation kept her voice steady and low. She barely recognized it as her own. "I'd cut you down before I would do such a thing to any plant. You take it back!"

Tanglewood felt the forces pulling at him with greater intensity. Turning inward was not giving him comfort any more, so he struggled to find another way. He turned to the big Taiko drum next to him. It had different parts, like he did, and it too was held together with rope. It even had a tight skin wrapped on it, like he had on his wrist. He flung himself at the drum, pushed his face up against the skin of the drumhead, and embraced the wooden barrel with his arms even as he held tightly to the *bachi*. Perhaps, Tanglewood hoped, the drum would understand, and explain, and hug him back.

"Take back what you said," Jen said to the man, slowly. She narrowed her eyes. She breathed through her nose, feeling jets of heat from her breath stream past her chin and onto her arms.

Coyote held her gaze as he added things up in his mind. The *kodama* who had danced into his drum circle was still here, and, although he seemed to be hugging the drum in a way that seemed a little sad, he didn't act scared. He wasn't running away from this Xena-being, who looked like she might be made from a tree herself. Coyote decided he must take her very seriously. Xena looked like she said only what she meant to say; there was nothing subtle about her. She wasn't a person; she was a force of nature.

Coyote held his hands flat toward her. "Forgive me, Xena. I couldn't allow myself to yield this *kodama* to The Woodcutter. I needed to be sure. I take back what I said. I can tell now that you are a Guardian."

Jen stepped sideways toward Tanglewood, keeping her eyes on the man in the long coat. She transferred the arrow into the same hand that held the stick, and then groped with her free hand until she had a grasp on Tanglewood.

Tanglewood felt Jen's tug, but he wasn't ready to leave the drum. He brushed the bound-together sticks of his head and hair against the tight skin of the drumhead, making a *shush-ka-shoop* sound.

Jen tugged at him. "We have to go now, Tanglewood."

"Is that what you call this *kodama*, Xena? Tanglewood?" Coyote said.

"Stay back!" Jen extended her arm that held the stick and arrow.

"I'm not going to stop you, Xena," Coyote said. "But please tell me its name."

"He's not an 'it', he's a he."

Coyote had never thought of a spirit of the woods as a boy or a girl — he always assumed that a spirit-being would be both at the same time. There was so much he wanted to know, and understand.

"How do you know that the *kodama* Tanglewood is a man?"

"I made him. And he's just a boy."

Coyote began to speak. "How—"

"We're done talking! Back away. I mean it."

Coyote took a step backwards. He was grateful to have had this experience and didn't want to anger Xena, who was clearly in charge of many things. If she had made the *kodama* named Tanglewood, as she said, that meant she was its mother. The dirt, or bark, that formed her face was in the shape of a young girl but if she was a mother then this force named Xena must be much older than she looked. Meeting a spirit of the woods and its mother was so much more than Coyote had been hoping for, or even imagined. He did not want to become a nuisance to the spirit world and have them abandon him, so he let go of all his questions.

Tanglewood let go of the drum, disappointed that it just sat there and did not hug him back, while the warmth of Jen's hand on his wrist did a much better job helping him feel like he wasn't alone anymore. So he moved with her.

"Thank you for sharing yourselves with us," Coyote said. "We know these woods and all within them are yours to wander. We hope you will both return to us. I am Coyote." He would never refer to himself as Senpai to a spirit and its mother. He had to be humble. It didn't matter to him if his students heard him say his real name. "I am Coyote," he said once more, "your servant."

"What a weird name," Jen thought, her eyes darting around her as she backed away from Coyote, holding Tanglewood by his banded wrist while wielding the stick-and-arrow with her other hand. She had forgotten that she was surrounded by the weirdly dressed kids; they had kept so quiet.

The kids were impressed with her, she could tell. Their eyes were wide, their mouths hung open. As she and Tanglewood made their way to the trees Coyote bowed low, and all the children did the same. They all bowed to her.

"This is more like it," Jen said to herself, and couldn't help thinking that this camp — if that's what it was — seemed like a better place than the one she had to return to.

She turned her mind to the need to move quickly, holding onto Tanglewood, who, she was glad, did not resist. She arrived at the spot where she had left Stones. But he was gone. Was she in the wrong spot? No. The greasy rock was right there and the pan next to it.

Jen panicked as she thought of Stones having a head start and getting back to Triple-Bar without her. And when he got there.... Her mind reeled; there was no telling what he would say or do after being tied to a tree all night only to be dragged by a leash down a hill and forced to eat bacon. And it would be so unfair if he made a big deal out of it after she had started to feel sorry for him!

This whole situation was becoming unbalanced, a brand new experience for Jen. She didn't like it. It messed with her confidence.

"Tanglewood, we gotta run, now!" She bolted up the slope, keeping a tight grip on everything she carried with her as she crossed back over to the other side.

SHAKEN

After breakfast had been served at Triple-Bar and most of the kids had left the dining hall, Nash went to the refrigerator, pulled out several plastic containers and put them into a plastic grocery bag. "I'm out until lunch prep," he told Ben. "Clean everything then shred that bin of carrots. I'll be back at 11." He exited through the screen door.

Ben went to the door, peeked outside and watched as Nash pulled a backpack from his truck bed then stuffed the grocery bag into it. Nash slung on the pack, hopped onto his dirt bike and roared off. He wasn't wearing a helmet.

When he was sure Nash had gone Ben looked at the clock. He had only two hours. He rushed to the sink, took out the pans that had been left to wash, and shoved them toward the back of a deep shelf. He tossed off his apron and left.

Once outside the kitchen, Ben took a roundabout path to keep a good distance from everyone. He made his way to the clothesline at the edge of the field. Sheets still hung from the line. By the trees beyond the sheets, where he had stowed it the night before, was a pile of Jen's clothes that Froggy had brought, including a pair of shoes. He stripped down to his underwear and put on a pair of her jeans with a cartoon monkey on the butt pocket. Ridiculous. The T-shirt was plain enough but it was bright red and uncomfortably baggy. He really wanted to tuck it in, but Jen wasn't a tucker.

The shoes were the most difficult. Jen had insisted on taking her "mixies" which consisted of one orange-white plaid high-top and another that had been pink until she had cross-hatched over it all over it with blue marker, making it a splotchy purple. Jen loved her mixies. Ben, however, had always told himself he would have to be dead before wearing these shoes.

"Now I know what it's like to be dead," Ben said out loud, trying to lighten his own mood as he tied the laces, but hearing his own voice say such a thing wasn't as funny as he had hoped.

Ben had also asked Froggy to grab the ziploc bag that held Jen's toiletries. He knew that Mom had included a bunch of elastic hair bands for her. Gathering up his hair, he snapped an elastic on to make a lopsided pony tail then folded his own clothes neatly and stashed them behind the tree. He took two steps toward the sheets and then stopped. He didn't want to do it, but at this point it would be stupid to overlook any detail, so he picked up a handful of dirt and rubbed it into his hair. Being Jen was a messy, messy job.

He decided to start his day as Jen by going to the infirmary, just in case she needed to make an appearance.

* * *

Nash stopped his dirt bike where Ginger Berger said she would meet him, in a group of trees behind the private cabin, which sat on a low rise apart from the main camp ground. As he cut the engine the oily perfume of exhaust disappeared, and all he could smell was the sticky odor of pine and oak. He pulled a bandana from his pocket and tied it around his face to filter out the stench.

"There's my bad cowboy," Ginger's voice rang out. "Ready for our picnic? Kind of a strange time for a picnic, I know, but the day will just get worse and drag me down with this problem and that. Might as well have fun when we can, right?"

"Did you eat breakfast?" Nash said.

"No, sir. I'm as hungry as I get."

"Here," he said, handing his backpack to Ginger, "The person in the back has to carry the pack. Climb aboard."

"Is it safe?" Ginger hopped onto the rear half of the seat.

"Safe for us." Nash stomped on the kick-starter and revved the bike.

At the first twist of the throttle Ginger wrapped her arms around his chest. He kicked the bike into gear.

As they roared into the woods Ginger let out a few squeals and whoops — nothing that suggested he should slow down or stop so Nash kept the speed as high as the engine could handle on the rising slope.

Nash tilted the bike left and right as he cut a course through the trees. God, how he hated these trees. He hated them from the highest top to the deepest root, and detested the dirt they grew in. He turned his mind to more calming thoughts. He thought of the bike's engine as it transferred explosive energy through the drive-train to the wheels, enabling them to grip and grind up the earth below. A big smile broke across his face as he pictured the dirt bike of his dreams, a combination dirt bike and chain saw, one that could shred a tree. The thought of wheels made of chain saw blades made his smile grow until every tooth showed.

Nash had no fear of these trees. They were woods trees, the dumbest and most docile of all trees, unlike the ones that grew where people lived — the ones that had snuck into civilization and successfully poisoned minds. People actually planted and protected them. Idiot humans, sacrificing their space and their water to plants of all kinds that then thrived at their expense, giving nothing back but leaves to rake up, branches that fell on roofs and cars, vines that pulled down walls and roots that buckled driveways and sidewalks. Unbelievable. Suburban and town plants were masters of witchcraft. But the trees up here? "Hell, I could cut any one of these down if I want to," Nash thought to himself. "No dirt-worshippers nearby enough to stop me."

"The clearing is over there," Ginger said in his ear. She used her elbow to point left. Nash appreciated that Ginger had chosen a spot that wasn't directly under the trees.

Nash unzipped the pack while she still wore it, and yanked out the plastic bag with the food. "Dig down into the pack," he told Ginger. "There's a rolled up blanket we can use to cover the grass." As she swung the pack off, Nash prepared an area for the blanket by stomping on the grass.

"What do you have for us?" Ginger asked.

"Double-mushroom breakfast burgers. Power food."

"Power food?"

"Mushrooms — THE power food. A plant that understands that the best thing to do is to eat other plants, and live off their corpses."

Ginger had never thought about mushrooms that way, but she found his passion for his own point of view irresistible. Her eye caught something in the backpack that she didn't expect — a bag of beef jerky.

"Well," she thought to herself, "this is good news."

"I was hoping you weren't so pure," Ginger Berger purred, her voice soft and low. "I knew those muscles had to come from somewhere other than turnips and beets." Nash had no idea what she was talking about.

Ginger snuck a piece of jerky from the bag and slipped it into her mouth, then turned to Nash and gave him a wink.

"What are you doing?" Nash said, flatly.

Ginger walked slowly toward Nash. The look on her face made Nash more than a little nervous. She lunged at Nash and smushed her face against his as she grabbed him by both biceps. He felt himself give in to Ginger's kiss — she was the kind of kisser who chews as she kisses. Then, as a strange flavor washed over his tongue, he went rigid with terror. He pushed Ginger back.

"Meat," he stammered.

"Aw c'mon," Ginger cooed. "You brought it. You must want it." She stuck another piece of jerky between her teeth. It looked like a dried-up, snake tongue. Ginger continued to stalk toward him.

Nash stepped backwards as he spat the meat taste out of his mouth.

"Don't worry. I won't tell anybody about your secrets if you don't tell anyone about mine. Personally, I like too much salt." She thought it was a funny thing to say, but Nash wasn't laughing, or even smiling. "I do love a man with self-control," Ginger thought.

Nash needed to get a grip on himself and sort out the frightful thoughts swirling inside his head. This woman seemed intent on drawing his energy away with meat and physical attention. She could be anything, from another lost human soul to a demon sent here to throw him off balance. Or worse, to ensnare him and eat him alive. And she might not be working alone so he didn't want to overreact and raise an alarm. The trees were stupid, but they were right here, watching, seeing it all.

SHAKEN

Ginger Berger swayed toward him step by step as he backed away. Nash was now under the shadow of a tree, and with the next step he heard a CRUNCH. He lifted his foot to see what he had stepped on, forcing himself to pick the thing up to get a closer look.

"What a cute little bamboo doll!" Ginger said. "How do you think it got all the way up here?"

For Nash, all possible answers to this question pointed toward a conspiracy. Nash's own thoughts assaulted him with horrible revelations. "The bamboo is working with this meat-eating woman. She's trying to hypnotize me and catch me off guard. And those damned kids from across the street, they're in on it, too. That boy, smooth-talking me, saying he lost a bet with Stones so he'd be working in the kitchen instead of him. How could I fall for that?"

"Hey, where are you going?" Ginger called out as Nash sidestepped her and ran to his dirt bike. In one clean move he hopped on, kick-started it, and roared off.

"What the hell, mister! You can't just leave me here!"

Nash could, and Nash did. This was no time to be with people he couldn't trust or control. He had to find Stones right away. If the plant demons got control of Stones before he could, that would mess with his options. "Never trust your neighbors! Never!" Nash yelled, as he gunned the throttle and careened downhill, heading back to camp.

* * *

Once she had doused the grease fire Anka checked the area to make sure no sparks had spread. That was how she found Stones. She called out to Justin — the camp's only staff person other than Coyote and herself — and had him help carry the boy into the cabin they used as an infirmary. Anka was both cook and nurse at Spirit of the Woods.

Stones felt as if he were inside and on top of a cloud all at the same time. His body was comfortable except for a cold sensation that began at his wrist and trickled up his arm. He opened his eyes and saw an unfamiliar ceiling.

"There you are," a calm voice said.

The kindest face he had ever seen leaned over and looked directly at him. There was something familiar about her.

"Mother? Is that you?" The words slipped out of his mouth.

Anka jerked backward. His words unnerved her. When she had first seen him, noticed how dirty he was, then found the emptied pan of bacon nearby she thought that the poor kid must have gotten himself lost and was wandering the woods, starving — that was the simple explanation. Then the first thing he asks is whether she's his mom! Theoretically, she could have been, and that's what shocked her.

She was nineteen when she had given a baby boy up for adoption. Other than the social worker assigned to her, Anka had never told anyone that she was pregnant or that she had ever given birth. She had insisted to the social worker that she didn't want the child, and whoever his parents would be, to know anything about her. Immediately after having given birth she had left the hospital before anyone could talk to her further, then took a bus to a different part of the country. It was the one part of her life she wished she could forget, and when it became clear that forgetting would take a long time, she had no choice but to pretend it had never happened. But that didn't work, and she was left wondering if she should have at least made sure that the baby was going to a good home. The boy would be about the age of this boy, the kid she'd found lying on the ground.

SHAKEN

Anka forced herself to stop thinking. There was no way anyone could have tracked her down. This was coincidence at work, and that was all. Coyote was the one who believed in impossible and unlikely things without the need for proof, not her. Anka's way was to seek rational explanations and then rule them all out, first.

I must look like this kid's mother, she thought as she exhaled slowly. She turned her attention toward figuring out how to help the boy. That was her job. She was a nurse.

"No, I'm not anyone's mom," Anka said. "Where did you last see your mother?"

"I've never met her," Stones said, "but I think she exists, somewhere."

Anka kept the conversation's focus on immediate, relevant issues. She had noticed the scrape on his cheek but didn't see any bumps or bruises on his head. Still, he might have suffered a concussion.

"Did you hit your head on anything?" Anka asked.

"No."

"Does your head hurt?"

"No."

Pounding drum beats came from outside.

"The drums," Stones said as he jerked himself upright.

"It's OK. We're a camp that just plays drums. You'll hear a lot of that around here. It's normal."

"I want to stay," Stones said.

"What's your name?" Anka asked.

"Rocky," Stones said. He had a vague memory that he used to be called "Rocky." Besides, he'd never liked the name Stones.

"Well, Rocky, you need your parents to sign you up if you want to go to this camp. In your case, I guess, that would be your dad. Where is your dad?"

"He's no good."

That made Anka nervous.

"Rocky, where did you come from?"

"I don't want to go back there," Stones said. "I want to stay here. I like the drums. And I liked the bacon. I think I may need more."

Anka didn't want to just call the police or turn this Rocky kid over to anyone else until she knew more about where she was sending him, and about whoever was going to take him back. If, in fact, he was wanted. To Anka he appeared to be the most innocent and vulnerable child in the whole world.

"OK, Rocky, for now, you're staying here. But I'm not promising for how long, and you have to listen to me. This place is a little odd, but it's a good place. You'll be safe here."

"Thanks, Mom," Stones said. "Can I call you 'Mom'?"

"No, Rocky, you cannot," Anka said. "My name is Anka."

Anka had spoken firmly. She had to keep this day from going completely out of bounds. It was already weird enough, having seen Coyote in the drum circle with a man made of sticks dancing around him. It would be all right with her if Coyote's beliefs about spirits turned out to be true, but she needed more proof. The grease fire had erupted before she had gotten a good enough look to see if that stick-man was really who Coyote thought he was. Coyote had plenty friends who would think it would be funny to camp out in a tree above the drum circle just waiting to drop a string-controlled, stick-man puppet, and then laugh at him later.

Then the fire erupted, which led her to Rocky, who must have arrived at Spirit of the Woods at the same moment as Coyote's stick-man. Rocky triggered all kinds of memories and impulses in her that she had walled off from herself years ago. It was truly beyond weird, all this happening at once. For all she knew, Rocky could be from the same alternative reality as Coyote's stick man. The kid had a detached way of talking, as if everything here was brand new to him, not just the Spirit of the Woods as a place, but everything. Like an alien who had dropped down from a spaceship. He even had the white skin, bony frame and long limbs that aliens were supposed to have.

Anka felt like a crack had opened up between two worlds, and the contents from each were all mixed up.

TORN

Jen needed to catch her breath and get her bearings. She was at the ridge but it looked different from the clearing where they had spent the night. Tanglewood had been keeping up with her and stopped when she did.

Jen's mouth was completely dried out. Her tongue felt like cardboard coated with chalk. She heard a burbling sound.

"This way," she said. The sound led into a dense line of low shrubs, tall grass, and trees. She held Tanglewood's hand as she pushed her way through, and found a creek.

Jen scooped a handful of water into her mouth then immediately spat out a spray of mud. "Blechh! Should have washed my hands first."

She rubbed her hands in the cool, slow-moving water until most of the dirt was rinsed off.

Tanglewood crouched down next to Jen, and turned to face her.

Jen suddenly realized that she never questioned whether Tanglewood could see. It was obvious that he could because of the way he walked and ran, but she hadn't fully noticed his eyes until now. They didn't look like regular eyes — that probably would have creeped her out. The interval of knots in the cord that tied the top of his head together, combined with pairs of bamboo leaves pinched around those knots appeared to her, now, as eyes with eyelids. But it wasn't the shape that convinced her she was looking into Tanglewood's eyes. She felt she was looking through a window into the deepest part of him. Like she could actually see his soul.

She knew that she had to get back to camp, but the feeling of connectedness between her and Tanglewood as they crouched by the creek held her to the spot. Jen wished he could talk. Jen needed to talk.

"What happened back there between you and that Coyote guy?"

Tanglewood held out the *bachi* sticks and moved his head in a way she could tell was meant to be a response, although she couldn't be sure if Tanglewood understood what she had asked. Even so, Jen felt certain the two of them were at least trying to have a conversation.

"I saw that Coyote gave you those sticks. But I mean, he acted like he knew you, which isn't possible. How could he know you?"

Tanglewood hugged both sticks close to his chest and rocked back and forth.

"Wait," Jen said, "how is that an answer?"

Tanglewood stood up, held the *bachi* firmly, then lowered himself into a half-crouch and began swinging the *bachi* in the same whole-body motion that the children used to strike their drums.

"What does playing the drums have to do with it?" Jen realized it was going to be difficult to come up with questions Tanglewood could answer using only pantomime, and even if she did, what did all his movements mean, exactly?

Tanglewood intensified his wordless drum-playing, putting his back into it and swinging his arms in bigger arcs. He began to twist and twirl.

"Whoa — slow down, buddy!" Jen said.

But Tanglewood's pretend drumming became more and more frenetic. His twirling became whirling. Then he overbalanced and had to flail to keep himself from falling. As his arms swept wildly the *bachi* struck several tree trunks and branches one after the other making a *k-tonk k-donk k-donk-donk-donk* rhythm that reversed and repeated as Tanglewood first swooped left, then swooped right, then left again before momentum and gravity tipped the scales and he went tumbling backward.

"Watch out!" she cried, but couldn't do anything to stop his fall. SPLASH! Into the creek he went.

"Oh my God, are you OK?" Jen feared that Tanglewood had hit his head or that he might drown even though the creek was shallow. She reached to grasp him by the shoulders to lift his head out of the water but he had already begun to get up by himself.

Water shed off him in sparkles as he thrust his arms upwards, pointing to the trees. He shimmied his hips into Jen's and tapped her repeatedly on the shoulder as he pointed again and again, like a child saying "Look! Look! Look!"

Jen looked up. The trees were moving. Not all of them, only five — the ones Tanglewood had hit just before he fell.

"That's weird," Jen said. She focused her attention on other trees, watching carefully for signs of movement but they all kept perfectly still except for the five whose branches moved in a way she had never seen branches move before. They moved up then down, up then down, slowly, together, in waves.

There was no wind, not even a breeze. The air was perfectly still.

"They look like they're breathing," Jen said, and she noticed that Tanglewood now appeared to be breathing. The leaves that filled the gaps between his bamboo bundles moved as well. Tanglewood's leaves rhythmically stretched outward, then inward. Were they growing? Was Tanglewood growing? Jen watched carefully, wondering if she would see him get taller or if bamboo stalks would begin to grow in all directions fast enough for her to see, the way she had described the plants growing around and into Brother Bones, but that was just a story she'd made up. She became worried about the power of her own imagination — what if everything she dreamed about or made up actually came true? And what if she couldn't control them once they had become true?

A grinding, roaring whine pierced the air in uneven bursts. The branches on the five trees came to a sudden halt. Tanglewood's body jerked and the movement of his leaves ceased.

Hairs rose on the back of Jen's neck as the grinding grew louder — a sound that reminded Jen of the chainsaw that had sliced through the bamboo while she could do nothing but watch it fall. She was gripped by the same physical impulse she'd had that day: the need to surround all the bamboo and shield it from being cut.

The sound penetrated Tanglewood, but not in the lively way that the vibrations of the drums had, or with the low, soft waves he had felt with the stick as he had touched it to the ground, or the warm pulse that emanated from the girl, Jen. No, this sound stopped all good sensations, and sent Tanglewood into a panic.

Tanglewood ran. Jen sprinted after him and grabbed him by the waist just as he was about to pass through a gap between trees. As she pulled Tanglewood back to the creek she caught a glimpse of a man on a motorcycle. He was heading toward them at full speed.

"Stay close to the ground and don't move," she whispered as she pulled Tanglewood close.

Nash, speeding away from his disastrous picnic in a state of high alert, had noticed strange movements in a line of trees. He thought he saw two small trees running by themselves. It was a disturbing sight but Nash wasn't about to ignore details that could give him further knowledge about any maneuvers his enemies were about to make. As he swerved over to get a closer look he cut the engine but stayed on his bike as it rolled to a stop a safe distance from the line of trees.

Jen found the sudden silence more distressing than the grinding noise. It meant there was no hope that the man on the motorcycle would just zip past them and be gone.

"Who's in there?" A growl that sounded barely human. Jen's recognized Nash's voice. Her heart sank. She felt Tanglewood tremble.

"Show yourselves you miserable demons!" Nash, pumped with adrenaline, was ready to tear plants apart with his bare hands.

Jen didn't like her options. Even though she could dodge and weave, making it difficult for a motorcycle to follow, Nash could just get off his motorcycle and run after her. She could handle the idea of her getting caught by Nash, but Stones had revealed enough of Nash's bizarre ideas about plants for her to know that if Nash found Tanglewood it would be a disaster. Nothing mattered more right now than figuring out a way to ensure that Tanglewood could escape.

On the other side of the tree line Nash waited. He wasn't about to get lured into a trap, and if the densely packed trees in front of him were anything, they were a trap. He had to draw out whoever or whatever was hiding. If he could force them to run into a more open area he could chase them down. This would be a good time to have a hand grenade, he thought to himself. And then he remembered the bamboo doll he had found. He had stuffed it into his pocket so that he could burn it and destroy any power it might have, but now he thought of a way to use it as a weapon for his own cause.

"I KNOW YOU'RE HERE," Nash roared, "And this is what's gonna happen to you if you don't show yourselves now!" He bit off the doll's head then tossed the body through a narrow gap between two trunks in the line of trees.

Jen saw something land on the ground nearby. It was Ben's Mini-T minus its head. Tanglewood saw it, too. To him it was his lost little-little one. His trembling turned to spasms that felt, to Jen, as if Tanglewood were sobbing. Sharp edges of Tanglewood's bamboo dug into her side, arms, and neck as he tightened his embrace. Jen felt as if the poor creature was trying to burrow until he was completely inside her. There was only one way she could think up to save Tanglewood. It was the most painful idea she'd ever had, but she had no choice.

"I'm coming out!" Jen shouted toward Nash.

She thrust at Tanglewood to separate him from her. She forced herself to face him, looking at him directly in the eyes and spoke firmly, quietly, coldly. "Get away from me. Go back to that place with the drums. Now. Go back to Coyote. GO." She pushed at Tanglewood again, this time hard enough that he had to let go of her. Tanglewood leaned back toward her, his arms seeking a hug but she shoved him again and pointed to the opposite side of the creek, mouthing, "Get out of here. Go. GO!"

To her dismay Tanglewood wasn't running away yet.

"I'm going to count to three," Nash boomed.

"Just give me a second to shake out a leg cramp. I'll be right there!" Jen shouted back.

Jen picked up the headless Mini-T, and threw it at Tanglewood, and that did it. Tanglewood ran into the trees on the other side of the creek.

Jen hated herself. She couldn't stop imagining what Tanglewood must be feeling. The image in her mind was vivid and disturbing, worse than just pushed away, worse than just chased away. Torn him off, thrown him away, and dynamited him with fear — that's what she did to Tanglewood. It was horrible. She didn't have time to explain that she had to do it because she wanted him to be safe. And it tormented her that she couldn't be sure if Coyote and his weird band of drummers was truly a safe place for Tanglewood. She felt like she had thrown a baby off a cliff to keep it from being eaten by a lion.

"Counting to three now. One..."

Jen decided that Nash was crazy enough that she should show up empty-handed, like a criminal emerging from a bank robbery that went wrong. But she didn't like the idea of being fully unarmed, so she dropped the stick on the ground and quickly threaded the arrow back into the hem of her poncho keeping the tip and feathers toward the inside. She squeezed between the tree trunks.

"Two..."

Jen contorted her face into a mask of hatred as she emerged and saw Nash. He stood boldly, arms crossed, his motorcycle underneath him. As Jen cleared the trees she lifted her arms straight to her sides causing the filthy poncho to spread like wings. She held her hands wide open, curling her fingers, wishing they were claws or talons. To her great pleasure Nash suddenly looked nervous, and gulped.

"There isn't just you." Nash was asking.

"I'm the only one here," Jen said.

Nash recognized her face. It was Ben's sister, which confirmed his belief that he was the target of a twisted conspiracy. New details began to crystallize in his mind as he looked at her. He was certain that he had just caught Jen in the act of turning herself into her tree-form. He wasn't sure what that meant, exactly, but the idea gave him such a chill that he decided it must be true. He needed to move this confrontation to an arena that was more under his control. These woods were much more deadly than he had thought.

He moved so fast that Jen didn't have time to react. Nash kicked the starter, zoomed at her, hooked his arm around her waist and swung her onto the motorcycle seat between himself and the handlebars as he twisted the throttle wide open. Suddenly, Jen found herself rocketing downhill through the woods at fifty miles an hour. If she hadn't been so angry at Nash and at herself she might have loved the thrill. As it was, she kept her eyes closed for most of the ride, peeking once every few seconds hoping to see signs that they were approaching Camp Triple-Bar and not heading for a sheer drop, or worse.

* * *

Ben entered the infirmary at Camp Triple-Bar. Wow, he thought, Froggy was right. The waiting area was filled with unhappy kids slumped in chairs. Most of them had their eyes closed.

The sign-up sheet was on a clipboard that hung next to a doorless entry that led into a corridor. As Ben neared it to check where Jen's name was on the list a hand reached around the doorway from the corridor and grabbed the clipboard.

A woman's voice said, "Okay. Jen— Uh, there's no last name. Jen, if there's only one of you out there, you're next."

No one else got up. Then it occurred to Ben that he hadn't prepared to actually see the nurse as Jen. What kind of problem would have brought her to the infirmary? That was the question he had to answer right away. It had to be something he could fake, nothing that would require blood and definitely nothing that would lead to the nurse examining him under his clothes, especially his pants.

The nurse sat at a desk filling in a form as he entered the examining room.

"Have a seat on the table. What seems to be the problem, Jen?"

"Uh...." A light bulb went off in Ben's head, just in time. "I hurt my wrist."

"Let's have a look, then. My name is Rip, by the way."

Ben thought that was a strange name for a nurse, but she seemed nice. Her hands were warm as she began to examine his wrist.

"No bumps, cuts, or bruises. What happened?"

"I was playing tetherball and I hit the ball too hard."

"Huh," Rip said, "I didn't know we had tetherball here. Well, you learn something new every day, right Jen? You'll be fine. I can put a bandage on it to help keep any swelling down. Plus it'll just remind you to keep it protected for a couple of days, OK?"

"That sounds good," Ben said.

"I have to go to the other room to get the bandage," Rip said. "Here, "munch on this in the meantime." She opened a drawer on her desk and handed him a Snickers bar. It tasted like heaven.

* * *

Ginger Berger could not remember a time when she had been more irritated and insulted, let alone as scratched up by underbrush or with ankles this sore. To save time she had taken a steep path that was the shortest route back to Triple-Bar from the clearing. It was painful.

As she descended the last bit of down-slope she heard a motorcycle. She forced herself to run the last stretch to the flat dirt road that circled the camp and arrived at the wooden cabins that housed the adult staff. She saw Nash enter his while brusquely ushering a child along with him.

Ginger hustled to the door and pounded on it while using her universal key to unlock the latch. She shoved the door open in time to see Nash parading Jen by her forearm and halting at the bedroom corridor as he hollered, "Stones!"

Ginger had enough self-control to keep her voice as low and calm as possible, not wanting to make a scene with a child present.

"What is going on here? I don't want to jump to any conclusions but what I am seeing concerns me deeply."

Nash wondered how Ginger had been able to get back so fast. Maybe she could fly. Demons and witches. He wondered if there was more than one of her, if she had duplicates stationed at different locations. He told himself to choose his words carefully, to act like he suspected nothing.

But before he could open his mouth Ginger took control of the conversation.

"I can see you're upset about something. But I'm sure whatever it is doesn't require dragging a child around with you. Now you just hold your horses while I do my job and make sure all our kids are safe and having fun. Let me start with this one right here, so why don't you just let go of her right away, I mean immediately, I mean NOW. She and I need to have a little chat."

Nash let go of Jen's arm.

"You come over here to Ginger, honey."

Jen walked over to Ginger.

"My goodness, what happened to you?"

"Nothing."

"Well I'm very happy to hear that. You're not hurt or anything, are you? Do you think you need to see the nurse?"

"I'm fine."

"Oh, good," Ginger breathed a sigh of relief. "You're the girl who told that story last night, aren't you? That was some story. You've got quite an imagination in that head of yours. Forgive me, sweetie, I've memorized faces but I haven't put names on everyone yet. Now what was your name?"

"It was Jen," Jen said.

"Well, Jen, I know kids your age don't love showers every day. It took me a while to appreciate the difference between clean and dirty — but you should go take one. How about you run along and do that? Whatcha say?"

"Do I have to?" Jen said.

"Yes, Jen. I think it would be a good idea." Ginger's voice lost that simpering talking-to-a-dog quality. "Now I don't want you to worry about this one over here," she pointed vaguely at Nash. "Ginger will make sure nothing like this happens again. But can you promise me something, Jen? If anything goes on around here that you don't like, you just come to me right away and I'll help. OK?"

"I'll do that," Jen said.

Ginger patted Jen on the head and opened the door. "Good girl. Don't forget to use lots of shampoo," Ginger said, wiping her hand on Nash's wall to wipe off the dirt from Jen's hair. Jen glared at Nash until Ginger cut off her view by closing the door.

Ginger swung her body around and confronted Nash without any sweetness in look or words. "You got some nerve ditching me like you did. Now I guess I'll just have to live with that humiliation but there is nothing acceptable about gripping a child like that as you froth at the mouth with whatever your dim intelligence thinks is going on. I don't know what your problem is but I swear if you don't stop acting like all your screws are loose I will fire you like a torpedo. You have a job to do, "Chef," and that's all I better see you doing from this moment on. Clear?"

"Not until I find Stones," Nash said.

"Find what?"

"My boy. What have you done with him?"

"Excuse me?"

"You. And that girl-thing, and her brother, or whatever he is, you've been misleading me all day. I can tell what's going on. You're all working together — with *IT*." Nash pulled the head of the Mini-T out of his pocket and held it up between two fingers.

Ginger's mouth dropped open. A grown man, his eyes practically spinning in their sockets, was pinching a doll's head and talking as if it were alive and in charge.

"Oh, my God, you are a mess." Ginger pulled at her hair, and thought out loud, "Not even the first week of summer behind us and I've got to deal with this kind of crap!" She was ready to fire him but not until she could be certain that no child was missing, even if that kid wasn't one of the official campers, and had the bad luck to belong to this awful man.

Nash began to yell out the window. "Stones! Stones! Where are you, boy?! STONES!"

Ginger had to shut him up. She slammed the window. "Now you listen to me, you bag of nuts, you are not going to get everyone around her all agitated, or ruin this camp's reputation, or mine. If you don't shut up and get control of yourself I will send you straight to hell."

Nash would gladly have gone to hell if it meant taking the trees and all the plants with him — especially the bamboo. It would be an honor to suffer eternity with the consolation that the bamboo burned alongside, and forever. But as much as he wanted to get into a real battle he first had to do what he could to find Stones. He cursed himself for not having the will to abandon Stones for the sake of his greater purpose — a perfect warrior would sacrifice all he loves for victory. Then again, a perfect warrior wouldn't have made the mistake of letting a child enter his life. Nash hated not being perfect, hated being only half of what he could be, and hated himself for caring about Stones.

"Did you hear what I just said?" Ginger poked him repeatedly on his chest with her finger. "Get a grip, mister!"

"Yes," Nash said, backing away.

"Good. Now, you and I are going to go find your boy, and then..."

"And then what?" Nash said, steeling himself for this plant-sympathizing flesh-eater to reveal the next stage of the plan she and her brood of demons had in store for him.

"And then you are going to make us all lunch," Ginger said simply. "Just like normal. It's a normal day around here and you better show me what normal looks like."

Nash was surrounded by an enemy that had the upper hand, but just for the moment. He had to play along and wait for an opportunity to seize control.

* * *

Jen had no intention whatsoever of wasting time by taking a shower. Before Ginger had burst into the house to rescue her from Nash's clutches he had demanded to know, "What have you done with Stones?" She had denied knowing anything about Stones but now that she had a moment to piece things together she figured that Nash must have been up in the woods looking for Stones, and for some reason felt that she was the reason he had gone missing.

Well, yes, there was truth to that, but too many things didn't add up. If Nash were looking for Stones then why wasn't he calling out his name when he was up in the woods? And why didn't he ask about Stones as soon as she'd showed herself? Why did he snatch her? And, if Stones had gotten a head start from the bacon spot, wouldn't he be back a camp? Maybe he was back, and Nash just hadn't seen him yet because he was on his motorcycle up in the woods looking for him. On the other hand.... Jen was going in circles, and then exited the loop as soon as she saw a copy of herself wearing clean clothes and her mixies, walking directly at her.

"There you are," Ben said. He didn't look as happy to see her as she would have expected. If anything he looked like he wanted his day to just end. He looked haggard, which he was, and his overall appearance was, well, very odd.

"Do I look that weird?" Jen asked.

Ben thought his sister looked several stages of weird beyond the dirt-encrusted appearance of any madwoman or destitute homeless person he had ever seen.

"Oh, my God," Ben said, looking her up and down. "You have no idea."

"No, I mean wearing that stuff you have on. My stuff. You're dressed like, I don't know, like a clown."

They were close to the edge of the dirt road and Ben wanted to get themselves into the boundary trees before anyone saw them. He grabbed his sister by her poncho and pulled her along as he answered.

"Jen, now is not the time for you to face up to your bizarre sense of fashion. Where's Stones?"

Jen didn't like to be dragged. She ducked to let the poncho slip off her head but kept following her brother. Once they reached the edge of trees, Ben repeated, "Where is Stones, Jen?"

Not only did she not have a simple answer, she was even more irritated that Stones seemed to be Ben's main concern.

"Aren't you worried about where Tanglewood is?"

"Yeah, but first things first."

"Stones comes before Tanglewood?"

"Stones is another human being, and not only that, if something happens to Stones it could cause us big problems."

Jen was mortified. "You think if something happened to Tanglewood that it wouldn't cause us big problems? You made him, Ben! You made him just as much as I did! And he's a living thing, not just some stupid plastic model you can glue together and forget about!"

Her words hurt, but Ben didn't want to get pulled into whatever argument Jen was pushing him into. He was tired of being pushed and pulled by Jen. He wasn't her puppet.

"Jen! Where. Is. Stones??"

"Isn't he back here?"

"If I knew that he was back here why would I be asking you where he is?"

"He must be back here."

"So you don't know where he is? Jen! What happened?"

Images of what had happened since waking up this morning overwhelmed her.

"A lot!" Jen began to sob. Tears streamed down her face, becoming muddy rivulets. "I feel— I— I f-feel—" Jen's chest heaved as she tried to speak through sobs that became deeper and impossible to stop.

Jen had never cried like this. In fact, Ben wasn't sure he had ever seen Jen cry, even once. And now he was the cause of her crying. Ben's mind swirled with guilt and confusion. What had actually happened? What was going on right now?

"I'm sorry! Jen! It's OK," Ben said, even though he didn't think that everything was actually OK. "It's going to be all right. We'll figure it out. Things will work out!" All Ben could think of to say were phrases he remembered his parents using when they had to console him, and, now that he was the one saying them, he realized that the words themselves were meaningless. But the sight of Jen upset was earth-shattering so he kept repeating the words. It was all he could think to do, except to hug her, which he did. She didn't resist the hug. In fact, she pressed herself into Ben with as much force as he used to hug her. This wasn't at all like Jen.

"I— feel— terrible!" Jen sobbed the words into his neck.

Ben worked hard to suppress his awareness that she was pasting him with dirt, muddy tears and snot as she hugged him. At least he wasn't wearing his own clothes.

"I don't know where Stones is!" Jen sobbed and continued in fragments accompanied by snuffling. "Tanglewood found another camp— there's drummers— and this Coyote— it's like they already knew him! Then I took him— away from there— I couldn't find Stones where the fire was— I thought he came back here— we hurried back— and Nash— on his motorcycle— he killed the Mini-T you made! And I had to do it— had to— scare him with Mini-T with no head— I didn't want him to get hurt! The sticks in his hands— made the trees move—" She wailed.

Ben felt nauseous. He had only thought that Jen looked crazy, but whatever she was saying, none of it made sense. Her mind was gone.

This is it, Ben thought. He remembered his oldest fear, that Jen would somehow disappear leaving him alone to face the world by himself. And without her all he could do was either die or turn himself into her in order to stay alive. Darkness grew inside him. Worse than darkness. Sadness. Loneliness. Emptiness.

The voice of a lisping cartoon cat punctured the expanding void within him and popped it like a toy balloon.

"Hey I was hoping I would find you guys so I kept looking and I did find you guys." It was Froggy. "You are you guys, right?"

Froggy's voice brought Ben back to himself and sent a wave of calm through Jen that halted her sobbing. She relaxed her grip on Ben. The two of them turned toward Froggy.

Froggy's eyes ping-ponged behind her glasses as she focused on each of them.

"OK. Phew, it is you guys. But I can't tell who is which. I think I see two Jens," Froggy said.

Jen giggled, which relieved Ben beyond belief because it probably meant that the world as he knew it was not ending. But he needed to make sure.

"Jen, tell me you're not going crazy." Ben said.

"No. I mean, I'm not. Everything I said is true, I swear."

"I couldn't really understand most of it. Or any of it," Ben said.

"Hey, where's Tangie?" Froggy interrupted.

Ben sighed.

"Ben, we're gonna have to explain it all to someone eventually," Jen said.

"OK. But we really have to find Stones. And Tanglewood," Ben added hastily, then turned to Froggy. "Froggy, Tanglewood is Tangie's real name."

"But yesterday you said that Tanglewood is Tangie's nickname. So it's really the opposite?"

"Actually, Froggy, Tangie doesn't exist," Ben said. "Only Tanglewood."

"Got it. Your cousin's name is really Tanglewood," Froggy said.

"Tanglewood isn't our cousin," Ben said. Then Jen interrupted.

"And he's a boy, not a girl," Jen said. "Froggy, you promised you would keep secrets, right?"

Ben interrupted Jen as gently as he could. "Jen, without Froggy, we'd already be in trouble. Trust me, she's with us."

That made Froggy smile, but it soon changed to a frown of confusion. "So, then, who is Tanglewood?"

"We'll get to that, Froggy, I promise," said Ben. "But we can't explain it right now. I don't know how much longer it will be before everybody here starts looking for missing kids."

"Oh believe me," Jen said, "It's going to be real soon."

"You have no idea where Stones is, do you," Ben said. It wasn't a question.

"He might be here?" Jen was hoping. Ben could tell. He rubbed his eyes. He was about to ask her where she had last seen Stones, but another trek into the woods — for a search this time — seemed unavoidable. He didn't want to waste time talking without moving.

"Froggy, Jen and I are going to be missing from this place starting now. I don't know for how long. If you want to come with us you can. But if you want to stay here, just pretend you know nothing."

"I do that pretty good," Froggy said. "But I think you guys may need my help. I mean, I don't know what you have to do, but I'm sure I can help."

"I'm sure you can, too," Ben said.

"Plus I don't think anyone here would miss me," Froggy said.

Jen gave Froggy a big hug.

"Wow. You're really covered with a lot of dirt," Froggy said.

"Yeah I'm a mess," Jen said.

"OK," Ben said as he began up the slope, "where was the last place you saw Stones?"

"By the bacon," Jen said. "Oh, hey I forgot!"

Jen reached into her pocket and pulled out a wad of bacon. She stuffed one piece in her mouth, then opened her hand so Ben and Froggy could take the rest.

Ben was so happy he put off asking how bacon connected to a lost Stones. He devoured it, ignoring the coating of lint from Jen's pockets and dirt from her hands.

"Go ahead, Froggy, have some," Jen said.

"That's OK, I don't eat meat," Froggy said.

"You don't?" Jen said. "How come?"

"I don't eat anything that has a face," Froggy said. "It makes me uncomfortable. But that's just me. I don't mind if you eat it."

Jen's appetite disappeared as she thought about faces and Tanglewood's frightened eyes as he ran away from her. "Ben," she said, "promise that we'll do everything we can to find Tanglewood."

"I promise," Ben said.

"Me, too," said Froggy.

BOND

Tanglewood ran through the woods, his mind like a messy pile of sticks, his thoughts clashing into each other at angles he could not follow.

The ground seemed to spread infinitely in all directions. He felt his legs spring away from the earth unable to connect to it, forced to leave it, then forced to return to it, over and over.

He thought of the girl, and the boy, and the other boy. He was just like them— But, no, he wasn't.

He saw the tree trunks embedded in the dirt as their tops stretched into the sky. He was like them— But, no, he wasn't.

He felt the *bachi* he clutched, as alive as he was even though they couldn't move by themselves. But when he moved them— The drum. The trees! Waves had flowed within him, through him and the *bachi* then into the trees. And they had moved! Moved with him. Moved by him!

Then that horrible noise had arrived, killing all other vibrations around it. No! Worse! It had turned the other vibrations against themselves. The noise halted the trees, and their sudden stillness expanded into a frightful silence. Then the girl, Jen, pushed and pushed until she threw him away from her. And now he ran, distancing himself from the crushing quiet and that terrible feeling of being torn apart.

Tanglewood's thoughts cut themselves to pieces, and cut into him from the inside, and all he could do is flee. But he had nowhere. He was nothing.

He ran into a meadow, and then it happened. A warm yellow light flashed on, a beam bathed him with an energy that replaced chaos with calm; and Tanglewood stopped running, and his mind came to rest.

His toes gripped the ground. He relaxed his arms, reached upward and turned his face toward the light of the sun. Its bright rays united all the broken, jagged thoughts that had skewered his mind, weaving them into a mesh that wrapped him, held him, and gave him strength.

He felt the tall grass curl around his legs as it joined him reaching toward the sun.

He remembered.

There was a time when he was never alone, when he had stood with the others — not just stood with them, he *was* the others, and the others were him. Separate and inseparable. They were one.

Tanglewood's thoughts flowed like a song.

We stand in the earth.

Drink the rain and sun.

Begin as nothing.

Become everything.

All in all...

All with all...

Tanglewood rustled in the breeze. Two birds landed on his head. He felt a tickle. A deer stood next to him, nibbling a leaf from his elbow. Tanglewood patted the deer on its head, then led it to a nearby bush bursting with red berries.

He saw five trees that grew in a circle near the center of the meadow. He entered the circle and sat on the ground in the middle of the five trees. Several squirrels, a family of rabbits, a raccoon and several more birds clustered around and on Tanglewood as he concentrated, his mind flowing freely, and clear, like water.

He believed there was a way to bring them all back together, to bring everything back together. More than believed, he knew. The rhythm that had made the trees breathe, back at the creek, it wasn't an accident; it was a call, something he had known since before he was born. And the trees had responded with a message of their own, a message they had carried for a long, long time. They had told him something. So Tanglewood turned inward, to remember the call, and to find the message.

* * *

At the Spirit of the Woods camp Anka gave instructions to her assistant. "I've got a situation to deal with so you're in charge of prepping lunch today, Justin," she said. "Just shape the meat into burger patties and cut up the tomatoes. The lettuce is already washed and in the fridge. I'll be back in time to help cook and assemble."

"No problem," Justin said. "There's only like, what, fifteen of us."

"Sixteen. Three adults and thirteen kids. Make plenty of extras for seconds. You know what," Anka paused, "I may be gone longer than I think so get the burgers started on the grill. Keep an eye on them, alright? No more fires."

Anka left the kitchen, entered the infirmary, and tapped Stones on the shoulder.

"It's time to meet Senpai," she said.

* * *

Jen, Ben and Froggy made their way up the slope from Triple-Bar. As they climbed Jen explained as much — and as little — as she could. She didn't want to waste breath talking, first of all, but just as important was to give Ben enough information while not freaking out Froggy.

She skipped the part about being snatched by Nash on a motorcycle and the weird interaction with him and then with Ginger Berger. Things were complicated enough, and as long as Ben was by her side she didn't need to fret about having caused any problem that would rain down on his head alone.

She explained how she and Stones had found another camp, how they had snatched some bacon because they were hungry, that Stones went missing, and that she had told Tanglewood to return to that camp because it seemed like a safer place. That was it.

They arrived at the big tree by the clearing where Jen, Tanglewood, and Stones had spent the night.

"Dang it," Jen said. "I was hoping at least one of those two would be here."

"Why would you think that?" Ben said.

"I don't know," Jen said, "Just because it was kind of like home for a little while."

"Home?" Ben said.

"Never mind," Jen said. "Stones really could be back at our camp, you know."

"I know," agreed Ben. "But if he is then they'll find him there, and then...."

"Then, what?"

"I don't know," Ben said. "But whether they find him first or we do, either way we're going to be real nice to him, Jen. Real nice."

Jen nodded. Negotiating with Stones about Tanglewood was too complicated to think about. What would they be negotiating for, exactly? For him to keep quiet, she guessed, same plan as always. She did not tell Ben that she had already tried to convince Stones that Tanglewood wasn't really a monster. Nor did she say anything about feeling sorry for Stones.

She still felt raw and miserable about sending Tanglewood away, but under the circumstances what choice did she have? And that decision could wind up being the best thing for him. Jen let herself imagine that everything would be all right, that she could sneak away from camp to visit Tanglewood at his new home. She let herself believe that Coyote would take good care of him. She couldn't bear imagining never seeing Tanglewood again. That was too painful. Maybe living in the woods was his destiny, and hers. She looked around at the deep woods and felt its endlessness surround her. The trees were so much bigger than she was. The woods, even bigger. People could disappear.

"Ben," Jen said, her voice so low he barely heard her. "What if we find Stones but he's...." She didn't finish the sentence, but Ben knew what she was thinking.

The idea of finding Stones dead in the woods sent a shiver down his spine.

"Stones is tough as nails, Jen. That might be bad for us, but it's good for him."

Jen did not want to explain that she had seen a side of Stones that was the opposite of tough, and that the whole story included that she had broken his will and forced him to eat bacon that left him unconscious. When he awoke he would be weak and confused, nowhere near tough as nails. If Stones was dead it would be all her fault.

"Guys!" Froggy hollered from the middle of the clearing, where she had wandered. "There's something lying here on the ground."

Jen and Ben both ran to where Froggy stood, their hearts and heads heavy with fear and remorse.

"Look," Froggy said as they arrived by her side. She pointed to a backpack that lay open on the ground.

Jen and Ben were in the middle of a huge sigh of relief when Froggy then said, "Uh oh."

Jen and Ben just closed their eyes.

"Litter-bugs," Froggy said, in a sing-song voice.

"What the hell, Froggy!" Jen yelped as she opened her eyes unable to take all the drama any more, even though all of it came from inside her own head.

Ben grabbed the familiar blue plastic grocery bag that Froggy had just picked up from the ground. He and Jen looked at one another as he removed a jumbo bag of beef jerky out from the bag. "It's open."

"Does that mean it's mine?" Jen said.

"There could be other bags of beef jerky in the world besides yours and mine," Ben replied. He sounded uncertain.

"Jumbo? And in a blue plastic grocery bag?"

"I think there must have been a picnic," Froggy said as she trotted over to a wadded-up blanket. She unfolded it, revealing several plastic containers with food still in them.

That was when Jen noticed that the soft, cushy grass near the blanket was split by two muddy stripes that extended back toward the woods. They looked like motorcycle tracks.

"We gotta get outta here!" Jen said, and grabbed Ben with one arm and Froggy with the other, pulling them toward the slope she had sped down with Stones down earlier that day.

"Jen!" Ben pleaded as he ran. "Talk to me!" He had to fling the bag of jerky away so he could use both arms to keep his balance as they careened down the uneven terrain. Ben felt like he kind of knew why they were running, but then again, kind of not.

"Nash!" Jen hollered. "He was there! He'll be back!"

Ben understood that was possible. That bag of jerky was the same brand as the one given them by their father, and was probably either the bag that Nash had confiscated or the one Ben had chucked blindly when he walked up for kitchen duty, having forgotten to ditch it in the woods. Nash could easily have found that one. But how did it wind up abandoned at a picnic with food containers, a blanket and a backpack all strewn about willy-nilly, not placed with a purpose. The whole scene back there was odd, disordered, and suspicious, all of which suggested Nash had something to do with it.

For Jen the logic was simpler because she knew the motorcycle tracks meant it was Nash's picnic. The idea of Nash, the marauder, grinding his way through every neck of the woods at high speed whenever and wherever he wanted weakened her hopes for Tanglewood and his safety.

"Where are we going?" Ben yelled.

"The drum camp!" Jen hollered back. "We're going there now! Watch out," she turned her head to shout at Froggy. "It gets pretty steep right up aheaaaaad AughHHH!"

Ben watched helplessly as Jen tripped and fell toward a tree trunk. She held her arms out in front of her to break the impact, smacked into the tree with her right wrist, and tumbled to the ground. Her poncho flared and twirled with her. The arrow she had threaded through the hem snagged on a fallen branch, which slowed her down as she dragged it. Her legs flailed as she dug her heels into the dirt, stopping just before the steep drop.

"Jen! Oh, God!" Ben was beside himself.

"Owwwww-uh!" Jen moaned.

"Are you OK?!?" Froggy butt-skid to a stop next to Jen.

"My wrist!" Jen yelled.

"Let me see!" Ben said. Jen held up her wounded wrist. As dirty as it was, Ben could clearly see that it was badly banged up. The white band of skin around her right wrist was now scraped and oozed blood.

He tried to channel his parents once more, unable to think of what, specifically, to do.

"Can you move it?" he asked.

"It hurts!" Jen yelped. But she was moving it.

"Can you hold my hand?" Ben said next.

"Hold your hand? I'm the one who's lying on the ground messed up!"

"I'm trying to see if something is broken!"

"I've felt worse," Jen said as she sat up. She cradled her wrist with her left hand. "Ow."

"Oh, wait!" Ben said excitedly as he stood up and reached into his back pocket. "I have this!" He held up the elastic cloth bandage that Rip had put on him. He had taken it off right after he had left the infirmary.

"I've had those." Froggy said. "I can put it on. I mean I can put it on Jen. I know how."

Ben was happy to let Froggy help.

"Careful," Jen said. She was nervous about Froggy putting on a bandage, unsure of what she could or could not see with those glasses. Froggy furrowed her brow into a serious look that was hard to take seriously.

"I'm going be a nurse," she said.

Jen closed her eyes as Froggy applied the bandage. Between the goggle glasses and the missing teeth an image of Froggy as a nurse was impossible to conjure. Jen could picture an older Froggy with front teeth. The teeth wound up overcompensating for the gap and were huge, turning Froggy from a cartoon cat into a cartoon rabbit.

"There," Froggy said, cheerily, "all done."

Jen opened her eyes. Froggy had done a good job. The bandage was neatly wrapped and tucked in so that it stayed on, not too tight, not too loose. And though her wrist stung and felt sore, having the feeling of a tight pressure on her wrist made her feel better than she had all day. She almost felt like Xena again.

"Why did you have this bandage?" Jen asked.

"Never mind," Ben said.

Jen accepted that. She removed the arrow from the poncho, pulling the tip from the notch in the branch that had snagged it, and then pointed it downhill and slightly to the left. "That way," Jen said. "I think."

Ben and Froggy chased after Jen down the slope.

* * *

Anka and Stones approached a large wooden platform next to the drum circle. A dozen children sat cross-legged on the platform facing Coyote who stood by a chalkboard with writing on it that he recited as he clapped out its rhythm: *"Don-Don-TsuKu-Tsu. DoRo-DoRo-Ka-KaRa."*

"Everyone, I'll be right back," Coyote said as Anka approached. "Practice speaking and clapping this rhythm together. Stay with each other as best you can. Remember: Many voices. One sound."

Anka got right to the point. "This is Rocky. He needs to stay here a while."

"OK," Coyote said.

They sat at a picnic table in the outdoor dining area, surrounded by tall trees.

"Do I get to know why?" Coyote asked.

"Not now. Later," Anka said.

Coyote nodded. In a situation like this, unlike Anka who would ask a lot of questions, he patiently observed, waiting for answers to reveal themselves.

"Rocky," Anka continued, "this is Senpai. He's the master teacher."

"Hi," Stones said. "I like the drumming here. Can you teach me how to play like this?"

Anka said to Coyote, "We have enough equipment for one more, right?"

"Not a problem," Coyote said. "Rocky, why do you want to play Taiko?"

"What's that?"

"Taiko is the name of the drumming we do here."

"Oh," Stones said. "Well I heard it coming from the trees, and it made me, I don't know, happy, I guess."

Coyote leaned forward and looked very closely at this mysterious new boy. "What do you mean," Coyote said, "that you heard it coming from the trees?"

"I suppose it was just you guys playing; it was kind of far from here, the first time I heard it, but it felt close, like the sound came from everywhere. But all there was, was trees." Stones said.

Coyote's attention riveted on Stones. "Where are you from, Rocky?" Out of the corner of his eye he noticed that Anka gently shook her head "no," without saying anything, like she didn't want him to ask that question.

"I'm not from anywhere, anymore," Stones said. "I live here, now."

Even for a person whose purpose in life was to become one with the universe, Coyote thought the answer was odd, coming from someone so young. Rocky looked, not only exhausted, but weary, especially in his eyes, as if he had been alive for a long time, wandering and lost, unable to find peace or wisdom.

"Rocky, do you know what *kodama* are?" Coyote asked.

"Nope."

Anka interrupted. "Coyote — I mean, Senpai — I don't think this is the time to go into that kind of stuff."

"I have to, Anka, after this morning." Coyote said, and pressed ahead, "Rocky, do you know who Xena is?"

"Who?"

"She's a girl about your age, but she's not really a girl. She looks almost like she's a tree herself, and she has a—"

Anka thought she knew the names of all the spirits Coyote was hoping to contact, but "Xena" wasn't one of them. She kept an eye on Stones for signs of distress. She didn't want this new setting and these strange questions to cause the boy to flip out.

Coyote continued. "Rocky, the Xena I'm talking about is, I think, a forest-dweller."

"A what?"

"She lives in the forest, and she guards over *kodama*, who are spirits that live in the trees, and sometimes these spirits show themselves. Xena has a *kodama* with her, made of bamboo."

"Oh. Them." Stones said, nodding. It was clear to him that Senpai had just described Jen and Tanglewood, only with different names. Names don't really matter, Stones thought to himself.

"So, you know Xena and her bamboo *kodama*?" Coyote said, pressing his hands onto the table and leaning forward.

Stones wondered if he shouldn't have said anything. But Jen and Tanglewood loomed large in his mind, and, although he was perfectly happy to forget his entire past, he found it impossible to completely deny the existence of those two.

Anka noticed that Rocky looked a little nervous, so she pushed her way into the conversation.

"Wait. Who exactly is Xena? That's a new one for me," Anka asked.

"She was new to me, too," Coyote said.

"Since when?" Anka said.

"Since this morning when she arrived shortly after the bamboo *kodama*," Coyote said. "Didn't you see her?"

"You mean there was a GIRL here, too?!?" Anka was shocked.

"She was a guardian spirit, not a regular girl," Coyote said.

"How do you know that?" Anka said.

"If you had seen and heard her you'd agree that she wasn't just an ordinary person," Coyote said.

Stones started to laugh.

"Did you see the bamboo *kodama*?" Coyote asked Anka.

"Not for long enough to believe that it wasn't just a puppet," Anka said, waggling her arms in a puppet-like way to emphasize her point.

Coyote looked hurt. "A puppet? How is it possible to think that that what happened today could be explained by a puppet?"

Stones's laughter intensified.

"What's so funny?" Coyote asked.

"Puh— puh— Puppet!" Stones said through his laughter. "That's a good one. Ha ha ha — only one problem — hee hee hee

— NO STRINGS ATTACHED! Maybe it's all done with mind control. But, no! It lives on its own!"

"What lives on its own?" Anka asked.

"Tanglewood! It's alive!" Stones couldn't stop himself.

Coyote jumped. "Tanglewood! That's what Xena called him! What do you know about Tanglewood?!"

"I thought he was gonna eat me!" Stones's clutched his stomach, and tears of laughter began to stream down his face.

Anka couldn't tell if Stones was really laughing, or if he was going insane right before her very eyes. She was suddenly overcome with worry, and threw her arms around Stones, holding him tightly, rocking him gently. "Oh my God! Rocky! It's going to be OK. Everything is going to work out, I promise! There's nothing to be afraid of!"

"Senpai! Senpai!" A girl ran up to the picnic table. "Senpai! Another spirit has arrived!" she cried out.

* * *

Jen, Ben, and Froggy had arrived at the slope that lay just above the Spirit of the Woods.

"Are you sure we're at the right place?" Ben asked his sister as they crouched behind the trees.

"Well I'd be more sure if I could hear drums instead of just clapping. Clapping is kind of like drumming, right?"

"I guess," Ben said. "I can't see anything through all these trees."

"Why don't we just walk down there and say 'hi'?" Froggy said, standing, ready to continue on.

"Maybe she's right," Ben said. "We're probably already in so much trouble that wandering into a place that doesn't even know us won't add to it."

"They know me!" Jen said. "And—"

"And what?" Ben said.

Jen whispered so that only Ben could hear, "I told them my name is Xena, and I kind of threatened the guy in charge."

"What?! Why?"

"Because I had to! To get Tanglewood back!"

Ben desperately wanted to know how much more Jen had been keeping from him before they marched into this next, deeper, circle of the unknown down there in Camp Clappity-clap. But time was running short.

"Froggy," Ben said, "I need you to move in closer. Get a good look at what's going on down there then tell us what you see. Stay crouched real low, OK?"

"OK," Froggy said, making her way through the trees in a crouch so low that her knees angled out to the sides. She used both hands and feet as she moved forward in small hops.

"That must be how she got the name Froggy," Jen said.

* * *

But Ben hadn't said anything to Froggy about staying hidden, so when Froggy had made her way to the last line of trees and saw a wooden platform with a bunch of kids about her age sitting and clapping, she followed her instincts and hopped in. Literally.

Cerise was the first of the platform kids to see the creature emerge from the trees. Its huge eyes stared at her as it landed on all fours.

"Hello." Froggy said.

"Frog spirit!" Cerise blurted out.

The other children gasped.

"Get Senpai!" one of them yelled.

Cerise ran off to do just that. The rest of the kids kept staring at Froggy, and Froggy stared back until the silence felt uncomfortable to her, which took about five seconds.

"My name is Froggy," said Froggy.

"Did our clapping bring you here?" Skylar asked.

"Kind of," Froggy answered.

"Are you a tree frog spirit?" Robin asked.

Coyote rushed forward with Cerise, Anka and Stones right behind them.

"Who are you?" Coyote asked Froggy.

Froggy jumped up, excited at seeing Stones. "Hey! We found you!"

"Huh?" Stones said. He recognized Froggy but only as some girl from Triple-Bar. He wasn't sure who she meant by "we." Worry flooded him. Now that he'd had the first taste of his new life, he wasn't ready to be found and forced to leave.

"Do you know him?" Anka asked Froggy.

"Yup," Froggy said, and before anyone could ask anything else she turned and shouted at the woods, "Hey, guys! I found him! He's down here!"

Jen was in the middle of explaining everything to Ben when they heard Froggy's call.

"Let's go!" She stood and pulled Ben by the hand as she rushed downhill. "Story time is over. Just follow my lead."

Coyote continued to throw questions at Froggy. "Is Xena with you?"

"Who?"

"Is Tanglewood with you?"

"Hey, you know Tanglewood?"

Jen and Ben arrived at the last line of trees. "Let me go in first, just wait for me to give you a signal," Jen told Ben. She burst through the trees and spread her arms to her sides making sure that the arrow was visible, but not pointed directly at anyone.

"Xena!" several platform kids shouted, and they all stood and bowed.

"Xena!" Coyote exclaimed, and bowed as well.

"Where is Tanglewood?" Jen said.

"Isn't he with you?" Coyote said.

Jen scanned all the faces in front of her, looking for Tanglewood, and saw Stones.

"You're alive!" Jen had to hold herself back from running to Stones and hugging him — she was so happy that she hadn't killed him.

"Hey there, Jen!" said Stones, smiling, relieved that it was Jen, another fugitive, and not some counselor or anyone who might be loyal to his father.

"'Jen'?" Coyote said, confused, looking up from his bow.

Anka stepped in. "So your name isn't Xena?"

"Well...." Jen hesitated.

"And you and Rocky — you know each other?" Anka pressed.

"Who's Rocky?" Jen said.

Ben had heard enough. He emerged from the woods, causing another student on the platform to gasp and point. "Look," she said, "another Xena!" The kids on the platform bowed once more, but kept their eyes on the unfolding scene.

"Ben! I didn't say to come out, yet!" Jen gave the ground a petulant stomp.

Ben ignored Jen's protest, "Which one is Coyote?"

"Him," Jen answered, pointing at Coyote.

"That's not Coyote, that's Senpai," several kids from the platform said at once.

Anka couldn't stand it any more. She raised her arms and spoke with a tone and volume that left no doubt that her patience was pushed to the brink, as if she was about to end the lives of everyone she'd fed and nurtured.

"All right, that is ENOUGH!"

Everyone instantly shut up.

"Now, if anyone or anything is still lurking in the woods around here, come out NOW!"

Nothing happened.

"Fine!" Anka roared and began circling the crowd like a mother lion. "As far as I can tell, nobody here knows anything. So we are going to take this slowly. We are going to figure out what is happening, and what is not happening, and who is who, and we are going to make sure that nobody gets hurt while we figure it out!"

Their full attention on Anka, all awaited her further instructions.

Just then Justin the assistant wandered in. "Hey, Anka, sorry to interrupt, but the food is ready."

Anka held everyone's gaze. She didn't miss a beat, "And we are going to figure all of this out while we eat lunch."

"This looks like more than sixteen people, Anka." Justin said.

"Then I guess you better throw a few more burgers on the grill," Anka told Justin.

Jen and Ben's eyes lit up.

RISE AND FALL

CRUNCH. Nash chomped into a carrot and a turnip at the same time. The tension inside him was at a breaking point. He had searched the entire camp and was now in the dining hall shoving tables with his boots out of frustration.

"Where's my kid?!?" Nash yelled at Ginger, who had stuck with him through the entire search, hoping to suppress any curiosity or concern Nash might trigger as he blustered through the camp. Few camp problems caused more hassle than a distressing rumor that someone was missing; it would spread like wildfire even if wasn't true, and sooner or later a parent would hear about it, later being worse because she would have less opportunity to correct a misperception, or tell her side of the story, or convince a mom or dad that "all's well that ends well" is a healthy approach to life's risks.

"Well, I am sure there's a reasonable explanation for all this. And a good outcome, of course," she added hastily. "Have you checked the kitchen yet?"

Before Nash could answer, Sarah, the head counselor, pushed open the door to the dining room and walked up to Ginger with a worried look.

"I'm sorry to interrupt but there's a question you should know about," Sarah said to Ginger.

"What is it?" Ginger took a deep breath.

"It looks like a couple of kids are missing?"

"Honey, that isn't really a question, is it?"

"No, ma'am," Sarah said apologetically. I guess it's more of a 'situation'."

That was the word for it, Ginger thought, hurrying out of the dining room, hollering at the sky, "Why don't you just drag me to hell over a gravel road while you're at it?"

Nash didn't follow. He entered the kitchen. Ben wasn't there and the lunch prep hadn't been done at all. That was proof enough for Nash that Ben and that hellion sister of his were responsible for Stones's disappearance. It was time to take matters entirely into his own hands.

He shoved open the screen door to head back to his motorcycle when he noticed something he had overlooked when he had gone to meet Ginger for their picnic. Several pots and buckets were on the side patio. He had thought at the time they were left by Stones to dry after washing them the night before. Now, suspiciously, they seemed to be set up as a drum kit. Nash's gaze lingered on the pot-and-bucket drums. When Stones had asked if he could bring his drums to camp Nash had told him, "No. Period. You'll be too busy working to have any free time." Nash disliked memories that triggered affection; he halted a tear from welling up by kicking the drumkit.

Then he saw pure bad news. On the ground, in front of the pots and buckets, lay several bamboo leaves. Their shape was unmistakable. He picked up a leaf and held it next to the head of the doll he still had in his pocket. He smashed the head between his fingers until it unraveled completely and a wad of leaves that formed the inside of the head unfolded. Same shape. Same color.

The bamboo was here, and not just as a doll. Jen had lied to him — there was something else with her behind that line of trees up in the woods. Nash looked at the trees surrounding him now and used every ounce of self control to hide his anger and fear from them. He must act dumb, as if he had no idea what was really going on. The bamboo would be in contact with all the trees by now, enslaving them to its destructive will. They had kidnapped Stones to get to him, Nash had no doubt. They had declared war.

Nash moved to his truck as casually as he could. He leaned into the bed to get the larger of his two chainsaws, then legged it to his dirt bike.

The oily perfume of the bike's engine filled his nostrils, and sent his blood pumping. His head filled with visions of bark and heartwood shredding under his saw, sap pouring out everywhere as he imagined the life draining out of every tree and plant in these woods, beginning with the bamboo, whatever form it took, if he had his way. Then Nash changed his mind — how much better it might be to cut the whole forest down first, leaving no place left for the bamboo to hide. It would be more like a game that way.

* * *

At Spirit of the Woods, when Jen and Ben sat down at the picnic table to eat lunch the first thing they did was open their hamburger buns and take off the lettuce and tomato.

"What are you doing?" Anka asked.

"Uh, well—" Jen began to explain.

"Vegetables are good for you, you have to eat them," Anka said.

"I'll eat theirs if they don't want to," Froggy said. "I don't eat meat anyway."

"Would you like a grilled cheese and tomato sandwich?" Anka asked Froggy.

"Yum!" said Froggy.

Anka told Justin to make a grilled cheese and tomato sandwich.

Jen said, "Can we at least have ketchup?"

"You can have all the ketchup you want," Anka said, handing Jen a ketchup bottle. "Ketchup is made from tomatoes, you know."

"It is?" Jen said.

"You know that it is," Ben said.

"Yeah but I like ketchup better when I don't think about what it's made of," Jen said. She took a bite of her burger and did her best to ignore the crunch of the lettuce. The flavor of the lettuce and tomatoes didn't bother her as much as the texture, which was true for Ben as well. Crunchy texture was difficult to handle because it sounded like bones breaking.

Anka kept the conversation uncomplicated for as long as she could. She didn't bother asking the four "new kids" what their real names were, she just used the names they had called each other back at the drum circle. Nor did she press for last names, or grill them about why Jen and Stones had given false ones. Anka knew that children instinctively protect themselves, which occasionally involved lying. She understood that forcing kids to admit that they've lied often leads to bigger lies, and she knew that any person's behavior — child or adult — revealed the truth so much better than their words. So, Anka was paying more attention to the way they spoke than to the things they said.

Anka asked Justin to bring Jen a washcloth. When Jen had rubbed off enough dirt that the skin of her face could show through, Coyote said, "You're fraternal twins, you and Ben, aren't you."

"Thanks for noticing," Ben said. He genuinely meant it, especially because he was wearing Jen's clothes.

"A lot of people say you're identical, I'll bet." Anka said.

"Yeah," Jen said, "it's like they can't tell the difference between a girl and a boy."

"That can be difficult, sometimes," Froggy said as she ate a leaf of lettuce. "Like I really thought that Tanglewood was a girl when that's what you told me. I couldn't tell he was really a boy. Don't we still need to find him? I wonder where he is?"

Everyone stared at Froggy. No one had mentioned Tanglewood since they had sat down. Coyote nodded at Froggy. He was definitely ready to talk about Tanglewood. Jen threw Froggy a peeved look. She wasn't certain how much she could trust Anka. Ben kept a close watch on everyone's faces, concerned that any talk about Tanglewood would cause Anka and Coyote to think they were lunatics and call the police. Anka was annoyed because she had lost control of the conversation to Froggy, but she quickly shifted her attention and concern toward Stones as she remembered him saying something about Tanglewood wanting to eat him.

"I'll bet Tanglewood will come back here if we play the drums," Stones said, calmly. "That's what I would do if I were him."

* * *

Encircled by the five trees Tanglewood sat as he tuned into the rhythms that lived deep inside him — messages both old and lost.

The crowd of animals around him had grown. Rabbits, squirrels, raccoons and birds moved with him as he stood up, making way for him as his limbs and body began to shift and sway. The movements seemed to arrive within him from nowhere, then radiated from the center of his chest outward to his hips, into his legs and arms. Tanglewood's whole body moved in swoops and steps that connected his feet to the earth and his hands to the *bachi*, giving voice to an ancient language, its symbols turning to sounds as the bachi struck the trunks of the five trees.

DoKo
DoKo
DoRo-DoRo
TzuKu TzuKu So-Zu SA!
KaRa KaRa Kon Kon Kon!
KaRa Kon! SA!
Kon Kon! SA!
DoKo DoKo DoKo DoKo DoKo DoKo

The branches on all five trees lifted and bowed in soft waves, rising and falling, pulling air upward, downward, breathing. Tanglewood could feel the air rising from the ground as it swept over and through him.

The animals around him felt it, too, and hopped and soared with Tanglewood.

Boom. Boom Ba Boom. Boom.

Tanglewood stopped.

Drums. The drums.

The drums would deliver the message, not to just five trees but to all of them.

Tanglewood was running to the drums, his chest bursting with a long lost light.

* * *

Nash saw it. He actually saw *it*.

He had made his way back to the dense line of trees where he found the devil child, Jen. He considered, once again, that the trees were a trap but then became enraged by the possibility that the dense growth was really a wall that hid secrets he needed to know so that he could undo them. He zoomed through a gap, cut across the shallow creek bed, and broke through the trees on the opposite side when he saw a spindly creature dashing across a meadow. It was the same sickening green color of the bamboo doll and the leaves he had found. Its head grew upward into spikes, or a crown. It was the Bamboo King.

Nash twisted the accelerator and roared into the meadow, then cursed and spat in frustration as the tall grass and soft earth slowed him down. He wished that he had a flame-thrower to scorch the earth dry and incinerate everything in his way. He felt a rush of adrenaline when the wheels finally gripped drier ground where the meadow yielded to the woods that the bamboo demon had entered. Nash knew he was heading in the right direction because the trees grew close together — a third line of defense after the tree-wall and the meadow quagmire. A third line of defense was a sure sign he had penetrated territory that held his enemy's most precious gifts — its heart and soul, and its hostages. And he would be the one to take them all, smiting the heart, crushing the soul and saving his son from tortures that could only have been born in the mind of the vilest of demon spirits, the Bamboo King. Nash swerved left and right to dodge the trees that were no match for his skill, determination, and violence.

The slope took a sharp angle. The ground fell away and Nash went flying over his handlebars as the chainsaw swung forward and pulled him with it. The teeth of the chainsaw bit into the ground. Nash felt the snap of the chainsaw's strap as it stopped him from tumbling any further, and watched as his motorcycle continued on its way downhill, without him, until it hit a rock, flipped and was swallowed by a sea of thorn bushes.

Nash got to his feet, checked the chainsaw to make sure it wasn't damaged. The enemy's defenses had turned his dirt bike into a casualty of war — a big mistake because it fueled his hunger for revenge and left him with no choice but to mount a stealth attack. The enemy had done him a favor. He sniffed the air and listened carefully.

"Drum beats," Nash whispered to himself. "They're sending out signals." He set out on foot, taking light, swift steps as he held the chainsaw low and out in front of him, like a machine gun.

* * *

The children of Spirit of the Woods, decked out in their belted jackets, loose pants, wrist straps and headbands, swung their *bachi* with a strength and coordination that Coyote did not expect this early in the month. The thunderous roll of the Taiko drums boomed and lifted. Jen, Ben, and Froggy were watching the surrounding woods but Stones was ready to play and couldn't help himself, banging away on one of the extra drums that Coyote kept near his central podium. Coyote wasn't prepared for Stones to jump in and was afraid, for a moment, that his lack of Taiko training would break the rhythm and set them all off track but Stones fell into the rhythm like he'd been born to it, using his bare hands.

"He's back!" Cerise shouted as Tanglewood shot into the drum circle, followed by a trail of forest creatures.

The excitement brought the drumming to a halt.

"Tanglewood!" Jen rushed up and threw her arms around him.

"Bunnies!" Froggy shouted.

"Froggy!" Ben yelped because he had completely forgotten that he had never fully explained to her who and what Tanglewood was. He froze, waiting for Froggy to scream as he watched her pick up a bunny and then face the unclothed Tanglewood.

"Hi," Froggy said to Tanglewood. "What happened to all the clothes you were wearing? I guess the sun isn't bad for you, either. I'm really happy about that."

"Froggy," Ben stepped in. "Just how bad is your eyesight? Can't you see that Tanglewood is made of bamboo? Doesn't that weird you out?!"

"Nah. That kind of stuff doesn't bother me."

"And what about the rest of you?" Ben said to the whole group. "Why isn't anyone flipping out at the sight of a pile of sticks that walks around by itself? How is this normal?!"

"Yeah, this is definitely not normal," Anka said.

"I know, right?" Stones said to Anka. "It's freaky."

"Ben," Coyote said, "some of us have been waiting a long time to meet Tanglewood, although we didn't know that was his name."

"Waiting? How?" Ben sputtered. "He didn't even exist until like a week ago!"

Coyote looked surprised. "Xena — I mean Jen — mentioned that she had made him, but I didn't know it was so recently."

"Hey!" Ben said, "Jen didn't make him! I'm the one who made him."

Jen stomped over. "Yeah, but he was my idea!"

"Hey!" Stones shouted above both of them. "You don't own him, neither one of you! Tanglewood is whoever he is, it isn't up to you! Even if you are his parents!"

"We're not his parents!" Jen fired back.

"Yeah!" Ben agreed.

"Then, who or what, exactly, is Tanglewood to you?" Coyote asked.

"He's our brother!" Jen and Ben said at the same time.

Everyone quietly absorbed this news. It didn't really change the fundamental situation but it did cause everyone's attention to shift to Jen and Ben for a few seconds.

Tanglewood now understood Jen and Ben well enough to know that they were settling some kind of dispute between themselves, but his focus was elsewhere. The pressure inside him was building up rapidly, and the big, double-headed drum that sat sideways on its stand was there, next to him, waiting to be used.

Tanglewood gripped the *bachi* firmly, set himself in front of the large drumhead and threw his whole body into it. The drum boomed.

DoKo
DoKo
DoRo-DoRo
TzuKu TzuKu So-Zu SA!
KaRa KaRa Kon Kon Kon!
KaRa Kon! SA!
Kon Kon! SA!
DoKo DoKo DoKo DoKo DoKo DoKo

The power of the rhythm caused mouths to open and lungs to expand. Everyone was mesmerized. The flow of Tanglewood as his limbs swayed and bent in long arcs — it was the most beautiful sight they had ever seen. No one could speak. No one could move.

Except for Stones. Tanglewood's drumming entered his soul. He had never felt so alive or so happy.

"I LOVE EVERYBODY!" Stones shouted as he ran to the drum and matched Tanglewood's movements perfectly, mirror images, as his arms connected to the opposite drumhead, hitting all the beats perfectly. The volume more than doubled.

* * *

Nash was forced to navigate down the hill using dead reckoning for a brief period when the drums fell silent, but now they were pounding away again, so loud that the leaves on the trees seemed to vibrate. He crouched low and maneuvered into a position where he'd have a clear sight-line through gaps in the trees.

There, about fifty feet below, was the worst sight he had ever seen. An encampment of humans, standing perfectly still like an army of the undead as the Bamboo King pounded out his evil instructions to them using a code that was probably forged in the icy pit at the bottom of hell. And there, banging the drum along with it, was his own son.

The trees around him began to move by themselves. Their limbs arced up and down causing updrafts and downdrafts. An emptiness was consuming Nash's insides, as the evil rhythms below were removing the breath from all living things that mattered to him, and giving it to the trees. Nash's will dissolved like iron in acid.

Then it came roaring back as he realized he was finally free of all attachments that restrained his inner warrior. Stones was gone; all that remained of him was a shell, possessed, already dead. There was no one to save, and nothing left to lose.

"The time has come, my friend," Nash said to the chainsaw. He pulled the rip cord and it sparked to life with the song of angels.

* * *

"The trees!" Jen said. "Ben! Look at what Tanglewood can do with the trees!"

"Tanglewood is doing this?" Ben wondered aloud.

Coyote felt a warm glow radiating from within. He was ecstatic. "It is happening! Anka! Children! The spirit of the woods has shown us how to talk to the trees! And we can hear their voices calling back to us!"

The wavelike motion of the trees held everyone in awe. The air rose and fell and rose again creating a melody through the trees that joined the Taiko drumming like flutes.

Then a strident noise ripped through the air that didn't sound musical at all. Or healthy.

Jen and Ben heard it first. That same tearing sound.

Jen grabbed Ben by the hand. The memory of the afternoon when they watched helplessly as the bamboo was severed from its roots came flooding back for both of them.

Tanglewood began to seize. Pain shot through every leaf and twig and stalk of his body.

A shroud of darkness enveloped Stones as that sound, terrible and familiar, came back to rip out his happiness.

The drumming ceased, the trees became stiff. The slashing growl of a chainsaw, unopposed, sucked the air away.

"The Woodcutter!" Jen yelled.

Everyone in the drum circle looked upward as a horrible, crunching CRACK! sent out a piercing shockwave. A tree on the slope above suddenly shifted to a sickening angle, then began to fall.

"Run, children! Run!" Coyote shouted, as he grabbed the kids within his reach and shoved them out of the circle away from the slope.

Anka sprinted to the furthest group of children — the ones closest to the slope — her arms spread wide as she swept in to move them all away.

Ben rushed to help Anka, pulling kids and shouting, "Move! Move! That way!"

And Froggy grabbed every rabbit she could lay her hands on.

Jen ran to Tanglewood. She had to, Ben knew, as he saw his sister run toward danger instead of away from it. He forced himself to watch as the tree continued its way down in a line that would intersect her path any moment now. She tackled Tanglewood like a linebacker and shoved him out of the way.

WHAM! The tree slammed into the drum circle, bursting drums and sending splinters in all directions.

Stones took it all in as if he were tied to a chair and forced to watch a movie he didn't like, but couldn't change.

"HAHAHA! DEATH TO THE PLANT KINGDOM!" Went the laughing roar of the maniac with a chainsaw.

Jen scrambled to her feet, lifting Tanglewood, imploring him, "Run! Tanglewood! Run before he can get you!" She pushed but Tanglewood wouldn't budge. He stood there looking up toward Nash as every individual fiber that made him wound itself around the others next to it. The voice inside him began to flow again.

Bamboo, cut and fallen down,
Roots torn from the ground,
Helpless then, but not alone,
We rose again and now we walk
Finding all who give life back.
But all who take without return
Who cut to end, who live to burn,
We stand to halt them in their tracks.

The Woodcutter must be stopped. Tanglewood marched past Jen. He marched directly to Stones who stood frozen at the big drum, which was still intact. He pounded on the drumhead with the *bachi* until he had shaken Stones out of his trance. Tanglewood tossed the *bachi* at Stones, and pointed at the drum. Stones understood.

Tanglewood hopped over the fallen tree and began to run up the slope.

"Tanglewood! Stop! Don't go there!" Jen pleaded. But Tanglewood kept going.

"Damn it, Tanglewood! Why you gotta be so stubborn?!" Jen hollered as she ran after him.

Stones began to pound the drumhead. Without Tanglewood there with him, he struggled to find the exact rhythm. But he had no choice; he had to find it. His purpose was clear: Whatever lived inside his father and had twisted him into such a rotten human being — that thing had to die.

RUPTURE

As the tree fell into the encampment, Nash's senses overloaded from the surge of victory. The tree had destroyed the Bamboo King, he was certain — bamboo shards had flown every direction as the tree whomped the ground. But the return of the mighty Taiko drum yanked him back to reality: this war had only just begun. The next bomb he delivered would destroy both the big drum and the human puppet left playing it — the puppet that used to be his son.

Nash quickly chose a nearby tree that looked as if it would fall in the right place and squeezed the trigger on the chainsaw. Wood chips sprayed out from the trunk as the saw's teeth did their work.

Then Nash felt fingers scratching his scalp.

He turned. The Bamboo King was right there. It waved hello, then darted away.

Nash yanked the chainsaw from the tree trunk and took off after the creature, but Tanglewood was faster and more nimble. Nash lost sight of him. He cut the motor of the chainsaw to listen for the rustling of bamboo.

"Grrr-Rawwwr!" Nash caught just a glimpse of the demon girl Jen as she rammed his chest with a long pole. He was top-heavy to begin with, and his attempt to keep his balance by lifting the chainsaw sent him backward even faster. The tree he had already cut down would have stopped him from falling further, but instead, his hip hit its stump, his body flipped and he rolled downhill.

Jen listened for a moment, but heard only the Taiko drum. She saw no sign that Nash was climbing his way back.

"Tanglewood!" Jen called out. "Tanglewood!"

She followed a *tonk-tonk-tonk* sound, and found Tanglewood many feet above her head. He stood on a branch that belonged to one of a cluster of tall trees — four separate trunks that came together as one at the very bottom.

"Are you all right, Tanglewood?" Jen asked as she grabbed a low branch. Her wrist hurt but she pulled through the pain as she reached for the second-level branch. Tanglewood freed up one hand and reached to help her. He grabbed her hand with his, and as he pulled her arm appeared to unravel.

The bandage on Jen's wrist unwound itself, taking dirt and dried blood with it as it peeled away. On her bare skin Tanglewood could see the pale outline that matched the shape of the band he wore on his own wrist. He saw the look of pain on her face as she struggled to pull herself upward. Tanglewood let go the *bachi* in his other hand, grasped both her arms and lowered her to the ground, then climbed down to kneel next to her. Jen cradled her wrist. He removed his wristband and gently attached it onto Jen's forearm.

"Don't, Tanglewood!" she implored him. "You need it more than I do."

Tanglewood shook his head "no," and put his hand to her cheek.

"Your hands," Jen said, "they're softer, and so warm."

He helped Jen to her feet. Jen didn't know why, but she began to cry. "Tanglewood...."

Tanglewood hugged her, slowly rocking her back and forth, and ran his fingers through her hair.

Jen pressed her head to Tanglewood. She let her tears flow. "Strong one…." a voice resonated from Tanglewood's chest. "Strong one…."

The chainsaw roared to life behind her. She turned and saw Nash making his way up the hill.

"Run! Tanglewood!" Jen shoved Tanglewood to the cluster tree and stood to face Nash.

"Tanglewood! Climb! Climb!"

Tanglewood climbed.

Nash flung Jen out of his path with such force that she almost flew. She landed on her back and her head hit the ground. Everything went dim.

Nash took a swipe at Tanglewood with the chainsaw, its teeth a blur as they sped their way around the blade bar but Tanglewood climbed fast. Nash whipped the saw into place and began tearing through the first trunk where it separated from the cluster. Tanglewood felt the tree cry in agony.

Tanglewood ascended to the top of the tree canopy leaping from the branches of one trunk to the next of the four. The first tree began to tilt away. Tanglewood gripped the severed tree and felt the tension cross through his body as he kept the tree from falling, anchoring his other limbs to the three remaining trunks.

The second tree sent out a cry of agony as the teeth bit into its bark. Darkness rose. Tanglewood used all his remaining strength to keep the darkness at bay, not giving in to it as it devoured the light. He concentrated his thoughts, "Stand tall, my sisters and brothers. Stand. Do not fall."

But the words, themselves, seemed useless.

He could see, inside himself, all the songs that needed to be sung — to be sent into the world. But the drum was unreachable, the *bachi* lay on the ground below, and all his limbs were stretched to their limit by the weight of the trees as The Woodcutter severed them from the earth one by one. Tanglewood heard the melody inside him — the song that could save them all but there was no way to play it.

The second tree began its tilt and the third began to send out waves of pain as the teeth relentlessly chewed and chewed.

If only the trees could breathe again. If only the air could move, but Stones, down below, was doing the best he could, and was struggling to find the beat and hold it steady.

* * *

Coyote ran to the large drum and joined Stones.

"Motomoto!" He shouted to Stones. "Follow me!" And he pulled Stones back to the rhythm.

DoRo-DoRo

TzuKu TzuKu So-Zu SA!

KaRa KaRa Kon Kon Kon!

KaRa Kon! SA!

Kon Kon! SA!

DoKo DoKo DoKo DoKo DoKo DoKo....

And the trees all around began to breathe once more. The air swirled and rushed across the ground and up the slope. It swept across Jen, and she came roaring back to consciousness.

Nash stood several yards in front of her, sweat-soaked, his arms vibrating to the chainsaw's terrible frequency. Jen scurried to the *bachi* that lay nearby and threw them at Nash's head, but Nash didn't budge and the grinding continued. The saw had made its way through three of the trunks and was halfway through the fourth — but they weren't falling.

She looked up. Far above the ground Tanglewood was stretched into an "X" in the middle of the four trunks, his limbs pulled straight and long. Even at this distance she could see that he was being pulled apart.

She pulled the arrow from the hem of her poncho. And thrust it deep into the back of Nash's knee.

"Arrrrgh!!!!" Nash grabbed at the arrow jammed into his joint but still kept a grip on the saw with his other hand, his finger squeezing the trigger, the blade unstopped.

He twisted toward her and let out a growl more terrifying than a bear, but Jen growled back with the fierceness of every bear that had ever walked the earth.

The volume of the Taiko drum doubled. The trees breathed deeper and deeper, their branches stretched up and down to their limit until the trees directly above Nash sacrificed branches they no longer needed, letting them break and fall away. The first one knocked Nash's arm off the saw. Then dozens more hit the ground around him, locking limbs with one another as they buried Nash in a pile that walled him off completely. Nash, in the darkness of the pile, felt tiny hands reach into him and pull at threads within, stitches sewn so deep they must have been what had held him together, or had binded him to his ghost, which the hands surrounded, and removed. Nash saw a shadow leave him, and he passed out.

The chain saw sat silent, but its damage had been done. The saw had only a few inches of the fourth trunk left to cut when it seized up, not enough trunk to stop it from tilting away, and the four trunks slowly separated like the spines of an umbrella.

RUPTURE

The stalks that formed Tanglewood's arms and legs began to slide over one another. He turned inward — going all the way, and he found a voice, his own, not just one that could speak to himself, but one that others could hear. The rising columns of air whooshed past his body and through his fibers, and the whole of him began to resonate with the soulful notes of a bamboo flute. Tanglewood sent out a melody both happy and sad. A song of healing; and a song of passage.

Zu Su

Rama Su

KoRa Rama Su Su

Rama Rama Rama Su

Over and over again.

Jen watched the four trunks reverse their fall and angle their way back to upright, the gaps sealing where they had been slashed. She looked upward as the trees became whole and strong again. But she could not see Tanglewood.

A wind blew. The drum fell silent. The sound of the bamboo flute echoed, and then left with the wind.

Then bamboo leaves fell like rain.

* * *

Ben scrambled up the slope calling for his sister. He found her sitting on her heels as she looked upward at the trees.

"Where's Tanglewood?" Ben asked.

Jen opened her hand to show Ben the bamboo leaves she held. "Everywhere," she said.

A muffled voice let out a moan. "Help me," it said.

It came from the pyramid of branches that stood not far from where Jen sat.

"There's someone inside this pile!" Ben yelped.

"It's Nash," Jen said.
"We have to get him out of there!"
"I know."

CIRCLE

Sylvanna, in her workshop over the garage, leaned over her worktable as she carefully sewed a seam that attached a sleeve to the shoulder of a dress. An intense contraction gripped her belly.

"Not now!" Sylvanna pleaded at the baby inside her. "I'm not ready!" Then she calmed down and let herself flow with events she had no control over. She called out for Ross who ran upstairs and helped her into the car.

* * *

Two days later Ginger Berger sat in the empty dining hall of Camp Triple-Bar. Anka and Coyote sat across from her.

"Are you sure you want to let that freak-show of an ex-cook of mine convalesce back at— what was the name of your camp, again?"

"Spirit of the Woods," Coyote said.

"It will be fine," Anka said. "Whatever was eating at him seems to be gone. When we visited him at the hospital this morning he was kinda sweet. Almost sad, really."

"Must have been the blow to the head," Ginger said. "But I

suppose if he's going to be in a wheel chair for the rest of the summer he won't be causing harm anytime soon."

"Oh, believe, me," Anka said, "Stones and I are going to keep a close eye on him. We'll make sure he gets better. Any sign of trouble and I'll fix it."

"You really want to keep him, too?" Ginger asked.

"Stones was made to play Taiko drums," Coyote said. "It will be an honor to teach him."

"It's your choice, honey. Now what about my offer? I'm short-staffed enough here as it is, and if I don't get another cook pronto I could have a full-scale rebellion on my hands."

"I'll take it," Anka said.

"You sure you can handle cooking for both camps?" Coyote asked her.

"Piece of cake," Anka said. "Justin can handle most of it, and I'll be there at least a couple hours during the day, and all night. Besides, we'll need the extra money now that we've had to replace all those drums."

"Thank God no one was hurt in all that," Ginger said.

"How are the kids doing?" Anka asked.

"Oh, they'll be fine," Ginger said. "You know kids — they always bounce back. It's the adults that'll crash and burn on you."

* * *

Jen sat on the ground by herself, at the edge of the field. Froggy walked up, sat down next to her and plunked a soft, white bunny in Jen's lap.

"You look like you need to hold a bunny for a little while," Froggy said.

Jen reluctantly began to skritch the bunny behind the ears.

"They like to eat carrots a lot," Froggy said, handing Jen a small carrot. "Just like in the cartoons."

Ben was running toward them from the other side of the field. "Jen!" He called.

Jen handed the bunny back to Froggy and stood up. She couldn't tell if Ben was excited or distressed but either way Jen was nervous. Strong emotions had worn her ragged.

Ben arrived, breathlessly. "Dad called! Mom had the baby!"

"What is it?" Jen said.

"It's a girl."

Jen leaped into the air. "Whoo-Hoo!"

* * *

A week later Camp Triple-Bar felt almost normal to Jen and Ben. They had each found their niche. The arts and crafts projects turned out to be so beneath Ben's skill level that he volunteered to be Anka's kitchen assistant for the rest of his stay. Kitchen duties enabled him to work with his hands all day, and Ben enjoyed cooking, which helped him appreciate that making a mess is sometimes the only way to get where you wanted to go.

Jen spent as much time as she could on the archery range. She was good; no one else came close to her ability to hit a bullseye. When other kids asked her how she was able to do it, she would hold up her forearm — the one with the band — and say, "It's all in the wrist."

Her counselor, Erin, came up to her.

"Jen-Jen" Erin said, "you have a visitor waiting for you over at the campfire circle."

Jen walked to the fire circle and saw Coyote sitting on the grass at the top of the embankment above the campfire. The wood was stacked in the pit, ready for that night's fire.

Coyote stood and bowed to Jen.

"You don't have to do that," Jen said.

"I want to," Coyote said.

"Have you told anyone about Tanglewood?" Jen asked.

"Tanglewood is your story to tell, Jen. For me, I am happy that the spirit of the woods is as real as I always wanted it to be."

"Not anymore," Jen said sadly.

"That isn't true," Coyote put his hand on Jen's shoulder.

"You're just saying that," Jen said.

"No, I'm not." Coyote said. "I've been observing these woods for a very long time. Not just these woods, but all plants. They are as alive as you or I, or anyone you know."

"And they die, too."

"Not the same way."

"What do you mean?" Jen looked up at Coyote.

"Plants live their lives attached to the ground. They know where they came from, and they know where they are going. Their lives follow a circle, and their ending always attaches itself to a new beginning."

"That would be nice if it was true," Jen said, dreamily.

"Trust me. It is. You should know. You and your brother made Tanglewood from fallen sticks, but the sticks still had life in them, and you helped them find it."

"What about the sticks down there," Jen said, pointing at the logs in the fire pit.

"There are many paths back to the beginning," Coyote said.

Jen stared at Coyote. "You are just as goofy as I thought you were the day I met you," Jen said.

"Anka says the same thing from time to time," Coyote said. "Anka also agrees with me that Tanglewood is real, and will find a way back, someday."

CIRCLE

Jen gave Coyote a hug.

"You have one more visitor besides me," Coyote said. "Look behind you."

"Hey," Stones said. He was walking toward her with Ben alongside him.

"Hey. You look pretty good like that," Jen said.

Stones was wearing his Taiko clothes.

"Yeah he does," Ben said. "I'm jealous."

"You wouldn't want to cook in these," Stones said, "and get them all dirty."

"Eh," Ben shrugged. "Dirt's part of life."

Stones cleared his throat.

"Guys," Stones said, "I wanted to apologize for, you know, all those things I did. I was mean."

"I'm pretty sure we're even," Jen said. "I'm sorry, too."

"You saved me, Jen. Both of you did." Stones put his arms around Ben and Jen. "The three of you did," Stones added.

They all fell silent for a bit. But it wasn't awkward.

"Is your dad OK?" Ben asked Stones.

"Yeah, I think so. It's weird. It's like he was never the way — you know — the way that he was. Senpai here thinks he was possessed by The Woodcutter."

"No way," Jen said.

"I'm not sure anything else explains what we all saw," Coyote said.

"And *that's* who you thought I was when we first met?" Jen said to Coyote. "You thought I was The Woodcutter, like *that?*"

"You were pretty scary," Coyote said.

"You sure were," Stones agreed.

Jen looked over to Ben, her eyes narrowing.

"Jen, I know you," Ben said without blinking.

"Meaning what?"

"Meaning, you know, you're amazing. And, also, there's the other side of you that's—"

"That's what?" Jen interrupted.

"Tough." Ben said.

"Wild." Stones said.

"Powerful." Coyote said.

"Good." Jen smiled, loving all these words used to describe her, especially Coyote's. And then it registered that Ben had used the phrase, *"the other side of you"*. She looked upward at Coyote. "Coyote," Jen said, "what makes me powerful?"

"It's not easy to know why things are the way they are," Coyote began, but Jen shot him a look he knew meant she had no patience for a soft answer, so he spoke his mind. "What I think, Jen, is that Tanglewood isn't the only one who has a spirit of nature inside him. I like to believe we all do, but I don't think that's true. Only a few of us are, well — two very different beings at once. I know that sounds nutty."

"The Other..." Jen breathed.

"Then you already understand what I'm talking about."

"My mother started to explain it. I thought it came from this," Jen held up her wrist.

"Your wristband is just a thing," Coyote said.

"So, part of me is like a plant?" Jen asked.

"From my point of view, yes," Coyote said, "But I'm new at all this stuff, and you'll eventually understand what's inside you better than I ever could."

Ben said to Coyote, "You're right. This all sounds nutty."

"That doesn't mean it isn't true," Jen said.

CIRCLE

"Well, it makes sense," Stones said. "Because if The Woodcutter was all tangled up inside my dad, then some other thing like it had to be what chased it away. It could have been you," he said to Jen.

"It was probably Tanglewood who did that" Coyote said, "along with the trees, and all the *kodama* living inside them. Jen did something else. She's like a protector, or a pathfinder, or both."

"What about Ben? We're twins. How could I have some spirit-whatever and him not?" Jen said.

"Who says he doesn't?" Coyote said. "Ben built Tanglewood — he could have a life-giver within him."

"Great." Ben said. "I'm the Doctor Frankenstein of plants. Sheesh."

"If any of this is true then my dad wasn't exactly crazy," Stones said.

"Well, he was right about plants being alive and aware — I mean, I believe that, too." Coyote said. "But the rest of what he believed and did was twisted by a dream of total destruction. Destruction is part of life. But total destruction is the exact opposite."

And then Jen asked Stones, very kindly, "Does Nash remember any of what happened?"

"Kind of," Stones replied. "He says it was like a nightmare that lasted for years and years. But he knows it was him that did those things, so, he's being extra nice."

"Really?" Ben said.

"Really. I told him that when we go back home at the end of the summer he has to replant all the bamboo."

"You did?!?" Jen said.

"Yep."

"And?" Ben said.

"He said he would. He had tears in his eyes when he said it."

"Thanks, Stones," Jen said.

"Actually, if it's all right with you, call me 'Rocky' from now on."

"You got it, Rocky," Jen said.

"I found something you should have." Stones picked up a long, drawstring bag that lay on the ground behind Coyote, and handed it to Jen. "I went for a walk and noticed them stuck in the branches up high in some trees."

Jen opened it, and saw a bundle of bamboo sticks.

"Tanglewood." Jen said.

* * *

Later that day, while the sun set over the ridge, Jen said to Ben, "I know what we should do with what's left of Tanglewood. And I'll need your help."

* * *

The month of camp went by faster than Jen and Ben ever thought that it could. And saying good-bye wasn't as easy as they'd expected, especially when they had to say good-bye to Froggy.

"Don't cry," Froggy said. "You'll see me again."

"How do you know?" Jen asked as she sniffed and wiped her nose on her sleeve.

"Because you want to," Froggy said.

* * *

Their father arrived and drove them home, where Mom had been eagerly waiting to scoop them both up.

"I love you two more than ever," Sylvanna told her children.

"Even though there's three of us now?" Jen said.

"Especially because there's three of you," Mom said.

"Jen made something for the baby," Ben announced.

"No, Ben actually made it."

"Well, it was Jen's idea."

"I can't wait!" Sylvanna said.

Jen and Ben left the room and returned a minute later carrying a small rocking crib. Its rails were green and smooth and its joints all carefully wound using cord that was the yellow-orange color of the sun.

Sylvanna gasped. "It's beautiful," she said.

"You kids hungry?" Ross asked Jen and Ben.

"I'll help you make dinner, Dad," Ben said. "What are we having?"

"Burgers — just the way you like them."

"Lettuce and tomato on yours, Jen?" Ben asked his twin sister.

"Yep," she said.

Ross's mouth dropped open. "What in the world happened to you two?"

* * *

Jen and Ben stood over their baby sister as she fell asleep in her new crib.

"She's so cute," Ben said.

"For now," Jen said. "But one day, she'll be tough stuff." Jen took off her Xena wristband and attached it to the crib.

"Good night, sis," Jen said as she and Ben left the room, leaving the door open just a crack.

The baby yawned, and stretched her tiny hand as far as she could, reaching toward one of the bamboo side posts. A small shoot emerged from the middle of the post, and unfolded into leaves that formed an equally tiny hand that entwined with the baby's. The two of them held onto each other as they fell into a deep, restful sleep, side by side, together, as one.

www.DamonWolfe.com

ABOUT THE AUTHOR

The entertainment arts and sciences have preoccupied me since age six when I decided I wanted to work for Bugs Bunny.

The first obstacle I ran into was typical: my family regarded my basic goal as nonsense, which explains why my occupational history began with medical school and then working as an actual doctor for a bit, which I did well, but there was a big problem: it turns out an ambition to work for Bugs Bunny isn't a thing you can just switch off and forget. I led a double life, filling sketchbooks with drawings and notebooks with the raw material of fiction. It was all part of my secret plan, which was built around two facts, one of them being: I like to make things.

My arts and entertainment career began with a sideways entry — my favorite approach to any problem. After devoting about a thousand nights teaching myself computer graphics I transitioned into graphic design and video games. Then I went to Vancouver Film School to learn character animation.

I spent the next ten years as an artist, technical director, and computer graphics supervisor at animation studios, including one of Disney's, where we made feature-length movies. Production is demanding work — much more difficult than being a doctor, but a lot more fun. It made me happy. But I continued to lead a double life because I wanted to build stories from the foundation. The second fact underlying my secret plan: I like to make things up, preferably out of nothing. Writing is one of the only ways to do that.

So I spent about a thousand nights writing three screenplays. This was practice. I love screenplays — they are compact and punchy. Screenplay number three was named *Tanglewood*. I was about to write its second draft to fix the usual problems in the telling of any story when a friend of mine advised, "If you want to find every weakness in your screenplay turn it into a novel." And, boy, did that work. Plus I discovered I like to write novels.

So I am writing more of those, in addition to building all the other components that are part of my secret plan, which I don't keep so secret anymore. You can watch it evolve on my web site:

www.damonwolfe.com

Made in the USA
San Bernardino, CA
26 July 2015